An Aunt Edwina
Christmas

A family history novel

Lynne Christensen

Published by Northleo Writing Inc.
studio@northleowriting.com

Northleo
WRITING INC.

First Edition - 2022

Hardcover ISBN: 978-1-7386517-0-2

Paperback ISBN: 978-1-7386517-1-9

eBook ISBN: 978-1-7386517-2-6

Dedication

———

To the Archivists, Genealogists and Family Historians
who toil for endless hours in dusty back rooms, often
without sufficient recognition, space, or lighting.

I see you.

I appreciate you.

Thank you for preserving the past for future generations.

This novel is for you.

Each book can be read as a standalone novel, however, do note that many characters recur throughout the series.

List of Characters (People)

————

Algernon 'Algy' Holgarth: Heir and proprietor of Holgarth Hall in Plumsden, Kent. Has penchant for tweed suits and formal estate living of yesteryear. Manages plant nursery and petting zoo at Holgarth Hall. Lance Holgarth's elder brother.

Bea Archibald: Professional archivist who gets priceless collections in order.

Bernard 'Bertie' Preswick, Fourteenth Duke of Conroy: Julie Fincher's aristocratic art patron. Incredibly wealthy owner of Scotford Castle estate near Oakhurst, Kent and a country house in Brambleford, near Medchester, Kent. Reliable friend of all family history adventurers who need help getting out of incredibly outrageous scrapes.

Clive Jakeman: Owner and sympathetic renovator of Torcwell House in Yorkshire. A decent human being who hosts Vikings and weddings with prosperous success. Generous with his high-limit credit card.

Constable Bud Snowdrop: Police constable trying to make his mark but forever blotting his copybook.

Daphne Florian: Circus acrobat and close friend of the law.

Donald Jerome Fincher: Julie Fincher's father. Retired furniture shop manager.

Dougal Galfinch: Gerald's father and Limousin cattle farmer.

Ewan Kilburn: Owner/operator of Kilburn's Outstanding Antiques in Plumsden, Kent. Kind, handsome Scotsman who serves as treasurer of the Plumsden Family History Society. Uncle to one piano-playing nephew and one highland-dancing niece.

Finn Severs: Bertie's ex-security service chauffeur trained in evasive driving techniques, bodyguard protection and rescuing his employer's friends.

Francine Junior Philmond: Widowed daughter of Francine Winloame. Lives in Carlingheath, Kent.

Frederick 'Fred' Aloysius St. John Todling: Pixleton, Devon-based, intellectual property solicitor who moonlights as a bookshop minder. Verbose with legalese and opinions. Owns potbellied pig named Barnaby and more.

Gerald Galfinch: Dougal's son and Limousin cattle farmer.

Gertrude 'Gertie' Porringer a.k.a. 'The Apricot Powerhouse': Boisterous female priest and slightly older cousin to Julie Fincher. Always available for a detailed pedigree chart review and exuberant karaoke.

Gwyneth: Archivist at a Yorkshire County museum and record office.

Harriet Tibbets: Antiques appraiser and Auctioneer. Classic beauty and quick as a whip.

Harvey Hartmore a.k.a. 'Old Two Two': Good friend of the Major and valued member of the Twenty-Second Cheshire Regiment. Lives in London and restores old military vehicles.

Hayleigh Grables-Muncton: Professional genealogist who needs a talking to and a client ethics course.

Jacques Lesabrioux: Stoic General Manager of the Greymore Hall estate. Has strong penchant for getting guest services just right.

Julie Fincher: Twenty-something bohemian style painter who married for family duty then quickly got off the wrong path. Daughter of Donald Jerome Fincher. Favorite of Lady Edwina Greymore. Lives in converted barn on Scotford Castle estate near Oakhurst, Kent.

Lancelot 'Lance' Holgarth: Younger brother to Algy Holgarth. Failed spicy chili-banana samosa kiosk owner. Now lives at Algy's beck and call for hound walking, vegetable rescuing, luggage heaving and general gopher duties. Resides at Holgarth Hall in Plumsden, Kent.

Landry Jackson: Tall Texan with a mysterious inheritance. Travels across the pond to meet new friends, solve a shocking chutney incident and compare ancestors' notes.

Major Barry Whitcombe: Retired military man who uses his pork chop sideburns, vast people network and army expertise to reunite families with their history. Hobby is buying vintage uniforms then rehoming them with proper regimental museums. Based in Medchester, Kent.

Maude Livingstone: President of Plumsden Family History Society. Director of Greymore Genealogy Research Site.

Mr. Neebles: Quiet gardener who has likely inhaled one too many aphids at Roycetonne House, Suffolk. Married to Mrs. Neebles. Enjoys scones with whiskey jam.

Mrs. Neebles: Strict and non-curious housekeeper at Roycetonne House, Suffolk. Married to Mr. Neebles.

Naomi Murphy: Professional archivist who works with Bea Archibald.

Oswald 'Ozzie' Boggs: Unforgettable Greymore Genealogy Research Site visitor who earned quite a reputation for thriftiness.

Pamela Fulham: Stylish Greymore Genealogy Research Site visitor who is now hooked on genealogy and family history research.

Peggy: Archivist who preserves the past with a focus on fancy greeting cards.

Rose: Enthusiastic donut maker at Greymore Hall.

Sherry Knox: Delightful eighty-three-year-old family history researcher who launches her battleships at precisely the right moment.

Steve Linham: Happy old codger from Yorkshire who volunteers down at the village archives when he's not abroad learning embroidery craft tips.

Tricia Belvedere: Small village volunteer with a fierce-looking dog.

Wally Dunstable: Unlikely friend of Ozzie Boggs.

And let's not forget the place where it all began:

Greymore Genealogy Research Site ('GGRS'): A wonderfully spacious, modern and welcoming place for family historians and genealogy researchers. Located on premises of Greymore Hall estate.

List of Characters (Furry Friends)

———

Barnaby: Potbellied pig often on the lam. Owned by Fred Todling.

Bingo: Eighteen-hand Shire draft horse teamed with Jim.

Gilligan: Caramel-blond-coated Afghan hound who herds lettuce and rabbits. Owned by Algy Holgarth.

Holophusicon 'Holly': Galumphing English Sheepdog owned by Fred Todling.

Jim: Eighteen-hand Shire draft horse teamed with Bingo.

Norris: Blue-grey coated Afghan hound puppy. Registered name 'Northern Thunder of the Gables'. Owned by Algy Holgarth.

Rex: Fierce looking German Shephard owned by Tricia Belvedere.

List of Characters (Ancestors, Infamous and Portraits)

Aunt Moyra: Landry Jackson's relative who left him a lot more than he expected.

Constable Bill Snowdrop: Bud Snowdrop's grandfather who ensured an innocent man wasn't unfairly punished.

John Cantonleigh, the Marquis of Estonburgh: A perfect society husband.

Keith Galfinch: Retired saddlemaker who kept a deep secret with an embroiderer friend.

Lady Adelaide Roycetonne: Unfortunate aristocrat who was unlucky in love yet found solace in her later years.

Lady Edwina Greymore: Helped raise Julie Fincher after Julie's mother died. Was family matriarch and aristocratic owner of Greymore Hall estate near Oakhurst, Kent. Community philanthropist connected to all the right people. Left a rich legacy to help anyone interested in researching their family history.

Lord Roycetonne: Lady Adelaide's father. Cruel, unyielding and strict Victorian man who built a mining empire yet never earned the love of his daughter.

Reginald Barr-Smythe: Chairman of the bank and leader of the local hunt club near Roycetonne House.

Sheridan Jackson: Founded a mail order catalog business in Texas, the Lone Star State.

Simon Chester: Expert horseman deemed below his true love's station.

Chapter 1

**Christmas Tree Farm, Oakhurst, Kent, England.
December 15. 3:31 p.m.**

The thirtyish Christmas tree vendor had royal blue, frizzy, shoulder-length hair, goopy coral lip-gloss, and wore quite the get-up.

Poufy, loud tartan parka with mustard yellow fake-fur trim. Check.

Leopard-print coveralls, skin tight, and shiny, zip up front. Check. Fuchsia pink, shortie wellies. Check.

At best, I needed sunglasses. At worst, we'd be caught staring—in a most unpolite manner—at the vendor. Ewan Kilburn, my dear friend and antiques shop owner, stood beside local solicitor Fred Todling. We'd all cleared our schedules for this annual festive ritual and it was easy to enjoy the scent of coniferous trees surrounding our frosty clouds of breath.

Fred was an amiable man with a slight paunch under his crisp shirt. He was also the most verbose man on the planet. "Ewan, I've got an illustrious friend who needs exquisitely expert help with a packed-to-the-gills house clearance sale up in Yorkshire.

Would you care to be granted a first, unhurried and unrushed look at her collection of antique eighteenth century silver and Art Deco furniture?"

It was music to an antiques dealer's ears. Ewan was raring to go on this one and responded with a quick nod of the head. "When and where, and I'll be there," he said. "I'm already salivating with that description."

I moaned. "Just don't do that over her Art Deco furniture, please," I said.

Ewan just grinned. He was like that. Enthusiastic yet restrained. He'd become a dear friend during our recent family history adventures and helping us to open the Greymore Genealogy Research Site ('GGRS') at our family's Greymore Hall estate. I'd founded the GGRS community facility with the generous inheritance Lady Edwina Greymore had left to me. I'd called her 'Aunt Edwina' but it was only for show and vanity; truth be told, the woman who helped my father raise me was actually my paternal grandmother. She was kind, a substitute mother to me after my own died when I was a very young girl. Aunt Edwina was also a family history devotee, absolutely fascinated with our ancestors and their worlds.

The three of us laughed and then snapped to attention when the oddly-clad vendor pranced over to where we stood. "Can I help?" she asked. Her eyes narrowed as she noticed Fred. "Oh. It's you."

Fred stood straighter. "Yes neighbor, indeed it is. I gave our evergreen object quest some quite serious thought and decided to perambulate in your proximity and support a local small business."

The tree seller took Fred on with gusto. "This isn't a 'small' business. My turnover is six figures and, well, never mind. Do you want a tree or what?" She stood there, hands on her hips. There was no Christmas spirit here, only the cost of true materialism.

"We're here to take a contemplative look at your vast inventory of coniferous greenery, hoping to find something that would satisfy our festive needs for the jolly holly season." Fred gave her a firm grin, as if he dared her to counter him. Half of me wondered if she was able to wade through that sea of adjectives. At least she wore rubber boots.

Ewan and I just blended into the background, pretending we were nonchalant customers who considered this verbal exchange rather blasé.

I supposed the woman wanted the sale more than the upper hand, so she issued one more frown at Fred and replied, "Suit yourself. There are twelve aisles, all arranged by species and tree height. If you find one you like, tear off the duplicate tag and bring it to the register."

"And is there someone here to help us carry our tree to the vehicle?" Fred asked, noting the cold rain that started to fall. Customers' coat hoods lifted and feet scurried for the sanctuary of warm vehicles.

"Nope. Self-service only." And with that, she stomped off without so much as a backward glance.

At this point, I was actually ready to go chop my own tree down in some licensed forest enterprise far away from here. Maybe even Canada.

I looked over at Ewan and noted that he registered the same look on his face. He leaned over to me. "Is she for real?"

"Unfortunately. What was it someone said to us once? The world doesn't *need* all types, it just *has* all types?" I looked into his kind eyes for solace. One thing about Ewan, he was a rock. Dependable, honest, loyal and good-looking to boot.

"That's about the long and short of it," Ewan said. "However, let's give her the benefit of the doubt. She may be dealing with an unspoken tragedy in her life."

I went silent, pondering his last statement. It was Christmastime, after all.

Ewan brightened and gave me a smile. "Never fear, we'll still keep up the Christmas spirit."

Fred leaned over the both of us. He spoke in a conspiratorial whisper. "I am so sorry to report that my neighbor is not well-versed in the niceties of the holiday season and helping one's fellow man. Or, in your case, Julie, fellow woman."

I thought for a moment then spoke. "Whatever happened to that nice old man who ran this place for what seemed like donkey's years?"

"He retired to Cornwall. He has two daughters and you just met one of them." Fred scowled. "No chip off the old block, as you just witnessed."

Ewan laughed. "Can't imagine meeting her in a dark alley at midnight."

"I'd bet five pounds she'd win," I said with a grin.

Fred snickered. "Ewan would likely bore her to death with an in-depth lecture on early modern pewter plates."

"Better than subjecting her to your fifteen-minute diatribe on the value of fourteenth century parchment land deed records," Ewan replied.

"Alright you two, enough. Let's go and find our tree. We have a ton of things to do back at Greymore Hall." I linked my arms through both of theirs and we all went off in search of a special tree.

***

Greymore Hall, Oakhurst. 6:00 p.m.

"She was wearing what?" my cousin Gertie Porringer asked me. She was the most street smart, effervescent vocal priest that I knew.

I explained. "It wasn't nearly enough, either for the cold or her job."

"Why was she so rude to Fred?" Gertie asked.

"Apparently they've got neighbor issues."

"Maybe he doesn't know the good old adage. A really high fence makes for a really good neighbor."

"In this case, I don't think a thirty-foot fence would be tall enough." I shrugged. "I didn't ask for details. All I wanted was our tree."

"It was that bad?"

"Let's just say I don't think she's made Fred's Christmas card list this year," I said.

Gertie laughed. My cousin could always bring a smile to my face. She'd done it so often in the recent past with her karaoke singing, encounters with Fred's potbellied pig, and viral social media videos.

"So, did you take separate vehicles?" she asked. "I don't see your partners from coniferous wonderland here."

"Oh, no. Fred and Ewan are around back unloading the tree. I told them to come in through the back hall entrance."

My comment was punctuated by a loud crash from the rear of Greymore Hall. That was saying a lot because we were standing in the front and this was an elegant estate home with massive square footage. I locked panicked eyes with Gertie, then we both raced to the back of the house. There was nothing in the back hall. No people, no tree.

"I think it came from outside," Gertie said. "My church youth group—there's eight members here today—was on standby to help." I surmised she thought the teenagers were up to no good with either the miniature goats, a farm implement or hijinks that got out of hand. I cast a glance outside to the back fields and saw nothing. There were heavy snow clouds above us, looking ready to burst their powdery explosions at any minute. We headed outside after donning quilted barn jackets from the hooks lining the wall. The crisp feel of a cold snap coming on met us as we left our warm hallway.

It actually wasn't any type of unexpected event involving youth. Rather, Fred and Ewan had got the wrong end of the stick. All we saw were boots, specifically the rubber soles of winter boots. Fred and Ewan were sprawled face down on top of the thirty-foot evergreen that lay on the ground like a fallen battering ram outside the machine shed. Fred was at the top, Ewan near the base. Both groaned.

They'd entered via the wrong door.

There was a great deal of scuffling and muttering between Fred and Ewan as they tried to untangle damp waxed jackets, scarves and gloves.

Gertie and I stood back and watched, wondering how both men had gotten impossibly tangled amongst the spiky branches of the healthy tree. It just didn't seem right. All our time spent selecting a beautiful evergreen, and now the men were flattening it.

"Ahem," I said, loudly clearing my throat. "Swimming usually involves a pool or the ocean." At the moment, both men were flailing arms and legs, trying to extricate themselves from the tree, using some type of wince-worthy breaststroke.

Ewan freed himself first. He stood up, covered in tree needles and pine cones. His look was one of surprise, especially when he saw the lawnmower where he'd expected the hall coat hooks. "It appears we were mistaken."

"I'm sure you entertained the miniature goats," I said, trying to conceal my laughter.

Gertie, on the other hand, didn't even try to hide her amusement and let out a hearty chortle.

"How on earth could you confuse the machine shed with the back hallway door?" I asked.

"Not that it helps us now, but I did ask Fred to make sure it was the right door. Come to think of it, there was a bit longer to walk than I remembered when I was helping your father move into his suite upstairs," Ewan said.

"There's your mistake. Following a solicitor more interested in ensuring no breath cloud is devoid of words, as opposed to watching where his feet are going," Gertie said. She turned and motioned over the church youth who were staring, goggle-eyed, at the two adult men who had deployed the impressive tree into the wrong building. An assortment of teenagers wandered over, jostling and joking with each other from underneath Nordic-style knitted hats, gloves and warm winter boots. They all had on the same style parka emblazoned with the youth choir's logo.

"They make for an inspiring bunch," I said to Gertie. "When's the next youth choir trip?"

"Norway in mid-January, hence the hats. They're trying to blend in when we let them loose on the town."

"And does that give you cause for concern?"

She shook her head. "Not half as much as those two over there buried in the Christmas tree."

The teenagers heard her snide remark and snickered.

Gertie smiled back at them. It was pretty hard to be mad when Fred and Ewan had made such complete, utter fools of themselves. "All right, Team. That's enough. Let's help Fred and Ewan get the tree into the front hall where it's supposed to be. Hopefully there aren't too many branch casualties as we go. You did leave it tied up, correct?" She stared at Ewan and Fred with a beady-eyed grin.

"Of course," Fred said, finally rising to a more coherent, vertical plane. "Both of us ensured that said evergreen remained firmly yet gently tied, around both limbs and boughs, thus preserving this exceptionally fine specimen of Mother Nature." He issued a furtive look at the teenagers. "Would it be appropriate to ask your flock for assistance?"

"They're not a bunch of turkeys, Fred," Gertie said, "and of course they're here to help. These teenagers comprise a group of high-achieving youth with far better things to do than stand around watching miniature goats all day. Once they've helped right the tree, they're going to put all the garlands up in the front hall plus hang the children's coloring contest entries underneath one of Greymore's portraits of Aunt Edwina."

"Those are lovely ideas," Ewan said, coming close. He looked like a genuine wrangler of a coniferous curmudgeon.

"It's a Greymore Hall tradition," I said, "but we'd better get a move on if we want that tree up today."

"And make sure it gets plenty of water. A live tree without water inside a house is a fire hazard," Gertie added.

One of the young men, he must've been about fifteen or sixteen years old, approached Gertie with a cheeky grin. "Some of us are wondering if this is going to be worse than the Gordon Mumbles Obstacle Course."

Gertie shook her head. "Don't worry about that. There's a clear path once the correct door to the correct building is opened. Straight shot in from the back, then right through to the front hall. Just don't snag the ropes on the coat hooks."

The young man gave her a smile and headed back towards the tree, motioning the others in his group to follow. It ended up being the eight teenagers carrying the tree inside Greymore Hall, while Fred and Ewan stood off to the side, watching like frustrated spectators.

Ewan came over to me. "Well, at least we got the tree onto the estate grounds."

There was that moment of uncomfortable which turned into hilarious silence. Gertie, Fred, Ewan and I all had a good laugh as we watched the tree disappear, foot by foot, inside the vast back hallway of the enormous Greymore Hall manor house. It looked like a green horticultural sausage bumping up and down with every footstep. There would be many more experiences like this I was sure. Still, if life wasn't an adventure, then it was dull. And no one wanted a dull life. Add our beloved family history into the mix, and it was definite: no day would ever be the same and we relished that fact.

Chapter 2

GGRS. Next Morning. 8:30 a.m.

"What's the Gordon Mumbles Obstacle Course, by the way?"
Ewan asked me at the information desk inside the research site.

"Oh, it's some outing Gertie took her youth group on, some
kind of physical stamina test. It gave them both a fun day out as
well as the opportunity to learn more about their physical and
mental health. It really encourages people to work together as a
team as they complete the obstacle course."

"Oh, I see."

"Here's a brochure," I said, pulling one out of our local attrac-
tions literature rack and handing it to him across the counter.

Ewan picked up the brochure and studied it. He saw the maze
of ropes, ladders, zip lines, tarpaulins and muddy ponds that
participants had to race through, all within sight of a pastoral
meadow background. I could tell what was going through his
mind: a) What a fun, legitimate reason to get all muddy; and b)
I wonder what the onsite café serves for tea?

"Don't look so smug. You couldn't handle it," I told him.

Ewan straightened. "You underestimate my team and I."

"Ewan, when you straightened up, your back clicked. You're not even forty years old yet already your physical prowess is starting to deteriorate." I narrowed my eyes. "What team?"

"Give us a chance and we'll prove you wrong," he promised.

At that moment, Maude Livingstone, President of the Plumsden Family History Society, came inside with Gertie. Maude was an organized woman in her seventies, with perfectly coiffed short silver hair and a penchant for pale purple cardigans and matching skirts. They were having an animated conversation about a nineteenth century census record.

"Ladies, Ewan is trying to tell me his team can complete and overachieve in the youth group's obstacle course," I said.

"Have you lost the plot, Ewan?" Gertie asked.

"No. Just determined," he said.

We had a brief staring contest.

"Okay, you're on," I said. "If you win, us three ladies will vacuum your car, mop your floors as well as organize your four new boxes of vintage postcards into categories using archival sleeves and labels. If you lose, you get to write the next GGRS newsletter, vacuum our three cars as well as spend an entire day transcribing a lengthy eighteenth century divorce court witness testimony record."

"Cursive or Olde English font?" he asked.

"Easy cursive. It's a fifty-page document that we haven't had the time to go through yet."

Ewan extended his hand. "Done."

I looked over my shoulders at Gertie and Maude, checking they were on board. I knew they'd been watching, eagle-eyed, to see if Ewan bothered to open the brochure. He did not. And what made our bet all the more delicious was the fact that inside the brochure it explained the obstacle course was designed by an eighteen-year veteran of the military service and was classified as tough as an expert downhill ski run.

We shook on it.

As Ewan walked away, I couldn't help but do a little happy dance behind the desk. Then I called out after him, "Oh, Ewan? Who's on your team? I'll need to know to make the booking."

He shrugged. "Just put down Constable Snowdrop, Fred and myself. The Major can coach us. I don't think we need to bother anyone else to win our little wager."

Oh, this was going to be good.

Major Barry Whitcombe, a prim and proper military man, now had the challenging task of getting an antiques dealer, pudgy police-man and verbose solicitor into the best athletic shape of their lives.

❀❀❀

Three Hours Later.

Thank goodness the hinges on the entrance door to the research site were well-oiled. The constant flow of visitors made it a necessity. The next visitor to enter was none other than Jacques Lesabrioux, a former bellman who was now general manager here at Greymore

Hall. He was somebody you could trust with your house keys, your mother or your deepest secret. He was like a vault, confidant, and banker all rolled into one, just the sort of person dear Aunt Edwina liked to have in her inner circle when she was alive.

The pert little man with the prim moustache strode up to the front desk, put both palms on the counter's edge and said in his efficient voice, "I am pleased to announce that the Christmas tree is now fully installed and decorated in the front hall. It has plenty of water tempering its roots."

"Wonderful. I'm eager to see it." I got up from the desk and numerous people trailed me outside into the front hall.

Jacques had dimmed the front lights for the specific occasion. Earlier today he'd curtained off the front hallway work area so no one could see the grand reveal until it was finished. A half-decorated Christmas tree didn't sit right in Greymore Hall. Aunt Edwina wouldn't have wanted it seen by visitors; she believed in offering only the finished product with all her genteel touches attached.

What a wondrous sight it was. We all stood in awe around Jacques' masterpiece. In front of us stood the thirty-foot-tall glorious tree, covered in white and icy blue lights. All the special ornaments Aunt Edwina had collected during her ninety-two years were hung. There were those that her children and grandchildren had made for her. I always looked to see where mine ended up on the tree because the location varied from year to year. I first saw Gertie's: a baked-clay horse and sleigh, obviously made by a child who hadn't quite yet achieved the finger dexterity needed to make it look like an elegant ride. I saw mine a couple of branches up higher, a lopsided snowman who had long ago lost the carrot from his nose. Yet Aunt Edwina always treated them like the crown jewels. She was very proud of her family and wanted to make sure that they knew. She was really grandmother to Gertie and I, but she insisted we call her 'aunt' so she never felt old.

Jacques leaned over towards me. "We left the angel for you and Gertie," he said. The look in his eye was calm and focused, as if he was telling me I had a duty to take on this role now that Aunt Edwina had passed the Greymore Hall torch to me. The tree sat in an alcove underneath the stairs that wrapped around it leading up to the second floor. It was a grand staircase, one that was carved centuries ago, yet it still bore the weight of its visitors with ease. My father was at the top of the stairs hold-ing the Christmas tree angel. I took Gertie's hand in mine, and together we went upstairs.

My father met us on the landing and handed me the angel. I took a quick look and saw that its scraped head was no longer bare. "Did you paint her?"

He nodded. "It was time to give her a fresh start."

I leaned over and gave him a hug. I passed the angel to Gertie. And together, both our hands touching the delightful ornament, we placed her on the apex of the tree. We plugged in the electric lights and watched the angel's wings and halo glow. There was great applause and appreciation below us on the first floor where our friends and visitors stood watching.

"It's amazing what one has time for in retirement," Dad replied, a small grin on his face. "My mother was using that angel when I was a little boy, so she was due for some T.L.C."

"It's lovely," Gertie said. "She looks good as new."

"Thanks, Dad," I said.

"I like to think she's looking down on us, happy with what we've done with Greymore Hall, so many family and friends here enjoying themselves," he said.

"I'm sure she's impressed," I said.

We all looked down as a gasp from our audience permeated the air. Jacques had just implemented phase two of his Christmas decoration plan for the estate. A wondrous glow of warm white and icy blue came in through the front windows. People rushed over to see what it looked like outside. Ewan threw open the front doors so everyone could walk out into the frosty air and glimpse what Jacques had created. He and I had, of course, discussed this earlier but this was going to be the grand reveal, our test of how it was going to look when we actually welcomed the public for tours over the Christmas season. We were one of the few grand estates in the area that was staying open until December twenty-fourth, closed for only a few short days before opening up again on December twenty-eighth to welcome family-friendly, safe New Year's celebrations on site. We wanted Greymore Hall to impress our guests, and there was a lot to be said for not overdoing it. I never wanted our decorations to be too plastic or too overdone. We'd stuck to a simple theme, and also maintained our love of nature by using as much fresh greenery as we could, items that could later be mulched and used for garden compost. Mother Nature would cooperate if one showed her sufficient respect.

Ewan and I followed the crowd outside the front doors. We emitted gasps of our own as we saw the beautiful winding drive aglow with the white and blue lights twinkling in all of the trees. Aunt Edwina's ancestors had planted these majestic oaks centuries ago, and they carried the lights beautifully well. This wasn't just a minor celebration; no, this was a gigantic celebration, within the boundaries of good taste, reminding everyone that Greymore Hall stood firmly for the principles of family, friendship and goodwill towards others. The fact that we were privileged enough to be part of this wonderful place made me feel all cozy inside. Right now nobody needed a coat; we were all feeling quite toasty thanks to the combination of collective body heat plus the sight of the beautiful lights. The Major, a good friend, was discreetly taking photographs of us outside the front door, and I nodded my appreciation. These would make wonderful pictures for our website as well as a couple to hang on the wall in the research site.

We needed some sort of comment to punctuate the moment and Maude stepped up with something less profound than intended. She turned to us, eyes glistening with excitement, and blurted out loud, "This is so lovely, I think I'm going to haunt the place forever!"

The crowd burst out into laughter and Maude quickly put a hand over her mouth, slightly embarrassed at her overenthusiastic and unplanned promise.

Ewan put a caring arm around her. "Never mind, we all understand what you meant." He looked out at the rest of the crowd. "I think the Major's taken enough surreptitious pictures. How about we all go inside for some hot chocolate?"

The Major look slightly perturbed that Ewan had called him out, but it was indeed hard to ignore the stealthy military man snapping away as people stood in awe of the lights. Still, nobody truly minded; everybody knew that Greymore was a safe place.

Everyone but Ewan and I trooped back inside, both of us lagging behind to close the front doors. "It's a beautiful light display," he said, coming close.

"Indeed it is. Jacques' decorations have exceeded expectations."

"Greymore is lucky to have all of his experience from the hospitality industry here on site."

Snow had started to fall and a couple of flakes got caught in my lashes. I tried to blink them away but the warmth of my skin melted them and needed a finger to wipe them off. I could feel my cheeks sting from the cold air. I looked over to the right and saw the old orangery that Aunt Edwina had renovated the year before she died. It was a large, glass-wall structure that we had turned into a charity Christmas tree display. Thirty different charities from around the County of Kent had put up their trees in support of worthy causes. We charged visitors admission and all proceeds would go to the three trees gaining the most votes. All thirty competitors benefitted from electronic signage on large screen displays throughout the building plus an information stand at their tree so people could learn more about their charity. I'd made sure that the charities' participation was free and that we heavily promoted their involvement on our social media platforms.

Ewan's eyes met mine. They held for a moment and then we shook off our unexpected locked stare. We refocused on closing the doors; it was especially important this time of year because we didn't want precious heat escaping from the drafty great hall. We never wanted our visitors and residents to be cold. Darkness would soon fall as these were the shortest days of the year. Our breath came out in small puffs and soon more snow would permeate the inky black night if anyone dared go outside later. I said 'dared' because with all the amazing family history resources, along with such a wonderful group of friends and family, there really was no reason to search for entertainment outside the research site. We had created something very special, a place worth holding onto and protecting forevermore.

I slipped my hand inside Ewan's. Together we walked back towards the grand Christmas tree.

Chapter 3

Grand Dining Room, Greymore Hall.
December 25. 5:30 p.m.

We started our Christmas dinner on the precise half-hour. People were already jolly from the pre-dinner sherry; those of us who were teetotalers were simply giddy with anticipation of the special meal ahead. We had a large assortment of family and friends at our Christmas dinner event this year: Gertie plus a few members of her church youth group; the Major with his pork chop sideburns and silver-tipped cane; the Major's military buddy Harvey a.k.a. 'Old Two Two'; my art patron, aristocrat and Scotford Castle owner Bertie Preswick, the Fourteenth Duke of Conroy; Maude plus my father and Fred; Pamela Fulham and her husband, both now avid newbie family history researchers; Francine Junior, daughter of the Marriage Bureau owner who had introduced Pamela's great-grandparents; over-eager and under-delivering Constable Bud Snowdrop and his new girlfriend; plus antiques store owner and all around good guy, Ewan.

The table easily sat forty people thanks to the umpteenth times great-grandfather of mine who once hosted King George the Second at Greymore Hall. I'm certain he was impressed with Greymore Hall dating back to 1629. The table was a large mahogany piece of furniture polished to a shine so bright one could actually see their face reflect off the table surface. There were two grand chandeliers hung over the table and miniature chandeliers in the form of wall sconces ringing the room; I suppose there were approximately twelve of them. I always got a kick out of how the wooden floors creaked as one walked inside. The noises reminded me that the centuries-old place had borne a lot of footsteps across its thresholds. The floor squeaks said to me, 'tread carefully so as not to disturb the memories of those who came before you'. I believed in good karma being earned, never doled out by chance. Live a good, clean life, and one would be rewarded.

The heavy velvet, wine-colored curtains were pulled back from the windows with golden braided cords ending in a flouncy tassel. I remembered playing with the tassels as a child and feeling how soft they were, their silky threads racing through my hands with wild abandon. I cast a glance out the window and saw two feet of snow outside on the grounds, an unusually large amount for England and particularly her southern counties. We'd all been watching the forecast with some trepidation. The first suggestion was that Harvey could bring one of his restored military vehicles up to the main house and shuttle everybody home on tank tracks. That suggestion was rapidly quashed by the ladies dressed in all their finery. I certainly didn't blame them; it made no sense to try and clamber over cold steel and down a narrow hatch while clad in sequins and high heels. So, Greymore Hall had once again stepped up to the challenge and took inventory. Rather, Jacques took inventory of the guestrooms available and reassured everybody that we could put them up for the evening or the next few days due to inclement weather conditions. The larder was fully stocked. On top of that, the last television report I heard stated that a large dump of snow had absolutely paralyzed the M25, the London orbital that connected all of the major roads leading into the capital city.

"They're now reporting a sixteen-vehicle pileup, including a couple of lorries," Maude said, whispering in my ear. She looked particularly stunning in a two-piece green evening dress covered with a delicate, feathered-sequined pattern. It was kind of like a shy peacock was wrapped around her body and it set off her lithe figure quite well.

"We have a full house tonight, Julie," my father exclaimed as he came over to clink glasses with me. "If you run out of beds, remember I've got a spare room in my suite too."

"That's very kind, Dad. Maybe I should get you to host Bertie. At least you know all of his aristocratic foibles and habits."

"Boiled eggs and toast in strips at precisely 7:45 a.m. every morning?" he teased.

"That's exactly what his butler brings him each day."

"Well, then he's going to rough it a bit if he's staying in my suite." My father took another look out the window. Thick, fat snowflakes barreled down on a collision course with each other. It wouldn't surprise me if we had another six inches before the evening was out. "Everyone had better stay. It's really bad out there."

I put an arm around him. "At least we have a lovely dinner ahead of us and it's going to be loads of fun!"

Francine Junior wheeled herself up to our little group, her eyes shining with delight. "I have a feeling it's you I need to thank, Julie," she said.

"I'm sorry?" I asked her.

"I received over one-hundred handwritten Christmas cards this year, far exceeding any hopes I had in this electronic communication age."

I gave her a little smile.

"I remember telling you about my Christmas card shortage when you came to visit me in Carlingheath," Francine Junior said.

"It was actually both Gertie and I who arranged it. We just thought it would cheer you up," I replied with a kind look. Inside, I was so pleased the gesture was appreciated.

"And it has my dear! Oh, how it has cheered me up!" She clasped her hands together with glee. "When I was a child, my mother would get so many cards. I would spend hours looking at all of them, reading the well wishes from couples she had introduced that now lived all over the world. I always had to wash my hands after holding those cards because of the glitter that got stuck to my fingers."

"I'm glad our Christmas card campaign brought back some good memories for you," I said.

Francine Junior took my hand in hers. "Oh, this will be such a wonderful Christmas!"

***

6:00 p.m.

Calligraphed, gilded place cards announced the seating locations so the crowd settled in without any drama. Jacques seated me at the head of the table, my father at the other end. Bertie was on my left, and the Major opposite him. It was the age-old courtesies, a plain deference to aristocrats and senior military man who had defended our country's honor. To the left of each of our forks and on top of a linen napkin embroidered with the Greymore Hall logo, sat a bright-foiled Christmas cracker, undoubtedly filled with a thin, paper hat cut to fit like a crown, a silly child's toy or game and a couple of irrefutably bad jokes translated into multiple languages. Our soup plates sat on top of creamy white linen napkins followed by a salad plate and the dinner plate. This stack weighted down hefty gold charger plates. Water, two wine and port glasses sat at the top right. Warm, crusty bread rolls with butter were stationed the length of the table. The centerpieces were comprised of holly, pinecones, gold tinsel, red berries and porcelain miniature goats. Goats? Yes, the very same ones that Aunt Edwina had reminded me of when she gifted me a stuffed toy miniature goat keychain ornament. It was the same one that Jacques had politely noted when I first met him at the Fizzleywick

Hotel for my ill-fated wedding. I looked back on those days with fondness now, able to laugh instead of cry.

We opened our crackers to much delight and hilarity. Paper hats were donned and signaled that our meal had begun.

"Speaking of Holly, how are Barnaby and she doing?" Ewan asked Fred, gently inquiring about his potbellied pig and galumphing English Sheepdog.

"How kind of you to ask about my esteemed companions on my relatively recently purchased homestead and abode. Barnaby is busy wallowing in his pen seeking truffles and whatever I can place in his trough. Holly, on the other hand, enjoys weekly sessions at the local doggie grooming salon and I take her out twice a day for walks ensuring that I clear up after her. We do, after all, have a duty to keep our streets clean."

Gertie leaned over to me and whispered, "I never thought I'd hear about somebody's potbellied pig being discussed at the Christmas dinner table."

"Just be glad there's no bun fights," I replied.

"Or pigs loose in the kitchen," she whispered back with a furtive glance. Barnaby's escapade into Ewan's aunt's holiday cottage on the moors was forever etched in her mind. It definitely was not her most favorite moment.

My favorite moment so far today was looking at all of our guests, including the aristocrat, clad in their traditional, flimsy, colorful paper crown hats. It was like we had all just finished a kindergarten class and wore our art projects on our heads. Bertie was busy spinning the top from his cracker on the tablecloth and Maude was trying to figure out how to untangle two small, twisted bits of metal from each other. My father was entertaining the Major with a really corny joke from his cracker. It was all very traditional and nobody questioned it; it was just a wonderful, lovely English Christmas.

The smells wafting in from the kitchen had already kept all of us hungry for hours. We'd kept the hunger pangs at bay snacking on mince pies, shortbread, mandarin oranges, and sugar cookies with sprinkles. Now came the exciting time where the big meal was due to take center stage. Jacques and his team had prepared an absolutely amazing Christmas dinner. After the lobster bisque and a small garden salad garnished with tomatoes, the main course was on deck. Catering staff brought out brussel sprouts, roast potatoes, cranberry sauce, pigs in a blanket, gravy, carrots and swedes followed by the grandest entrance of them all, and carried by two sous chefs: a 26-pound gargantuan turkey. Everybody oohed and aahed at the sight of this wonderful feast.

Harvey turned to Constable Snowdrop's girlfriend, Daphne Florian, on his right. She was a pretty young thing, petite and blond, but no one knew much about her. Harvey was about to change all that and asked, "And what do you do for a living?"

She gave him a firm look. "I'm an acrobat. I travel with a small gypsy circus and its fairground rides."

"A gypsy circus. That must be an interesting way to make a living," Harvey said.

She giggled. "One thing is for sure. It makes a woman strong and tough."

"I see. So you're on the trapeze, riding elephants, that sort of thing?" he asked.

"Well, I'm certainly not working the miniature donut stall." She held up her arm and made a bicep curl. She was a sinewy athlete, and appeared quite able to hold her own.

Constable Snowdrop had stars in his eyes. "Daphne's been with the circus since she was fifteen. Got picked out of a gymnastics class at her school for exceptional achievement."

"You mean she was recruited by gypsies?" Ewan asked, slightly amazed.

All eyes now focused on Daphne. This story was just too intriguing.

She shook her head. "No, that's not quite how it happened." She patted the back of Constable Snowdrop's hand. "I won my school's gymnastics competition and proudly wore the medal to a circus performance I was going to with my parents the next day. A gypsy's daughter was in my class at school and the medal made her remember me. She introduced me to her dad after their performance, and that was that."

"Much to the horror of your parents, I would suppose?" the Major asked.

I looked at Bertie with much amusement. He was all ears on this conversation, and as I passed him the dish of carrots and swedes, I could see that he was fascinated by this world that his privileged upbringing never, ever allowed him to experience. The closest he'd ever come to a circus was when his family had to get Scotford Castle ready for a royal visit.

"My parents expected me to be a housewife, good at sewing and scrubbing floors. I decided not to go that route, and as soon as I brought home my first circus paycheck, they were satisfied," Daphne said.

"But what about your long-term prospects?" Fred asked. "Certainly one cannot be leprechauning around on the trapeze at the age of fifty-two?"

"Correction, Fred," Gertie replied. "<u>You</u> will definitely not be leprechauning around on a trapeze at the age of fifty-two."

Everybody laughed. The idea of verbose solicitor Fred Todling larking about on a shiny steel bar suspended from the ceiling by two narrow chains just didn't add up. He was much better suited to his legal tomes, pinstripe suits and fancy briefcase. Yes, dear Fred Todling had come a long way from his part-time bookshop minding and ill-fated toga costume at Bertie's summer solstice party. What hadn't changed was his verbosity.

It.

Still.

Was.

Unbearable.

Fred harrumphed. "On that particularly astute note, I would agree with you, kind friend."

Nothing ruffled the man. Amazing.

"Say, did you two plaster up the cubbyhole door between your law office and antiques store in Plumsden?" my father asked.

Everyone now watched a tennis match. We zoomed to Fred and then back to Ewan.

Ewan took this one on. "Of course we did."

His answer came a little too quickly for my liking. I needed more clarification. "How soon?"

Fred looked to Ewan. We watched the tennis match a few seconds longer. Back to Ewan. Then to Fred. Back to Ewan again.

Both men sighed. Ewan straightened up in his chair as he served himself some brussel sprouts. "Fine, guilty as charged. We left the tiny door unhindered for a few weeks longer because both of us developed a slight addiction to the new samosa stand that opened up a block and a half down the road."

"Was Lance Holgarth involved?" I asked, dredging up fun memories of Earl Algernon 'Algy' Holgarth's little brother who lived at his elder brother's beck and call at their sprawling Holgarth Hall estate in Plumsden.

Everybody at the table laughed. Lance's escapades with their dashing Afghan hounds, Gilligan and Norris, plus petting zoo fauna were legendary. Algy spent most of his days in the library writing history books while tasking unfortunate Lance to handle the estate's bed-and-breakfast, petting zoo and horticultural nursery operations. Lance had come crawling back to his elder brother when his spicy samosa business had failed. Perhaps Ewan and Fred had stumbled onto a new marketplace opportunity.

Ewan shook his head. "No, I don't think Lance would want part of this. The samosas were only a sideline of a plant-dyed fabric business. We were willing to brave the owner to obtain the yummy food, but I don't think many other people were."

"What do you mean 'brave the owner'?" Gertie asked. "It wasn't a true restaurant?"

Fred cleared his throat. "Not exactly. It had a takeaway counter and the man running the takeaway counter wore an ankle monitor bracelet."

"Prison food?" Gertie said. She waited until the astonishment around the table had subsided. "Well, there's nothing wrong with a convict trying to put his life back together. Besides, 'tis the season, goodwill towards everyone and all that."

Fred gave a slight cough. "That is, ahem, a slightly delicate issue. You see, the last time we went to purchase four said samosas, we were accused of leaving without paying which was actually and completely untrue. I had Barnaby along with me and when he sensed that a personal affront was being laid upon my precise person, well, he got his bristling hackles up."

My father leaned in from a few chairs down the table. "Don't tell me you are now walking your potbellied pig down Plumsden high street?"

"Of course I was. Barnaby is quite a popular character amongst all the high street merchants. Children flock to him, even the bank manager comes out and gives Barnaby his favorite biscuits when he sees me ambling by."

Jacques was now carving the turkey and putting the meat onto two separate platters that waiters were carrying up and down the length of the table on either side. It was getting to be a difficult decision: focus on the wondrous dishes passing before me or get to the bottom of what had delayed Ewan and Fred from plastering up the secret cubbyhole door between their two respective businesses.

"So Barnaby got mad at the convict serving you samosas. What does that have to do with the door between your businesses?" I asked.

"Isn't it obvious?" Ewan asked. "We couldn't go back to the samosas stand because of how we were ill-treated. That meant we weren't able to share samosas through the cubbyhole door. Henceforth, we didn't need it anymore."

"I see."

The solicitor tried to sell us a bit harder. "It was the right thing to do, until a divine fish and chip shop opened up two blocks at the other end of the street," Fred lamented.

Ewan looked a bit sheepish as well. "I think we should quit while we're ahead."

"You should quit while you're only a mile or so behind the rest of us," I quipped.

Everybody chortled with laughter as we tucked into a delicious meal.

Seconds and thirds were plentiful. I announced a respectful interlude between the main course and dessert. Gertie and her youth choir had met with me a few weeks earlier and offered to provide some Christmas carols as surprise entertainment. They had wonderful voices and their a cappella versions of our favorite Christmas songs were well appreciated by all. The Major even videoed it, ensuring Gertie had more for her social media postings.

I beckoned for Jacques to approach me at the table. "I think we're ready for the Christmas pudding now."

"Yes, of course, Julie. Luckily, we made quite a large one this year. I'll go and check it's properly warmed–"

His comment was interrupted by a fervent pounding on the front door. I knew it took a lot of strength to make that much noise; Greymore's front doors were quite thick.

"Who on earth could that be, here on Christmas day, in a snowstorm?" Maude asked.

"Are we missing anyone at the table?" Gertie asked.

"Not that I'm aware of," I said. "How odd."

Jacques excused himself and went to investigate the doorstep commotion.

Chapter 4

_____

Front Hall. One Minute Later.

I joined Jacques after his frantic motioning from the other end of the dining room. We'd all heard the front doors open and close, followed by a strange man's muffled voice filling the hall.

"Pardon me a moment, please," I said, blotting my mouth with a napkin and pushing my chair back. The Major leapt up with alacrity to help me out of my chair; I was grateful for I didn't want to snag the hem of my beaded gown.

I looked around the table at all my family and friends. "Please, continue. Don't let your meals get cold."

A waiter appeared out of nowhere and put a cover over my plate to keep it warm.

I left the room as elegantly as I could without tripping in my special occasion heels. I felt the rush of cool air as I entered the front hall, knowing winter had invaded merely due to Greymore Hall's front doors being opened for a short period of time.

I stopped and had to blink a couple of times to process what—or rather, who—was standing on our front door bristle mat. It was a lone cowboy, his shoulders dusted with snow. He wore a tall, beige cowboy hat with snow all around the brim as well as inside the hat's top divot. He shook off the snow like a large buffalo on the open plains. His face was ruddy and his blue eyes kind. The cowboy took off his hat when he saw me enter the room, showing us his short buzz haircut. What 'Cowboy Buzz' was doing here in our little part of England on Christmas Day mystified me. I could see it also mystified Jacques, the attentive estate manager dealing with our unexpected visitor.

"Howdy folks!" boomed through the front hall, likely a bit louder than intended. The cowboy stood up straight, shook himself off once again and extended his right hand to Jacques. "Thanks for letting me in, sir."

"Welcome to Greymore Hall. How may I help you?" was Jacques' pert and standard answer.

I came up to my manager's side, curious, and also to help my friend with our most unusual arrival on this blessed day.

"I do apologize for barging in like this on Christmas Day. My rental vehicle broke down a mile back up the road," the cowboy explained.

"Oh dear, you must be frozen through," I said. "Let us take your coat and then you can come in and have something to eat."

"Ma'am, I wouldn't dream of disrupting your Christmas dinner more than I already have. I just need to get to a phone so I can call auto repair. My cell's out of juice, forgot to charge it before I hopped across the pond."

Jacques and I looked at each other, processing the lingo. I spoke first. "Your cell?"

"My apologies, again. I believe you call it a 'mobile phone' over here?"

"Oh, that's right," I said. I noticed Jacques was busy taking the big man's coat off. The cowboy towered over me, about six-foot, two-inches in height. He looked safe enough. Besides, it hardly was plausible someone would show up on Christmas Day looking for anything else other than help. Aunt Edwina would expect us to help this stranded traveler.

I handed him a clean hand towel from the umbrella stand, ones we kept there to wipe the backs of our guests' necks when they came in from a particularly damp walk.

Our unexpected visitor looked at me curiously.

I smiled back. "To wipe the back of your neck? So you don't catch chill."

"Gotcha. Much obliged." He did the dutiful thing and then tried to fold the towel up with his large hands. It was like a giant trying to roll elegant marzipan treats. "I'm afraid I'm not too much good with all this dainty stuff, ma'am," he admitted.

"Never mind. And it's Julie, please."

Jacques came up beside us with a silver tray and the tall stranger deposited his half-folded towel on top. He gave me a focused grin. "Mercy me. Where are my manners! My name is Landry Jackson and I come from Fort Worth, Texas." He thrust out a meaty palm and it met mine with a firm grip. One could tell a lot about a person by the feel of their handshake: sweaty or not, limp or firm.

Landry's was cool and firm, so he passed the test. I also could tell by his large bejeweled belt buckle and diamond pinky ring that he wasn't here to rob the place. No, this was certainly a desperate traveler who needed our help.

And he stood there, looking at me, and then back to Jacques. We were back to playing eyeball tennis again. I decided to break the ice. "Landry, please, I'd like you to join the festivities. You shouldn't be out there all by yourself in the snow. The auto-clubs have already announced forty-six hour delays for roadside assistance on the television and radio."

"I'd feel like I was imposing. Us Texans believe in hospitality but also we don't ever want to be impolite."

I threaded my arm through his and gestured with my head that he should follow. "Nonsense. We have lots of food and there's a real party going on with some great people. Allow me to introduce you."

❈❈❈

Dining Room. Thirty Minutes Later.

"You call a cell phone a mobile phone. You call the restroom a toilet. A truck is a lorry. And underwear is pants." Landry's face crumpled up in a scowl. "First time I heard your word for truck I expected to see a woman named 'Lori' in the room."

My father smiled at him. "You look like a man confused by your new friends across the pond."

"Well, not confused, exactly, but I do have one question," Landry replied.

"And what would that be?"

"What the heck does a man call what he wears on his legs if you can't call them pants?"

"We call them trousers," my father said.

"Even jeans?" Landry asked, astonished.

"Denim."

"Facecloth?"

"Washcloth," Dad said.

"Just don't ask a lady for her vital stats," Gertie piped up.

"What? Doesn't that just mean her birth certificate?" Landry asked.

My father shook his head, amused at this one. "Over here, it means you're asking for her body measurements."

"Well shucks. Okay, here's one: Christmas dinner." Landry tossed it out like this one was a real challenge.

"Christmas dinner," my father responded. It was like the two of them had invented their own game of verbal sparring, much to the amusement of everyone else at the table. Gregarious Landry was received with open arms; because we had extra room at our table it was no problem for the waiters to find him a space. So far, Landry had entertained all of us with jolly stories about his twelve-hour flight delay en route here and then how his SUV got stuck in the snow despite it having four-wheel-drive. The tall Texan had ingratiated himself with ease here tonight, and he actually made an incredibly welcome addition to the table.

"Okay, here's another one. Why is Newmarket not even on the map? I looked it up once and couldn't even find it in Suffolk," Landry asked.

"Ah, that's because Newmarket is a border town and it may be listed in Cambridgeshire. From a genealogy perspective, also remember that since 1964 whole counties have disappeared altogether. Rutland is one of them." Maude nodded in a prim manner. "We consider a lot of these details when doing family history research."

Gertie chimed in. "Knowing the social history of the time is really important; relating it to your genealogy research is critical. It will help explain why people aren't on the census. For example, maybe they're away at the hop harvest. Perhaps they're not in a church record or records were missing due to the Civil War, or even they were bombed out during World War Two. Perhaps your relatives went to live with another family during a depression or the record office flooded in a great weather event and the specific details were lost. There are so many things one has to consider when doing research. I even found a man who appeared on the census twice in two different towns. Turns out he was a travelling salesman who moved lodgings every two days and the census taker was none the wiser."

Landry took all this in with a serious expression. "You folks know an awful lot about family history research, much more than I ever expected needed to be known."

There were gentle murmurs and nods around the room.

"My Aunt Moyra was interested in her own family history, and was doing some kind of research. But she never told me what exactly she was looking for," Landry said.

"Understood," Gertie said. "It can be quite frustrating at times."

"Could be."

I looked up in horror. "We forgot the Christmas pudding."

Landry's face fell. "I'm afraid I'm to blame for that. Let me hustle into the kitchen and help Jacques." Landry moved faster than I could speak to politely decline his offer. He turned back as he walked. "I didn't know you folks here in England ate chocolate pudding at Christmas."

"It's a dense fruit pudding," I replied, "with some added, er, special ingredients."

Landry looked intrigued. "This I've got to see." He headed for the kitchen.

Ewan leaned over to me, "You can't make this stuff up. If you'd told me two hours ago that we'd be celebrating Christmas dinner with a tall Texan with equally tall tales, I wouldn't have believed you."

"This from the man who insisted on having a cubbyhole between his office and his neighbor just so they could coordinate their hot lunch purchases," Gertie said with a smirk.

"Just leave the samosas alone. They're in the past now." Ewan gave her a mock glare.

Moments later, there was a bunch of chortling that emerged from the kitchen. We all looked up to see Landry trailing Jacques, both men showcasing equally large grins on their faces.

"Alright gents, what now?" I asked.

Jacques went first. "There was some unfortunate confusion in the kitchen over how much was a 'gill'."

"A gill? It's a shot glass-sized amount of alcohol you pour at the base of the Christmas pudding to set it alight," I said.

"That would be the problem. I don't know that term, so I guessed," Landry said.

"You upended the entire bottle of brandy over the Christmas pudding, didn't you?" I asked.

"Good grief, man! We're lighting a pudding, not a bonfire for Guy Fawkes night!" the Major said.

Landry nodded. "I hope I haven't ruined things for the second time this evening."

"Not to worry. I'm sure you've made the festivities a little bit more jolly," Bertie said, oozing his usual aristocratic charm.

Indeed, Landry had. After the Christmas pudding was shared out with dollops of thick cream over the rich dessert, people started to forget their troubles and felt extra warm and cozy inside. This was a special time of year when glad tidings and good memories needed to be at the forefront of everyone's minds. Not every day was going to be perfect and no year was going to be full of ups without downs. But here tonight, with all my friends and family in this room, I knew that I could count on their laughter, support, and gratitude in the months and years to come.

"We'll put you in the one of the spare guestrooms for the night, Landry," I said.

"It's either that or he sleeps outside a mile down the road in his frozen vehicle," Ewan teased. "That is, if you can find it underneath the snow drift."

"I'm very grateful," Landry said. "How soon do you think I can get back on the road again?"

"The Major's been watching the news on and off all day. I think we're all going to be stuck here for at least thirty-six more hours. England isn't exactly known for plowing out its small villages in rapid time," I said.

"Shucks. And here I was thinking I'd make Newmarket by late tonight."

"Why Newmarket?" Ewan asked.

"I'm here to clear up my Aunt Moyra's estate."

"That's a long way to travel to serve as executor," I said. "I remember what I had to do for Aunt Edwina's estate and it was no small feat."

"It is a bit complicated," Landry explained. "My Aunt Moyra was a recluse, as was the woman who left her the property years ago. Perhaps you've heard of it? It's called Roycetonne House, up near the racehorse training stables?"

"Good grief, you don't mean Lady Adelaide Roycetonne?" Bertie piped up, his spoon uncharacteristically clattering to its saucer.

Landry nodded. "The very same. It's been an odd few decades with those two. They squirreled themselves up in the house all alone and virtually had no contact with the outside world apart from the internet, three staff and the mailman. Oh, and once when one of them caught pneumonia. Then they let a doctor in to prescribe medication."

Bertie's eyes were nearly bugging out of his head. "I don't believe it. I just don't believe it."

"What, were they some sort of legends around those parts?" Landry asked. "I've heard Newmarket is where horse racing started."

Bertie smiled. "Roycetonne House is very close to the Newmarket racecourse in Suffolk. King Charles the Second actually used to ride in the Rowley Mile races. The Rowley Mile was named after a stallion that was particularly good at siring offspring. Due to the king's rather, ahem, randy reputation, they also gave the nickname 'Old Rowley' to the king himself who had over ten illegitimate children."

"How far away is Newmarket from here?" Landry asked.

"A good hour and a half on a fine driving day," Bertie said.

"I wonder if I've gone a bit off course. I was supposed to be heading north from Heathrow but I looked at my phone just before I ditched the vehicle and it said I was heading west."

"You're in the Kentish Weald at the moment, directly south of London and, yes, a bit west in Oakhurst," Bertie confirmed.

Landry sighed. "All the little villages over here in England. There's often more than one with the same name. I think I counted six Ashford's while I was still stateside."

"That's one of our endearing qualities," I explained. "Never underestimate the power of the English to concoct numerous places with the same name, spread all over multiple counties!"

Gertie smiled. "Don't worry. Once the roads clear up, we'll get you on the right path."

It was obvious Bertie was immensely curious. "So are you the executor or the inheritor of the estate, if you don't mind me asking?"

"I'm both. Aunt Moyra wanted me to process the contents of her house, keeping an eye on the solicitors who are signing over the estate to her small group of legatees. I was her only relative and main legatee, but it's important to me that her friends and house staff are given their proper inheritances once any debts, taxes and legal bills are paid."

"I doubt there'd be any debts; the Roycetonne family was very wealthy. My set has tried for decades to figure out what happened to Lady Adelaide after her father passed away. All we know is that she became a recluse," Bertie said. "She trusted very few people near her."

"My Aunt Moyra was Lady Adelaide's constant companion for twenty-three years. She came back to nurse Lady Adelaide when she fell ill and after Adelaide passed away, my auntie found out she'd inherited the lot. Didn't expect it at all, but that's what happened." Landry smiled then looked puzzled. "What do you mean by 'wealthy' by the way. A couple hundred grand in the bank?"

"Dear me," Bertie said, shaking his head. "Try a couple hundred million. Her father was a leading copper and gem miner in the Edwardian age."

"No." Landry was shocked.

Bertie nodded. "Friend, the estate you've just inherited was valued in 2001 at £217,000,000. Approximately $300,000,000 American, and that's not counting inflation or compound interest."

Landry was caught at a loss for words.

I shot a warning glance over at Fred, knowing he was already mentally rubbing his hands together with glee at the prospect of yet another well-to-do client possibly in need of a solicitor.

Chapter 5

Everyone retreated into the drawing room for canasta and charades after dinner. The Major and Constable Snowdrop had over-imbibed. Thanks to the copious amounts of food, drink and turkey enzymes, the men automatically loosened their belts and fell asleep in two of the many comfortable chairs scattered around the room. Gertie and I both played a mean game of cards, so we were up for whomever wanted to challenge our prowess at the canasta table.

With Constable Snowdrop dozing in a corner, we took the opportunity to cozy up to his new girlfriend.

"So Daphne," Gertie started, "do you have family in town?"

"One sister. She runs our family's Christmas tree nursery business."

Well, this was a shocker.

"Really. Whereabouts is she located?"

"Not too far from here, actually. She took it over from our father when he retired."

Ah, the leopard-print-coveralls, fuchsia-pink-wellies-wearing wonder.

The follow up conversation was bound to be awkward.

"I think we may have gotten Greymore's tree from her this year," I said. "Your sister is rather–"

I felt a hand on my elbow and then Bertie's posh voice in my ear, "Julie, a word please."

Saved by the diplomatic aristocrat. Again.

I'd lost count of the times Bertie had rescued us from a rather delicate situation. Bertie guided me away from our little conversation group, leaving Gertie to find out more about Daphne's opinion of her own sister.

Once Bertie and I were alone in the wood-paneled library, he turned to face me with a solemn expression. "Julie, I can't emphasize this enough. Roycetonne House has been a mystery for decades. All of society's outreach was rejected at the front gates. Lady Adelaide's solicitor even sent me a registered letter when I tried to intervene to do a wellness check." His eyes looked hurt, and I knew his heart was never anywhere but in the right place.

"It's like Landry said, she was a recluse. She obviously wanted his Aunt Moyra to carry on the tradition and granted her the estate to do so."

"But the rumors, you cannot ignore the rumors," he replied.

"About what? Two old ladies living in a house together? Maybe they just preferred each other's company. There's lots about the real world today that I certainly don't want to face. Turn on the television and you get streams of violence, profanity–"

Bertie shook his head. "Julie, this isn't an episode of a detective show. Lady Adelaide had a very controlling father and it was rumored she'd set the house ablaze all these years ago now."

"Set her own house on fire? What's that all about?" I asked.

"To escape her father's imposing nature." He shrugged. "She was away at a ship launching ceremony on her father's behalf when the fire actually broke out. Her husband and her two daughters all perished in the flames. Rumor was, she only wanted her father and husband dead, and didn't know her daughters had changed their travel plans at the last minute. Still, nothing was ever proven."

"Did your family go to the funerals?" I asked.

"My father told me about it. At the time, they claimed that the house would be rebuilt to the exact way it was prior to the fire. Her father insisted on all the mirrors being covered in black cloth to ensure the souls of the departed wouldn't get stuck here on earth. Quite a sad business, really. Lady Adelaide's father was a very odd, controlling man, wealthy but eccentric," Bertie said.

"Are there any other types of wealthy men?" I shot back, thinking of how eccentrically enthused Bertie was about his mango chutney sales tours.

"Very amusing," he crooned in his elegant voice. "I just want to warn you to be prepared for the unexpected. Be careful."

"What do mean 'be prepared'?"

"For when you travel to Newmarket and help Landry open up a house that's been shut away from society for decades." He nodded then smiled. "It's going to be Gertie, Ewan, yourself plus any other hanger-on expert who can wheedle themselves an invite."

He was right. One hundred percent right. After both our recent excursions to help researchers Ozzie Boggs and Pamela Fulham, my destiny and life had become quite clear: to go on field trips with family history researchers to unravel the mysteries their ancestors had left. I was effectively busted, outed, and discovered by none other than my wise art patron. Bertie was like a kind, older brother to me.

"You win. I can't deny I'm incredibly curious about what Landry's going to find in the house," I said.

"As is everyone from the lowest parlor maid right up to the upper echelons of society," he replied.

"Her father had that much influence?"

"Indeed he did. But it's what Lady Adelaide did that really shocked the world. She tried to marry below her station and when that went south, Roycetonne House, well part of it at least, went up in flames years later so she could escape the marriage her father forced her into taking. Nobody knew the end of the story, no one knew what happened to the man she truly, deeply loved. People have died waiting to know what went on."

"How sad. But Landry told us Lady Adelaide died well before his Aunt Moyra."

"And that creates the biggest question of all. What pieces did Moyra pick up and what others did she leave to simply fade away? Think of the genealogical and family history possibilities, Julie. A house locked up for decades, no one knows what's happened. A wealthy family, no news in or out ..." He gave me a wistful look, one that settled on me first and then went past me to settle on a set of twelve eighteenth century poetry tomes behind my left shoulder.

Bertie was right.

And there it was; the poignant family history question that needed an answer. Any genealogist worth their salt would expect it.

I gave Bertie a determined look. "If anyone can figure this out, it's the team from GGRS."

***

Greymore Hall, Caretaker's Cottage (Under Renovation). 2:00 a.m.

Ewan agreed to sleep in the caretaker's cottage so we could put Landry up in a main house guestroom. We'd lost many guestrooms when my father and Maude chose to live in their respective, newly renovated suites on the top floor where I'd repurposed the space for two large flats. That meant that with our large guest list for the Christmas dinner, we were one room short once Landry showed up. Ewan had not yet unpacked his overnight bag so it all made perfect sense. He didn't mind that the caretaker's cottage had one room still needing plastering and a couple of light fixtures were still missing.

Unfortunately, we soon had more to worry about than some tacky plaster and a couple of holes in the wall.

It was like déjà vu in Ewan's aunt's holiday cottage as I stood together with Gertie, both in our bathrobes, looking at something very odd. We stared up at a huge hole in the ceiling. The problem was, the water pipes were older than we knew and gave way once they froze and burst in the cold. That meant that a load of semi-icy water had rained down upon poor Ewan, asleep in bed, making for a rather rude awakening.

We had his feet in a bucket of hot water, and wrapped him in warm towels and blankets. We sat him in the rocking chair by the gas fireplace turned on high.

"I'm sure I'd have a snide comment or two, but my teeth are chattering so much I don't think I'd be able to emit a coherent sentence," Ewan said.

"Oh, come on. You don't look that cold," Gertie said in a mocking tone.

"How would you like to be tucked up in bed, just drifting off into blissful sleep after a wonderful Christmas dinner and then Wham! A bathtub full–"

"It wasn't a bathtub, only pipes–"

"Of cold water splashes down over your duvet, soaking you right through." Ewan looked downcast, obviously trolling for sympathy.

Aunt Edwina would be shocked.

I was sympathetic. "I'm just glad nothing fell on you except for the water. What if a piece of heavy pipe had come loose and–"

Ewan, the sturdy, strong and reliable, took it all in good stride. He issued me a calm grin. "Well, it didn't. And it gave me a chance to see you two lovely ladies one more time this evening."

"Try morning," I said. I peered outside the curtains and saw that it was still pitch black outside.

"Happy Boxing Day!" we all chorused together. It was impossible not to laugh.

"So what are we going to do now?" I asked.

"Ewan's certainly not coming into my room," Gertie said. "I know, he can bunk with Fred. His room has two twin beds and he didn't bring a plus one, so you're all set."

Ewan's face fell. "You give me a choice of having my ear talked off the entire night or sleeping on the pullout sofa in the former servants' hall? I'm taking the pullout sofa."

More laughter. It actually wasn't that bad in the end because my father had a spare room in his suite and was more than happy to put Ewan up. It was interesting how Ewan could only take a limited amount of Fred's nonstop verbiage; I just found it to be an interesting background patter after a while and let it run, kind of like comforting background music. Fred's topics were always interesting, they were just punctuated with far too many effervescent adjectives than necessary.

Once we delivered Ewan to my father's suite's front door, Gertie and I headed back to the guest rooms we were occupying over Christmas. I turned to her and said, "That was an unexpected surprise. It means only one more to go."

"Between Landry's arrival and Ewan's waterbed experience, what else could happen?" She looked at me with focused eyes.

"Harvey and the Major are doing something special for all of us later this morning. I don't know anything more than that."

The last time Harvey and the Major had helped us out with a genealogy research trip, I'd ended up coming home with Pamela Fulham in the back of a troop transport vehicle converted into a luxury motorhome.

"Right then. We're all sorted." Gertie tied her bathrobe belt around herself a bit tighter. I could tell she was tired because her eyes looked slightly puffy. She was too tired to even question the pending surprise for Boxing Day. It was likely a wise decision.

It was time for all of us to get back into our beds.

***

Dining Room. Boxing Day. 11:37 a.m.

"So Boxing Day was actually created because it meant that the masters of the manor house would box up leftovers from their dinner plus a small money gift and give it to the servants for their own day off?" Landry looked incredulous.

"That is correct." Jacques had patiently explained it to him twice already.

"Well, I'll be schnookered. I had no idea. I just thought it was a time to clear away the boxes from opened presents," Landry said.

"No, I'm afraid that North American holiday is based upon deep-rooted English aristocratic tradition," Jacques replied.

"I don't know if it's a holiday in the United States, but I know in Canada most people take it off as a stat." Landry leaned back and pushed his plate away, emitting a gentle sigh of satisfaction. The kitchen staff had outdone themselves yet again with an incredible breakfast, both hot and continental meals were on offer. Everyone had their fill and it was now just down to finishing up beverages and planning to lift anchor for what was next.

Jacques looked confused. "Pardon me, but a 'stat'? Did you mean statistic?"

Landry chuckled. "No, not statistic. Statutory holiday. I think over here you called them bank holidays?"

"I see. Here I was thinking that you took some odd tally of days of the year in your part of the world."

"No, sir. It's just a holiday as far as I know. But nothing like a Thanksgiving," Landry said.

"In Canada they celebrate their Thanksgiving mid-October but America's is later November, correct?" Ewan asked.

"Correct," Landry said. "In the US, Thanksgiving is nearly as big as Christmas. We take the last Thursday of every November for Thanksgiving and then on Friday we go shopping for Christmas presents."

"People get a day off to go shopping?" Maude was stunned.

"Many do. It's called 'Black Friday' because that's the day retailers expect to get their bottom lines into the black for their year because of all the shopping done that day."

"Home of the doorbuster sales, correct?" I asked with a smile. "Gertie and I were at boarding school in America."

"You got it. It used to be jampacked at the malls, but nowadays folks do a lot of online shopping. It cuts down the arguments between customers scuffling over that green argyle sweater marked down ninety-percent."

The contrast between two cultures, actually three cultures, all of which spoke the English language, had become rapidly apparent to us. I think that's what I liked about family history so much: one always learned things about other people and places through delving into ancestors' backgrounds. And it wasn't enough to just make a cursory note and say 'yes he was from Minnesota' or 'she once owned a fishing vessel based in Nova Scotia'. To do right and proper genealogy, one had to go beyond merely mentioning the place name. To learn more about what one's ancestor found, felt, and discovered as they lived, albeit in far less technologically advanced times, it was important to learn about the town itself. One must learn about the state or the province, understand the country and its customs. Learning these things helped researchers understand what their ancestors embraced and resisted when they were in a strange land. Foreign cultures could explain why an ancestor never celebrated birthdays, preferred to travel by bicycle instead of train, and never wanted their photo taken. On a bit of the smaller scale, I now understood why one of my great-grandfather's diaries went on and on about the importance of proper animal husbandry. As it turned out, he spent time in a tiny village in France with a world-renowned veterinarian who frequently lectured to encourage the decent and humane treatment of all animals, whether they were working on the farm or merely pets. Family history research also helped explain why the Major's dearly departed mother had a fondness for embroidered cushion making; she'd spent time in Portugal with a craftswoman who taught her top notch skills. All of my ancestors' portraits that hung at Greymore Hall carried a feather quill in their hand. It signified that they were learned, well-traveled people who enjoyed writing while away on their grand tours of Europe and Africa. This passion for travel was passed along from generation to generation. Bertie's family, on the other hand, happened to be extremely interested in astronomy and that's why his family portraits showed starry skies, maps and globes, both on tables and in various backgrounds. All of this was simply fascinating and literally millions of untold family histories awaited discovery by our GGRS team right here at Greymore Hall. Technology and sound research made it all possible.

I couldn't be quite certain, but thought I heard the sound of bells outside.

I wasn't the only one.

A few heads leaned to the side, followed by people getting up and going to the window. Everyone was excited to see the Major and Harvey draw up with two large black Shire horses, each with four white stockings and white blaze, pulling a hay wagon filled with loose straw, rolling along on snow-defying studded tires. The horses' harnesses had bells all over and they both looked quite content.

Each Shire had a blanket clip, meaning the winter coat was shorn under the horse's chin, neck, chest and belly to ensure he didn't get dangerously sweaty while working. A blanket would keep them warm when the horses weren't working.

The Major waved at us through the window and beckoned for us to come outside.

"Hats, scarves, and gloves everyone!" I called out, turning to face the eager group of people.

The throng of people murmured excitedly. I smiled as I saw the long row of nose prints they'd left on the windowpane, the seniors among us leaving the best impressions of all.

It was a crowd filled with good cheer that headed for the outdoor gear stored in the mud room. I knew the Major had already been around the fields a couple of times this morning with the tractor, heavy chains around its tires. He said he was clearing a path for the walkers, affectionately known as the 'Terrified Trotters' ever since he and Harvey had brought in an unexpected World War Two tank headed directly for them under its own steam. Now I knew the real reason for his early-morning work. He'd been out clearing the results of our incredibly large snowstorm so we could all enjoy a sleigh ride complete with bells, straw, and authentic draft horses.

Ewan and I were left alone in the room for a slight moment, the others having literally stampeded out like little children to get ready for their surprise sleigh ride.

"I hope you got some sleep last night once we rescued you from your waterbed," I offered.

"No problem. I managed to get about six hours sleep, so I'll survive."

"I feel absolutely terrible. You've been so helpful, a real friend for us on our family history adventures."

A thought ran across his face. "You could make it up to me," Ewan said.

"I'd like to. Very much," I said.

"Come with me to Yorkshire."

"Yorkshire?" His suggestion was rather unexpected.

"Yes, I'd like a second opinion on that pre-house clearance inventory Fred's put me on to."

"I don't know, Ewan. Gertie has more knowledge of old silver than I do."

"I think you'd be better company." His eyes were kind. "For me."

"That's not a day trip. We'd have to stay overnight."

"Of course. And I'd book the hotel." Our eyes caught in a lock. He realized what he'd just implied. "Goodness, two separate rooms of course." He cleared his throat as if for emphasis.

I just stared back at him. Pondering. Wondering. Curious. Anxious. Shy. Jaded. Enticed?

"I've got a load of furniture to deliver up to a dealer in the city of York. We'll go along and then look at the house clearance inventory the next day."

I held out my right hand. "And this cleans the slate?"

Ewan nodded. "I will never again mention the word 'waterbed' in your presence."

"Done."

We shook on it.

He smiled. "The whole event made for a most memorable evening."

"It certainly wasn't intentional. I hope you know that."

He moved closer towards me standing by the window. "Of course it wasn't." For some inexplicable reason—maybe it was the sunlight, maybe it was a shadow dancing off the glass pane—we both saw the mistletoe at the same time. It was one of those stolen moments when we found ourselves alone, away from the visitor chaos and holiday cheer. It was easy for Ewan to bend his head down towards mine and I knew what was coming next. I smiled back up at him and …

"Now where the heck did I put my hat?" Landry's booming voice announced.

Ewan and I each took a startled step backwards.

"Um, I think you left it over on the side table, just to the right of that wingback chair," I said.

"You're right. I see it now. Gotcha!" Landry picked up his hat then came over to shake my hand. "I can't thank you enough for rescuing me last night. You showed me some real hospitality, without even knowing my name or where I was from."

I stared down at the big cowboy hat in his hand. "I kind of had an inkling."

"There's lots of other places besides Texas that use cowboy hats," Landry said.

"Call it a lucky guess," Ewan offered.

"Am I that obvious?" Landry asked.

"Let's just say if there was one stranded traveler in the world that I could choose to show up on Greymore Hall's doorstep on Christmas Day, I would choose you." I gave Landry a friendly smile back.

"That's mighty kind of you." Landry put on his hat, touching the brim as he nodded at both Ewan and I. "And now, I'll let you two get back to whatever you were doing." He gave us both a wink. Then he slipped out of the room.

I called out after him. "Landry, we weren't doing anything, we were just–"

Ewan held my hands. "Julie. Let it go. He's gone."

"Are we that obvious?" I looked up at him with wide open eyes.

"And if we were, what's wrong with that?" Ewan asked.

"Nothing, I suppose."

Ewan looked heavenward. "Julie, I don't want to be your 'supposed' anything. I want to be your choice. But as I've said before, let me know when you're ready for more. You're one-hundred percent in the driver's seat."

I put a gentle hand to his cheek. "Oh, Ewan. Thank you for being you."

Chapter 6

─────

Behind Greymore Hall. 1:37 p.m.

Shire horses, sleigh, driver and rosy-cheeked passengers traveled around the back meadow circuit three times. The miniature goats likely thought we were all a bit daft going round and round with no final destination in mind. Never mind. All of us fell off the hay wagon, that is, except for Maude and Bertie who were the elegant ones right up front, clinging steadfast onto the wagon's frame.

Everyone had a fantastic time and straw was everywhere. Of course there were a few hijinks along the route; somehow my boots got filled with straw and Gertie had straw jammed inside the collar of her coat. Ewan had straw inside his gloves and the Major found some tucked inside his ear-flapped shearling hat. All the fresh air made us thirsty. When we drew into the back courtyard, everyone sensed that it was a good time to end the ride.

A couple of us stood up front with the Shire horses, patting their necks as a thank you for all of their hard work.

"What are their names, Harvey?" I asked, smiling at the bells jingling on the horses' harnesses.

"Bingo and Jim." Harvey joined us up front with the horses after making sure the wagon's brake was set. He also started patting the horses' necks in appreciation.

"I'll see if Jacques can rustle up an apple or two for them," I said.

"They'd like that. I'll make sure they both get a nice warm bran mash with their feed this afternoon too."

"They both certainly worked for it. I didn't know you kept horses at your place." Steam rose from the horses' flanks and Bingo emitted a soft sigh as the Major put a blanket over each equine's hindquarters to prevent their backs from seizing up in the cold.

"I don't. Just kept them as a boy back at my family's farm in Yorkshire. They're on loan from the local brewery. Sad though, it's now just down to Bingo and Jim here. They're both in their twenties now and have given a good lifetime of service to their owners."

"Draft horses are such kind, gentle giants. What are they, about eighteen hands tall?"

"Something like that."

I knew a hand was four inches and any horse over about sixteen and a half was considered quite tall. Eighteen hands and over was positively stratospheric.

"I hope everybody enjoyed themselves today," the Major offered.

"We all had a wonderful time. Did you want to join us for hot chocolate and some snacks?"

The men exchanged glances. There was some militaryesque telepathy going on, something I knew not to ask about because it was secret.

"We'll take a hot chocolate in a to-go cup. We've got to get these boys cooled down and then back home."

"On these roads?"

"I thought you knew," the Major said. "We trailered them in right before the storm. Their temporary home is inside the old Greymore stables out back. We bedded down a couple of spare looseboxes."

I smiled. "Oh, how fun. I thought I recognized the wagon. I remember Grandpa taking Gertie and I out in it when we were children."

"She finally notices. The Major and I've been tinkering with it for weeks now as a surprise. All we needed was the horsepower," Harvey said, eliciting a grin from the Major at the same time.

I looked at them, sunlight shining in my eyes. "Gentlemen, thank you. This was a wonderful Boxing Day idea." I caught a glimpse of a snowed-under horse trailer off in the distance at the corner of the yard.

"No sense in trying to haul the horses home today."

"You'd get about six feet outside the drive and then have to turn back." I knew the Major had done a great job with the estate's tractor clearing our yard and drive, but Oakhurst's roads were a different story. A call to the local roadworks wouldn't be appropriate if we could survive without them; the crews were just too busy at the moment. We could cope.

"Exactly." Harvey tipped his shearling hat at me.

The Major did the same.

"No worries. It's rather cozy here with all our guests. Bingo and Jim are very welcome, too."

Both men had shared a delightful experience with all of the guests snowbound at Greymore Hall. Thanks to them, we'd all enjoyed an incredibly pleasant time together.

Back inside the manor house, everyone clambered out of boots, coats, hats, gloves and scarves, retreating back into the large drawing room where Jacques had set up refreshment stations.

"Do you celebrate Christmas, Jacques?" Ewan asked, looking concerned at how busy Jacques appeared. Ewan took a tray of warm cookies from him and helped arrange it with the others on a nearby table covered in an embroidered cloth showcasing bright wildflowers.

"I have no family here in England except for the people at Greymore Hall. I am very happy to share the day with them," he said with a pert little smile.

"But you're working," Ewan said.

"I'm helping people enjoy themselves. I look at it in a different way. I shall take some time off after the holiday season and once the snow has left. Two weeks in Barbados." He beamed.

"Now that sounds like fun," I said.

"Yes, my sister lives there with her family and I visit once a year."

Maude shushed everybody, then increased the volume on the television so we could hear what the announcer in her bright emerald green business suit was sharing with the world:

"Southern England is in for a big melt starting later this afternoon, with temperatures zooming up thermometers and expecting to be in high melt territory for the rest of the week. Expect flooding in low-lying areas and after an enormous Christmas delay, perhaps people can start finding their vehicles that were abandoned in so many snowdrifts all over multiple counties. City works yards are reporting schedules slowly getting back to normal ..."

"Well, finally I'll be able to get my vehicle back on the road again," Landry said with a contented sigh. "Although, I will be sad to leave you folks. You've been awfully kind."

Ewan smiled, as did the rest of us.

"What?" Landry was a bit confused.

Fred decided to tackle it. "My Texan friend, permit me to explain it in this manner. The radio, not precisely two minutes and forty seconds gone by, reported an enormous snowstorm which yielded unheard of sized snowdrifts. Therefore, I put it to you that it is simply not possible to expect to depart our fair lands for at least another two days. Even if we had exceedingly tropical weather starting in the next five minutes, there is simply too much of the frozen, white powdery stuff on the ground to disappear with such unbidden haste."

Landry narrowed his eyes and then chuckled. "In other words, I'm stuck here for another forty-eight hours."

Fred nodded, likely amazed that Landry had consolidated his last paragraph into a few words on the fly.

It wasn't hard to do, yet one had to give it full attention.

That said, I'd actually been quite impressed with Fred on the sleigh ride; he wasn't exactly the rough-and-tumble type, but he got right in on the fun stuffing straw down Constable Snowdrop's back. Win one for the good guys. I was still smarting at the ridiculous parking ticket Constable Snowdrop issued me when an unexpected museum exhibit army tank was parked on Greymore's back meadow, apparently without the proper permit.

"Well, there's nothing wrong with that. I'm sure we can find a few things to do," Landry said in a jolly voice.

Maude straightened up and gave an expectant look to Bertie. It was obvious they'd concocted something between them, in a quiet, behind-the-scenes manner.

Bertie stood up, cup of warm hot chocolate in his hand. "Landry, I would highly recommend that you seize the opportunity to avail yourself of the wonderful resources at the Greymore Genealogy Research Site."

Landry put up both his palms as if to shield himself. "Hey, I'm no researcher. I know my way around computers and security systems, but I have high respect for those people who get into the old census records and such. I would have no clue where to start."

"You are a bright young man. You can certainly learn the basics in no time at all," Maude said with an encouraging voice.

"Give this lady a new diamond necklace. Call me a bright young man any day and you'll be my friend forever." Landry gave Maude an incredibly kind grin. Perhaps it was too much of an over-compliment?

Maude smiled, yet wasn't rattled or deterred. That was why she was so effective at managing the research site, keeping things on an even keel no matter the research panic, discovery or disappointment. "Indeed. And don't underestimate your skills. If you have computer knowledge, it will make your learning even easier because a lot of the research is done online these days. Just don't think that everything's available at the touch of a button. You have to put in the hours, days, months and many years to assemble a full family tree."

"There are some things you need to find out immediately," Bertie said. He had that look about him, the one that said 'please do take my sage advice and heed it'. I'd seen that look before, when he was helping me out of a jam, either with my ex, a painting that was going a bit south or an architectural drawing change for the renovations done at Greymore Hall in need of a bit more revision.

"I appreciate your hospitality but I didn't come here looking to do a family tree. I'm here to clear up my aunt's estate. I'm happy to do that, but I have my own mobile cybersecurity business that I have to run while I'm here," Landry admitted.

"You're a cybersecurity consultant?" I asked.

Landry nodded. "Job security for life."

Now other ears were wagging.

"So you prevent all the nefarious people trying to hack into systems and steal personal data, credit card information, things like that?" Fred asked.

"Yes, among other things. I mainly deal with large public companies looking to be proactive rather than reactive with their IT systems," Landry said.

"I'll bet there's no shortage of demand for your services," Ewan said.

"As I said, job security for life. So long as I have a laptop and internet connection, I can work from anywhere in the world. It's a sweet gig." Landry smiled.

"We had a local expert come and look at Greymore's systems before opening because of all the personal data here at the research site. We've also trained staff on respecting the privacy policy enforced in Europe and other countries," I said.

"Mistakes can happen, but generally you're on the right track." Landry said. He'd likely given that spiel about a thousand and nineteen times.

"I should hire you for the antiques shop website. It's in dire need of an overhaul," Ewan said.

Landry chuckled. "I don't do web design, just prevent the bad guys from gaining access. I could refer you to a great vendor who can help ..."

"Fine. I have to get my online store up to the next level, take credit card payments, blogging, things like that."

"Sure. There's a number of payment apps you can–"

"Gentlemen ..." Bertie interrupted using his gentle, aristocratic persuasion that was always very effective. "I would highly recommend you look for any marriage records of Lady Adelaide and also of your Aunt Moyra."

"The two mysterious ladies," Landry said. He then shot a puzzled look at Bertie. "Why marriage records?"

"Because of the circumstances. An executor doing his job would want to ensure no one claims later on that they would have contested the will, had they known their true lineage."

"Don't I just place an ad in the local paper?" Landry asked.

"You can. But I always say better to be forewarned, than in for a nasty surprise," Maude added.

Gertie added her two cents. "Perhaps the parish priest knew their secrets and recorded their marriages in his register without broadcasting it to the world."

"Could people marry under assumed names in the twentieth century?" Ewan asked.

Gertie nodded. "It was harder to do once the population as a whole could read and write, but it still happened. Like you said, mistakes can happen and documents can be forged."

"I'll bet there's some kind of records left," I said. "For a love that runs that deep, one that's worth defying your wealthy father who will subsequently disinherit you ... I would expect at least some kind of letters were kept."

"You mean between Lady Adelaide and the man she loved?" Ewan asked.

"Yes. Perhaps they did marry in secret," I said.

"But there was a society wedding at her father's behest," Bertie added.

"Who knows. This could be quite a romantic saga," Gertie observed, "and all happening decades ago when life was so much more innocent than it is today."

"I agree. A deep love makes people keeps letters. It begs for mementos and souvenirs to be squirreled away," Maude said. "No true heart can deny it."

Gertie and I swooned with delight at the prospect of such a committed love. It was rare in any century for a deep love to transcend social class, status, money, family and friends.

Bertie sealed the deal. "Landry, you need to know if either woman married in order to properly carry out your duties. And remember, there is an additional duty to record the detailed family lives of aristocrats running a large estate. Think of all the workers on the estate, the people who rented land and cottages, how the village economy depended upon the lord and lady of the manor. It's critical social history."

Landry slumped down in the computer chair he occupied and raised his hands in defeat. "All right, y'all convinced me beyond a reasonable doubt. Let me work at a computer some more, and with your help, let's see what we can find."

"Excellent!" we all replied in unison. It was wonderful to hear how the GGRS team all thought alike on this important commitment to family history research.

❖❖❖

Research Site. 2:57 p.m.

Jacques approached me with trepidation.

I was deep into a fascinating article about 1950s women's industrial factory work. I looked up when I heard his polite cough, giving him an inquisitive glance. "You look like a man who's just seen the ghost of turkeys past," I teased.

"It's rather unfortunate, Julie. I'm afraid we have an incident in the kitchen."

I jumped up like I was in a hot seat, scurrying alongside Jacques to find out what the drama was about. "I take it there is something quite serious going on, I mean, for you to come and get me for a kitchen matter–"

He sighed. "It is far more serious than a soggy Victoria sponge cake."

"Oh dear."

"It's donuts."

"Donuts?"

He gave me a solemn look. "I'm afraid one of our rather overenthusiastic staff trainees has overfilled the batter container for the donut machine."

"I see."

"You will momentarily. We have avoided a huge mess, largely due to the efforts of a willing kitchen team. However, I'm afraid we have rather a lot of donuts to consume in rapid fashion."

"You're not just talking the 'royal we', as in you and I, are you?" I teased.

"I am sorry to report it's far worse than Christmas feast leftovers requiring consumption," he said in a glum voice.

I narrowed my eyes. "Just how many donuts are we talking?"

"I think you should judge for yourself," he said. Jacques led me into the kitchen and I then saw how serious the excessive batter issue really was.

Jacques protectively stood next to a woman in her late sixties who looked rather guilty. She was a kindly woman, her hair in a low, netted bun at the back of her neck, pleasant smile and hazel eyes. Her name tag said 'Rose'.

Rose spoke with a trembling voice. "I-I didn't want to waste any. I didn't have my glasses on and my cataracts are getting worse, so I accidentally quadrupled the amount of flour. Once I realized what I'd done, I had to make up all the other ingredients. It means we have far more donuts than we need. I'm so very sorry."

It was impossible to be angry. This was simply, well … 'donutgate'.

"Mistakes happen. It's good of you to be here over the holidays. Now let's just focus on not letting this food go to waste," I said.

I gestured to the stacks of donuts that they had stabilized by running through vertically anchored stainless steel rods from the barbecue shelves we used in the summer. There must've been hundreds and they were everywhere. Donuts on the counter. Donuts on the tables. Donuts double-stacked on cooling racks over the stove. There were donuts on chairs, donuts hanging from coat hooks and for all I knew there were probably donuts in the freezer jostling for space amongst premade lasagna and casseroles. It was too many donuts. All of them were plain sugar-glazed and definitely needed to be eaten while they were fresh. There was only one thing I could do to fix this problem.

I turned to Jacques and said, "Let's package all these up in bakery boxes. Find Constable Snowdrop and tell him he has a delivery to make to the local police detachment, retirement homes, youth clubs and food bank. Harvey can take him there with the big farm tractor if he needs help keeping safe on the snowy roads."

"I was worried sick I'd be fired over this donut fiasco," Rose said. Her face looked so relieved.

"You've just made a lot of law enforcement officers exceedingly happy," I said.

"It just got out of hand. Once I started increasing ingredients, it took over and then this happened. I'm ever so sorry."

"It's alright, Rose. Let's just focus on getting the donuts to a good home." I put a kind hand on her shoulder.

Shades of Lettucegate with Lance and Algy Holgarth at Holgarth Hall during our recent trip to carry out Aunt Edwina's family history treasure hunt.

The kitchen phone rang and I happened to be close by, so I answered it.

"Julie?" I heard my father's voice.

"Hi Dad. Is everything all right?"

"Oh yes, everything's fine. I just have a rather odd visitor in my room."

"Fred didn't bring Barnaby along and forget to tell us, did he?" I wouldn't put it past the long-talking solicitor to try and smuggle in his potbellied pig for the holiday. We all knew how fond he was of his pet.

"No, no. Nothing like that," my father said.

Come to think of it, Fred had his own guestroom here at Greymore to wait out the storm, so it didn't seem likely that Barnaby would be in my father's suite on a different floor. However the pig was quite adept at opening doors, so I wouldn't put it past him to figure out the elevator. But Fred hadn't brought Barnaby along in his car. What on earth?

Julie, you are now expending mental energy deciphering the perambulations of a potbellied pig.

Fred likely had someone from the ballet school in Plumsden taking care of Barnaby and Holly over Christmas.

"So what's the actual problem, Dad?" I was thinking burned-out lightbulb or leaky faucet.

What I got was a complete surprise.

"Well, you see, it's like this. There is an owl in my room."

A person could have knocked me over with a stack of glazed donuts. "An owl. A live owl? I'll be right there."

Two minutes later I was up on the top floor of Greymore Hall, standing beside my father and looking at an owl with very yellow eyes, blinking at each opportune moment. It had a bright orange beak, and a mottled brown and grey body, one that would blend in perfectly with tree bark.

"How fascinating. And what a beautiful bird. But how on earth did it get inside your suite?" At present the bird was perched on top of the ceiling fan, looking down on us all. Luckily the ceiling fan wasn't turned on due to it being winter time, and I was thankful for that small mercy. I didn't believe the owl would appreciate being spun around like a vinyl record on an unforgiving turntable.

My father shook his head and spread his hands wide. "Well, I noticed that the owl was roosting on a tree very close to my window. I enjoyed watching it every night, and then when I opened the window for a few moments this afternoon just to get some fresh air inside, he unexpectedly flew in."

"Just like that?"

"Just like that. Silently glided in. I promise."

"Well, he cannot stay in your room."

"Thank you, Miss Obvious."

At this very moment, the owl, about a foot tall, blinked his yellow eyes. The bird of prey then let loose a quick, violent river of white liquid from his bottom that landed on the spanking new carpet below.

"I can't imagine that's going to be easy to get out of the rug," my father said using his dry wit.

"No, I imagine it's not. Is it vinegar, water, hairspray?" I wondered aloud.

"Hairspray's for ballpoint pen. I don't think water would be strong enough and acidic vinegar might fade the carpet," he said.

It was a deep subject to ponder.

The bird blinked his yellow eyes once again. It was amazing how wise these birds looked, without even uttering a single sentence or sound. They were majestic creatures and our first-order of business was to get him back outside in the wild where he belonged.

"Have you opened the window again to try and get him to fly outside?" I asked.

"No. He was just sitting up there all quietly and I thought I'd phone you first."

"Thanks for that."

My father got an impish smile at the side of his face. "I thought it would be rather interesting to see who you considered phoning first to resolve this matter."

"Well it's not Fred Todling or Constable Snowdrop. My money's on Jacques or Maude. They're the most sensible, experienced people we've got on site. Ewan's a good choice as well."

My father settled down in an armchair. He looked a bit tired. "I'll leave you to it. I don't want anywhere near those talons."

"I don't think he's going to attack you, Dad."

He waved the suggestion away. "Get somebody younger in here to handle this one. Please."

I thought I would try the obvious first, and wandered over to the window and pulled it open. I looked back up at the owl, and then over to the window, then back to the owl again. No dice. The owl's eyes were now shut and it looked like he was happy roosting there in his nice, new warm spot, high up near the ceiling.

I picked up the phone and rang down to donut-fest. "Jacques? Can you please bring Maude upstairs to my father's suite on the double? Yes, the donuts are going to have to wait."

***

Greymore Hall's Front Drive. 10:37 p.m.

The tow truck's bright headlights broke the darkness. We didn't leave the Christmas lights on all night because it was a waste of electricity. Apart from Christmas Day and New Year's Eve, they were turned off promptly at 10:00 p.m. each night.

One creature that I knew wouldn't be impeded by the darkness was our new friend, the owl. After a bit of cajoling using a couple of large potted palm leaves, we'd managed to coax the owl safely outside. I instructed Jacques to get screens reinstalled on my father's windows as soon as possible. When we'd done the initial renovations, the screens were there but my father had insisted on removing a couple of them, claiming they were obscuring his pastoral view. His choice now was to either enjoy the view from a non-opening picture window that didn't have a screen or deal with the owl's next up-close and personal visit on his own. Funnily enough, it turned out that Dad was now amenable to the screens. Maude had addressed the carpet goo using some type of homemade cleaning concoction she'd learned from her mother. All was well again. It had been quite the day.

I ended up on the front steps with Ewan, both of us doing last minute security checks for the building. I went down to greet the tow truck driver, assuming that he had Landry's SUV hitched up behind him. I was right on the money, and spoke to the tow truck driver, a pleasant man with a plaid cap and scarf. We agreed he should deposit the SUV in a spare parking space off to the left of the building. Apart from being covered in a bit of icy snow, the vehicle didn't look that worse for wear. I sure wouldn't want to sit on those stiff leather seats though; they looked awfully cold.

The big melt was starting and it wasn't super freezing cold outside anymore during the day. However, it would be a day before longer distance travel would be safe. There was still a lot of white stuff cloaking our estate, the countryside and the nation.

Ewan came up next to me. "So, they finally located Landry's vehicle?"

"Apparently it was caught inside a six-foot snowdrift, at least that's what the driver claimed. Landry must've just parked in the wrong place at the wrong time. He left it in a high wind area that was susceptible to tall drifts."

"I suppose it didn't help too much that he's a tourist."

"Exactly. People from around here wouldn't drive west from London to get to Newmarket in Suffolk."

We watched the tow truck driver expertly deposit Landry's rental SUV exactly where we agreed. I went over and gave him our thanks, offering him a cup of tea. He pointed to the thermos beside him and politely refused, claiming he had twelve other stranded vehicles to deal with in the next eight hours. He would be busy.

"At least take some donuts, please," I implored, thinking that this was an incredible opportunity to get rid of about fifty-three thousand of them from our kitchen.

The driver waited as I dashed inside and made up a generous care package for him. The roads were starting to get a little bit slushy and although the air was slightly crisp, I knew that even better, clearer days were ahead.

Ewan and I watched the tow truck driver depart. We both turned towards each other at the same time, trying to get back inside the building and lock the last set of doors. We ended up bumping heads and stumbled back, groaning. It wasn't elegant, but as Ewan put his hands on my shoulders to steady us both, I felt a warm rush of friendship go through me. I also felt something else I couldn't quite put my finger on ... but I knew it was good.

"So, a sleigh ride, an overabundance of donuts and a visiting wild owl. Not exactly what you expected at Greymore Hall today, did you?" he asked with a smile.

I loved the way his eyes got crinkly in the corners when he smiled.

"No. Every day is turning out to be an adventure here at Greymore."

"You missed all the excitement in the drawing room when you left to deal with the owl upstairs."

"What? Did you win at charades?"

He shook his head. "Nope. Fred announced that he has a speaking role in the upcoming ballet company performance." Ewan couldn't wipe off his grin.

Fred had generously sponsored the ballet company through his law firm, but I had no idea he was taking on a more active role besides wearing a flashy logo'd leisure suit outside of office hours.

"He says he has to rehearse, and it's very important he gets into character before treading the boards." Ewan got a glint in his eye. "I'd pay a month's shop revenue to see him in a leotard. Do you think he has to wear tights?"

"What role, exactly, is Fred taking on?" I asked.

"Actually, there's two. He's playing a tree and a dead body."

"And I'm assuming the talking part goes to the tree?" I asked.

"Apparently so."

"You are so making that up."

"No, I am not. Go ask the man yourself."

"It's late. There's no way I'm going hunting for a solicitor right now to ask about his extracurricular activities. It's time to call it a night."

Ewan held the door for me like the gentleman he was, and we went inside. Both of us were more than ready to go to our respective rooms and prepare for whatever tomorrow might bring.

Chapter 7

————

GGRS. Next Morning.

We took our midmorning break with goats, specifically marzipan goats. They were Maude's special holiday treat and she made one for each of us. The sweet almond paste, formed into plump, individual figurines, made for an amusing and delectable snack.

"I've heard of peppermint pigs and Christmas crackers, but not marzipan goats. What's with this?" Landry asked.

Maude smiled. "It's a leftover from Lady Edwina's Sherry Club's holiday tradition. I made them once, and only on a lark, but they were so popular that I just continued from year to year. I also do parrots, llamas and clown fish."

"What are you smiling about?" Gertie asked me.

"Too many things. The donuts, the owl, Fred's ballet role, or rather dual role," I said.

"Yes, that came out over canasta and carbohydrates yesterday. You weren't in the room at the time."

"I expect we'll receive free tickets?"

"Are you going to go?" Gertie asked. "I, for one, wouldn't miss it for the world."

I looked over at Landry and saw that he was smiling about it as well. "So what's your family background?" I asked our larger-than-life Texan visitor.

He leaned back in his chair and put his fingers over his wide belt buckle. "I come from an old department store family. My grandfather, Sheridan Jackson, opened up one of the early mail-order catalog businesses in Texas in 1925. He sold everything under the sun including stoves, ladies undergarments, combs, projectors, and seed storage equipment. Some of the old catalogs are just fascinating reading. Everything in the catalog was hand-drawn, the women's faces cut out of studio model photos and pasted over top of garment drawings. Kind of freaky, actually."

This was fascinating stuff, kind of like a twentieth century smorgasbord of retailing.

"Do you still have the store?" Gertie asked.

"Not as it was. Big Daddy, er, that's my father, Travis, actually closed the store when he saw online shopping taking over. Now it's just a heritage boutique selling our forty-nine most popular items including almond bark, cashmere scarves, cotton socks, and tent fly sheets. Dad retired a few years ago and we've got good management in place."

"That's quite an eclectic mix of products for sale." Gertie looked impressed. She always liked oddities and a mixture of candy, clothes and camping definitely qualified.

"You could say that. I like the fact that we kept the tradition going and evolved with the times. We knew we couldn't keep going as we were, so we just put the bestsellers online." He popped his marzipan miniature goat into his mouth. The look of rapture on his face was something all of us had experienced that morning consuming our own marzipan treats.

I was still stuck at 'Big Daddy'. Ewan mouthed the two words at me. I glared back at his goofy expression. One had to be respectful of local names, no matter from where the person originated.

"And how did you get to be so close with your Aunt Moyra?" I asked Landry.

"My father said I should make the effort because she was special. I wasn't told anything else. As it turned out, Aunt Moyra was a fine woman. I sent her a Christmas card and a detailed letter three times a year, just like clockwork. We did speak online throughout the year, but I never saw more than her mantelpiece and a couple of bookshelves with some knickknacks behind her. That's why I had no idea how big the estate was, or even the house was. All I ever knew was that she was caring for an older lady. The solicitors told me nothing about the estate, just that they'd reveal all when we met face to face."

"You thought your Aunt Moyra was just working as a nurse in a private home?" Gertie asked.

"Exactly. Middle-class, clean and somebody that needed caring for, but none of this aristocratic estate nonsense." Landry looked over at Bertie with a guilty expression on his face and gave a sheepish grin. "No offense intended."

"Certainly none taken. We're trying to figure out a family mystery, and that usually entails putting all of one's cards on the table," Bertie said.

"I appreciate you being so generous with your time and your knowledge. All of you." Landry spread his hands wide. "You've really taken me under your collective wing, so to speak."

"It's important to understand that Lady Adelaide Roycetonne of Roycetonne House was likely the most famed recluse in this county, if not the country. She lost her family—her husband was a rich Marquis and they had two daughters—in an horrific fire at Roycetonne House in 1941. Lady Adelaide herself was last seen in public in 1961. The rumor was she shut herself off from society to mourn what she lost and then the world never saw the wealthy, elegant lady ever again." Bertie's succinct explanation revealed more of what Aunt Moyra dealt with as she cared for Lady Adelaide. The emotional aftermath must have been awful.

We left the breakroom, heading out to the research area. Maude gestured for us to come over to a computer where she had a picture from a 1940s newspaper up on screen. "I found one of Lady Adelaide. The newspaper ran a photo of her the day after the fire in 1941 and it was captioned, 'Lady Adelaide was photographed crying over the smoldering ruins of the burned section of the house'."

"Meaning not all of the house went up in flames?" I asked.

"No, it did not. Which is why she could keep on living there. There were some workmen who moved in and out right after the fire, but no one knows what state the house is in today. The paper ran a follow up piece in 2015 but was refused all interview requests. The solicitor even sent a stern cease and desist letter when the newspaper flew a drone over the manor house."

"Does anyone know how big the house is?" Landry asked.

All eyes went to Bertie. He nodded. Of course he would know. "When Roycetonne House was built, the plan showed 112 rooms, thirty-four of which were bedrooms."

"Thirty-four bedrooms?" Landry asked.

"Indeed. But apart from what the family showed outside the front gates, what went on inside the house remains a mystery." I could tell Bertie was both intrigued and saddened at what happened to one of his set.

"Did you ever meet Lady Adelaide?" I asked Bertie.

"My grandfather did, when she was quite young. My father only ever saw her from afar and I certainly never did. No one even knew she had a nurse later in life."

"It's sad how some seniors drift away from society and just don't want to engage anymore," Gertie said.

My father nodded. "Seniors need a good group of friends, family, and activities to make them feel welcome and useful. It's tough when you're on your own, your spouse and friends have already passed away, and you don't really have any hobbies. You're retired from work and perhaps live out in the country all by yourself. That's when visits from the postman and the milkmen get to be the highlights of your week."

We all pondered that for a moment. It wasn't right for people to be lonely. "Well, we try really hard at GGRS to engage our seniors. Everyone's welcome," Gertie said in her jolly voice.

"And a fine job y'all are doing," Landry said. "This place is a real boon for the community."

My heart swelled with joy. I was so happy to be fulfilling Aunt Edwina's legacy. It was just proven right in front of me by a complete stranger, a member of the public we'd hoped to help. Well, I supposed we couldn't call Landry a stranger any longer, but it wasn't like we'd planned his visit on our recent, snowy Christmas day.

"Come on Landry. Let's try and get this mystery figured out," I said.

"Yes, ma'am. Any and all guidance is greatly appreciated. I'm dreading what's up at the house for me to sift through. It sounds like I'll be there for five years." He looked at us guiltily. "Not that I don't love England, it's just that I've got a business to run. I don't know anything about old letters, genealogy, family history or the social history of the place ..."

Gertie and I exchanged a glance. Music—no, a symphony—to our ears. Landry's family history mystery was our golden opportunity and we were super curious. We both looked back at Landry the same time, saying in unison, "Can we come with you to help?"

"I couldn't possibly ask you to do that," Landry said.

"No, really, it's fine. It's what we do," I said.

"You mean you take in tall, snowy strangers for Christmas, give them a wonderful time and festive meals, a hayride, and then offer to help them research their own personal family history crisis all with a big smile and grin?"

The group of us from GGRS looked at each other and then we all looked back at Landry.

"Of course. It's just what we do," Gertie said with firm conviction.

❋❋❋

Maude gave us an overview of what she'd found online after an initial search. "The 1939 wartime register for all citizens and residents for ration booklets shows that Roycetonne House was primarily requisitioned for the duration of World War Two for artwork storage from London museums. No one was bombing the racetrack in Newmarket; the enemy was more keen on bombing armaments and plane-building factories much closer to London and right here in Kent."

"No noblesse oblige?" Bertie asked, referring to how many aris-tocrats felt they had to step up and offer their manor houses for as great a purpose as possible.

Maude nodded. "Not everyone in the wealthy set wanted to be part of the war effort housing soldiers in their homes."

"I believe Roycetonne House was used as an officers' respite. It didn't have extreme proximity to London so it wasn't requisitioned as a hospital or for regular troop relaxation. However, they did do something to help out by storing priceless, gilded canvases," Bertie said. "Scotford Castle did the same, but apparently Roycetonne House had more room for storing art than we did."

"Jealous a bit, Mister Aristo?" Gertie teased.

"Rather surprised, that's all," Bertie replied. "I didn't understand how they calculated their square footage, that's all."

"Oh look here. The article explains that the fire was caused by an army officer there on leave who was smoking a pipe," Maude said. "He left it unattended and the curtains caught on fire. Thank goodness the artwork was saved."

Bertie shook his head. "That's not what society said happened."

Landry straightened up in the rolling-caster computer chair he currently occupied. "That sounds like a convenient excuse."

"How do you mean?" Gertie asked.

"He means this," Bertie said, bringing over a book from one of Greymore's shelves. It was a large coffee-table book that profiled the fifty largest homes in the nation. Roycetonne House was on page eight.

Landry took the book from him and whistled between his teeth, a low, admiring sound. "I had no idea. I know you name all your houses and cottages over here, even the tiny ones, so I didn't think anything of the name 'Roycetonne House'. Our family's certainly never had any grandiose airs. Like I said before, all my conversations with my aunt were her sitting in front of a bookshelf with maybe a couple of framed photographs and a slew of trinkets behind the desk."

"It's important to note what the book says about the fire. It actually blames Lady Adelaide. They say it was arson she committed to get rid of her cruel husband, a man handpicked for her by her father. The fire killed her husband, the Marquis, all right, but it also snuffed life out of her two beloved daughters who weren't supposed to be at home that night. And that's when Lady Adelaide's reclusiveness began," Maude said.

"Did she suffer from mental illness?" I asked in a quiet voice.

"It's too early to see if she was branded a lunatic by her father. Those census records won't be released until a hundred years after they were taken, so 2041," Ewan said.

I shook my head. "You won't find them. The 1941 census wasn't taken because of the war."

"You're quite right, Julie," Gertie said.

I started, "We could try the local archives, her solicitor, her doctor–"

"Who may stonewall us due to doctor-patient confidentiality and attorney-client privilege," Gertie said.

Bertie looked up into the air, shaking his head. He simply couldn't relate to a life turned so sad. "It's all just so tragic."

"It was a doomed arranged marriage purely for the benefit of society," Ewan said. "People should be allowed to marry for love." His eyes held mine.

"I agree," Gertie said.

"Well, what's done is done. I don't know if we'll ever know the truth at this point," Bertie said. "Lady Adelaide and Moyra likely took that secret to their graves."

Landry was busy scrolling through his phone. He looked up at all of us clustered around the computer carrell. "There's one way to find out. Who wants to come with me on a road trip to Newmarket tomorrow?"

Chapter 8

Landry Jackson's SUV. Next Morning.

Another family history field trip. Bertie, Gertie and I were snugly settled against the heated seats in Landry's SUV. In case of an unexpected return blast of winter, we'd loaded up with a huge amount of emergency supplies, blankets and even emergency rations. Not that we had much to worry about; the roads were now all slushy and the big snowdrifts had melted down to half-size. It always bothered me looking at the aftermath of what was salted and gritted during storms; no one liked looking at the ugly brown mess once the melting started.

"Severs is meeting you there?" I asked Bertie, referring to his ex-security service driver.

"Yes. He'll be at Roycetonne House at noon with a hot meal. No one knows if any staff are there taking care of the kitchen right now, so the meal options may be slim pickings."

"Well, that's very kind of you, thank you," I said. I could tell Bertie was along partly out of curiosity and partly because he didn't want Gertie and I to be absconded by the tall Texan down some narrow little dark road. Of course, Landry appeared to be totally safe, but we had only known him for a few days, so it paid to be careful in today's world. Bless Bertie's dear heart for looking out for my cousin and I.

We were on the M11 which turned into the A11 road on our route northward. Over an hour later, we started to see signs for the Newmarket racecourse and knew that we were close. Apparently, Roycetonne House was tucked away a few miles from racehorse central in the nearby village of Denslough. It was a well-to-do place with a proper high street winding through the village that only had the toniest of shops and cafés. Everything was neat and tidy, right down to the flower boxes that were on hibernation from winter, all wrapped up in their layers of burlap. Even the melted snow somehow looked cleaner and fresher here than what we'd driven past en route. It offered the sense of country fresh and dedication to the land, enhanced by the sport of kings. There were a couple of random piles of horse manure swept off to the side of the road, no doubt left over from early morning gallops. I imagined it would be quite the thing to see racehorses walk by with their exercise riders, ever so early in the morning. The horses would be champing at the bit, their breath emitting frosty puffs as they danced, eager to get to the soft turf. They'd all wear quarter sheets over their loins to keep their muscles from seizing up in the chilly, damp air. Once they reached the exercise track, racehorses would explode in a ball of speed just like they were bred to do. They truly were majestic animals, and if you worked with horses, they became friends too.

Once we'd driven through the main part of the village, we turned down a good-sized country lane surrounded by well-clipped, tall laurel hedges. The lane ended after about a mile, up against two tall wrought-iron gates surrounded by a stone wall that surrounded the entire estate. The wall must have stood twelve-feet tall. The cost of that wall alone would be exorbitant, even back in the nineteenth century when it was originally constructed. I had read the entire chapter Bertie pointed out in the coffee-table book, and the construction cost statistics for this house were absolutely staggering. Hundreds of laborers. No expense was spared according to those graced with coveted invitations to elegant balls and dinners back in the days when Roycetonne House once welcomed society across its threshold.

"Imagine us actually driving through these gates," Bertie murmured as we drove along.

We drove up a paved path and it became hard to speak. A huge, stone-clad Victorian mansion loomed in front of us like a stone ghost. It had a steep grey roof, two mismatched turret towers, and a plethora of gingerbread lattice wood finishing. It was a dollhouse on steroids, a hodge podge of asymmetry built by someone with more money than sense. This was the house that Lady Adelaide's father had built using the fortune amassed from his global copper and gem mining empire. Surely this grotesque, sprawling, cold stone monstrosity wasn't a home. It looked like a showpiece manor house that screamed wealth, reserved demeanors, and above all else, stifling of emotions. The black pollution from the air that fixed itself into the carved crevices of stone only underscored that message.

Despite there obviously being a gardener still working on site, no amount of perfectly clipped topiary would ever warm the place up. The front and side gardens had masses of intricately sculpted box hedges and of course not a single one of them would dare to ever get box blight. Thorny roses were in the center of rings of dark green hedges, each rose a perfect, dark crimson. We saw an expertly-tended kitchen garden peeking from around back, through an open wooden gate inside a pale-grey brick wall. The garden was bare in many spots now because of winter, but seeing the cold frames and greenhouses revealed the utmost care put into this space. In the spring and summertime it would simply be glorious.

We drove around to the port cochere and saw that it still had brass rings on hitching posts for horses. There was also a water trough. After we parked and emerged from the vehicle, the clock tower just off to the left played an eerie song, sounding quite tinny because no doubt the mechanics were quite old. With these imposing stone walls, the Roycetonne Family signaled how much it valued its privacy. In fact, it appeared to have some deep, dark secrets to keep. Overall, the place looked frozen in time and absolutely deserted.

"This place already gives me the willies," Landry said.

"The style may be cold, but remember there once was love inside this house," I said.

"And here I was thinking Aunt Moyra was living in some cozy cottage in a pretty little village," Landry said.

"I wouldn't call this house 'cozy' by any means," Bertie said.

I turned to Bertie. "Have you ever been inside?" I asked.

He shook his head. "I only heard stories about it from my father back when he was still alive. I've seen the same coffee-table book that you have. That's why this is so alarming."

Landry frowned. "What do you mean alarming? I don't see any bodies anywhere."

"No, of course not. I meant it's just sad that two old ladies had to die without any human contact besides the likely two or three staff they had left. I'm sure the local community would've rallied to help them. There's all sorts of local charities that offer friendly visitor programs, bring hot meals and ensure home healthcare is provided. That's what our community village back home is all about. I just find it disconcerting that they shut everyone else out." Bertie looked genuinely concerned. He was a caring man, and to see people of his set just push all of the outreach away obviously didn't make sense to him.

"I'm sure they had good reason," I said. "And Bertie, you shouldn't feel guilty at all, because we all know you tried."

He sighed. "I did. My father did. I wonder who found your Aunt Moyra, Landry."

"I got an email from the solicitor. Apparently Aunt Moyra passed away while speaking on the telephone with him. He had power of attorney and had the local police batter the door down."

His comment made all of us turn to look at the oak front doors. They looked solid, as if they'd been in place for centuries. At each side sat a weathered, life-sized statue of a bird hunting dog, greened with time except for each dog's shiny nose.

Bertie made a point to rub each nose. "Legend has it, Lady Adelaide's father held extravagant hunting parties here. Each rider rubbed both dogs' noses for good luck."

"To prevent them from falling off their horses?" I asked.

"Exactly," Bertie replied.

"I thought you said the doors were battered down?" Gertie asked.

"Yes. Staff were all out at the time. The solicitor then had the doors replaced immediately, and artificially aged," Landry said. "That much I was told."

"It's all just so curious," I said. "Roycetonne House would serve as a perfect backdrop to a Halloween function when the skies got dark and the wind started to howl."

There was no answer at the front door, so Landry pulled out a set of jangling keys from inside an overseas courier pouch. He slid them inside the well-oiled hardware and it turned with a heavy click. We were inside, setting our eyes upon a central hall that was ornately decorated. The room was completely overstuffed with everything the Victorians loved: wicker furniture, intense bric-a-brac, taxidermy animals and dried plants under tall glass domes, an enormous array of silver plate behind glass, plus dozens of countryside and botanical watercolor paintings on the wall. It was supposed to be an elegantly curated collection, but through today's eyes it looked like clutter. Dust collectors. Out of date. All of it was poignant and sad.

We stood in a circular area with a parquet floor comprised of elegantly polished hardwood in three different tones. A labyrinth of four passageways all radiated out from the central hall. Presumably, each passageway led to a wing of the house. There was a giant metal balustraded staircase and what looked like a modern elevator. Each wing was labelled with a discrete brass plaque and I read 'to dairy', 'to conservatory', 'to drawing room' and 'to guest quarters'. Down the hallway to the drawing room was a passage lined with family portraits. It also appeared that some of the painted panels on the walls were covered with thin plywood. Perhaps a leftover from its art storage days during World War Two? I was beginning to feel like we were wandering through a place frozen in time. This level was extremely clean, but there was a difference between having dust and having modern conveniences and fixtures. Roycetonne House was a grand old lady indeed.

This place was extremely curious as well as being mysterious. A circular window was off to the right, beside a large closet for guests' coats. A stained glass window hung high above; inside the glass was a stylized capital 'R' intertwined with images of miners at work, laborers working by candlelight in the cold, damp caves in Victorian times. Much had changed, yet we all had a duty to remember the past.

I was curious and walked over to look outside. I saw a well-trimmed hedge maze.

"What's with the fountain?" Gertie asked.

We all focused on the eight-foot wide marble fountain in the center, towards the back of the hall. We went over and saw the insides of all three basins, graduating from large to medium up to small; each basin's interior was decorated in tiny little squares of stone, a mosaic pattern just like an ancient Roman temple. The mosaic formed an intricate paisley pattern surrounding the stylized Roycetonne name that was repeated twice in each basin.

"See here." Landry walked over to the side of the room and flicked on a brass switch marked 'fountain'. The plumbing dutifully responded, and a tall spray of water shot up eight-feet and landed elegantly down below, not spraying a single drop outside the fountain's three basins as it cascaded from top to bottom. This was craftsmanship at its height of elegance.

"I can see Lady Adelaide's father reaming out the engineers if a single bit of mist got onto his fancy-pressed suit," Landry said.

"I take it he wasn't a very nice man," Gertie said.

Bertie shook his head. "No, he wasn't. Extremely controlling and he always wanted his daughter under his thumb. I can't say she really had much of a life to herself."

"All sad. So incredibly sad," I said.

"May I enquire as to whom you might be?" a clipped voice said behind us.

We turned to see a tall, immensely thin Scandinavian woman covered in wood shavings. Stand her sideways and her shadow would disappear. She wore dirty tan overalls, a man's waffle work shirt and safety goggles perched on top of her head. Over her shoulder she carried a transparent dry cleaning bag containing two long black dresses, each with a high collar of starched white.

Landry stepped forward, cowboy hat in hand. "Ma'am, I'm Landry Jackson, Moyra's nephew. You've been expecting me."

The woman drew herself up to her full angular height. She looked like a cross between a lumberjack, bug exterminator and steampunk ghost hunter. "Dear man. You're a day earlier than we expected, arriving on my day off. I ask that you please excuse my appearance and wayward wood shavings shedding. I'm the housekeeper, Mrs. Neebles."

"My friends are with me from the Greymore Genealogy Research Site. Julie Fincher, her cousin Gertie Porringer and Bertie Preswick, Duke of Conroy."

I supposed Landry should have called Bertie 'His Grace' but it just would seem out of place right now. I never used it.

"Thank goodness you've arrived." Mrs. Neebles' stoic face looked ever so relieved. She gestured for us to follow her. "Now, there is a lot to be done. Please follow me."

Chapter 9

———

"Whatever did she mean by all that?" I whispered to the group as we quickly hustled behind Mrs. Neebles to keep up.

Mrs. Neebles rapidly shed curly wood shavings with every stride. We'd obviously interrupted her in the middle of a project and I was sure a dedicated vacuum and its operator would clean up all these little bits post haste once us visitors were seen to.

Landry bent down towards me. "Aunt Moyra told me that the housekeeper had an unusual hobby. Mrs. Neebles is into chainsaw wood sculpture carving."

"Hence all the wood shavings," Gertie said as we nearly had to jog to keep up with our hostess.

This place got more and more curious by the minute. I was waiting to hear about the ghosts or pirates who frequented the place next.

Mrs. Neebles led us upstairs with all the efficiency of a steam engine recently loaded with a fresh supply of coal. I could almost feel the smuts hit my face as she mounted the stairs two at a time. It was a big, long staircase, at least forty steps to reach the second floor landing. I supposed the elevator was too small to accommodate us all. Likely, Mrs. Neebles was also checking that we were up to the task ahead. Whatever we were in for, I knew it would not be easy. And just how did I know this? Because of what appeared on the top floor. It was a hallway with a series of eight doors, all shut, four on the left, facing four on the right. They were graciously-burnished wood doors, intricately carved, and as we approached, I saw that each one had a different flower and fruit combination gently carved into the wood. I thought back to the antiques auction Gertie and I once attended with Ewan. The wood carving sold at the auction was of master craftsman level and these doors weren't far behind. Of course, the creators lived centuries apart, but the style and talent of Grinling Gibbons was repeated inside this Victorian-era house.

Mrs. Neebles halted just outside doors number one and two. She took a deep breath, clasped her hands together in front of her stomach then gave us a serious look. She exhaled. "You are now about to walk into eight rooms that have not been seen by anyone other than Lady Adelaide and Aunt Moyra for a very long time. I know not if they meet up to my standards of cleanliness nor if they are in a shambles. I assume the construction is still solid but I would mind your step."

"What do you mean no one has seen inside?" Landry asked. "You're the housekeeper."

Mrs. Neebles shook her head. "I was never allowed to work this portion of the upper floor. The twenty-three guest suites, yes, but never Moyra or Lady Adelaide's private rooms. When I started working here so long ago, the rooms were already locked and I had no access. It just became a part of the house that I never bothered with."

"Twenty-three guest suites?" Landry whistled low. "That's some guest list."

"What about the fire in 1941?" Bertie asked.

"It mainly affected the guest wing, the library, the study and some mechanical rooms. There were workmen in right after the fire to repair it, but goodness knows what happened to the Roycetonne Family's wonderful book collection and private papers," she said.

"Now come on, Mrs. Neebles, weren't you ever a little bit curious about the locked rooms?" Landry teased.

Mrs. Neebles drew herself up to her full height. "Certainly not. I have my duties and I respect my employer's direction. What is within my purvey is done to perfection. Anything outside of that is beyond my realm and focus."

Gertie jabbed me in the ribs. "I'll bet this place has a few skeletons in its closets."

I shot her a withering glance. Looking over at Bertie, I could tell he was fascinated. "I'm sure there's going to be some surprises behind those locked doors, everyone. Are we all going to go in together or just let Landry look first?"

Landry shook his head. "There's nothing that I'm anticipating. It was just two old ladies living together, one taking care of the other. Didn't my aunt let you in any of these rooms after Lady Adelaide passed away?" he asked Mrs. Neebles.

"No, she certainly did not," the housekeeper replied.

"So you just let them be squirreled away up here? All day, every day?"

"My duties included delivering their meals on a rolling cart to be left at the top of the hallway outside the first door. When they were done eating, they would roll it out of the room and leave it for me to collect, precisely one hour and two minutes after I had delivered it. That timeframe never wavered. Well, until the day Lady Adelaide died."

Mrs. Neebles was perfunctory and factual with everything that she said.

"It fits with what society knew of them," Bertie said. "They locked themselves away from the world and didn't let anyone in."

"But why? Were they ill? Disfigured?" Gertie asked the obvious.

"Not that I knew of," Landry replied.

"It doesn't make sense," I said. "There's got to be a reason why they didn't want any contact with the outside world. Usually if someone is secretive it means they have a secret."

"My thoughts exactly," Gertie said.

Mrs. Neebles focused on the ring of keys Landry had in his hand. "Sir, if you'd like to do the honors? I can make myself scarce if you would prefer?"

"Not necessary, Mrs. Neebles. You'll probably know more about what's going on behind these locked doors than I do," he said.

We all held our breath as he dialed through the keys, kind of like selecting a favorite candy out of a chocolate box. He tried a few and failed. Then he tried another one, put it in the lock and heard the satisfying click as he turned it. "Open Sesame," Landry said, turning back to look at us with a grin. "Anybody nervous? Do we expect ghosts to come tumbling out of this room?" He let out a big-hearted chortle.

"I really don't know what to expect," Bertie said. "This has been an English secret for absolutely donkey's years."

Landry got a quizzical look on his face. "Donkey's years? What do you mean?"

Gertie, Bertie and I looked at each other. Mrs. Neebles wanted no part of this discussion.

"It means a long time," Gertie rapidly explained.

"So why don't you just say 'a long time'?" Landry asked.

"Like Americans say 'it took me forever to get here' when that in itself is always untrue?" Bertie retorted.

"But donkey's years?" Landry shook his head.

"Fred Todling would know the origin of that saying," I said with confidence. "We can ask him when we get back. Better yet, I'll just text Ewan."

Bertie decided to fix this once and for all. "Donkey's years means a long time because no one ever recalls seeing a dead donkey. They seem to live forever."

"Interesting," Gertie said.

"Might we get on with the task at hand?" Bertie asked in his slightly irritated, posh voice.

"Apologies. Now everybody stand back for a moment, because I have no idea what we're going to walk in on here," Landry said in a confident, booming voice. His voice filled whatever room it was in, and at this point in time it was nice somebody was in control before we all stepped over the mysterious threshold.

And what a threshold it was.

We peeked in on a vast drawing room absolutely stuffed and crammed with excessively ornate Victorian furniture including sofas, chairs, multiple small tables, an intricately painted harpsichord and a pair of porcelain Staffordshire dogs, each showing the detailed faces that indicated the pair were genuine. This odd room rivalled any great palace with a thriving mirror collection. There must have been a dozen or so scattered around the room, some hung on the walls, some tilted on wide wooden feet as they covered floor space. The mirrors were of all shapes and sizes. It was eerie because all the mirrors were covered with heavy black crêpe.

Gertie dug an elbow into my side. She was rather effective at doing it, never failing to get my attention. "This signifies the family's in mourning, Victorian-style."

"It seems rather odd, in modern day," I said. "But maybe her father's orders were for them never to be removed and she was just being respectful." I cast a glance around the room again and shuddered. It was as if someone had banished all the light from the surroundings and then covered it with a dark veil of gloom. This was no easy passage onto the other side. Those whom this person or persons left behind would be forever lost without them. The sadness pervaded the room. Even the air hung heavily around us.

Bertie ran a finger over the mantelpiece that surrounded a pristine clean fire grate. He came away with a thick layer of grey dust. "I wouldn't call this modern day. Rather, it's frozen in time. She's mourning the family she lost in the fire." He thought on it. "Or, perhaps, as rumored, just her daughters."

"The whole place looks like it's stuck in a time warp," Landry said.

"That dust is not my responsibility, just so everyone's clear," Mrs. Neebles said. She looked haughty and worried at the same time, concerned that we thought she wasn't doing her housekeeping job to the utmost proper standard.

Landry gave her a grin. "It would be very unfair of us to hold this dust against you. How could you keep on top of it if you were never allowed inside?" He gave her a friendly nod.

Mrs. Neebles exhaled, as if a great weight had just been lifted from her shoulders. "I am glad you understand. However, it has always been my belief that the best housekeepers are not curious people."

"Especially around the eccentric aristocracy," Bertie said. "However, you cannot do your job without access to ninety-five percent of the house. I can see an owner keeping five-percent private, but no more."

Gertie and I exchanged a glance. Landry was brave enough to say it. "And I'm assuming that five-percent means occupied restrooms or as you Brits say, loos?"

He'd caught Bertie off guard. My favorite aristocrat straightened up and issued a firm look. "Yes, plus the safe room. All great houses should have one and those are strictly off-limits to staff for good reason."

"Are you worried about them pilfering the family silver?" Gertie joked.

"Not the silver, so much as family secrets, business plans and everything that families with hundreds of years of history would rather not lay out on display to anyone but their closest inner circle."

"Is there a safe room here?" Gertie asked.

"Not to my knowledge. But perhaps it is in one of these rooms up here," Mrs. Neebles said. "We still have seven to go."

"Wouldn't a safe room normally be on the main floor?" I asked. "They're usually reinforced with some pretty thick steel walls. Pretty heavy for a second floor, weight-wise."

Landry looked at me, impressed. "I didn't know you were familiar with construction details. I'm impressed."

I shrugged. "I had to learn a lot—and very quickly—when we renovated Greymore Hall to accommodate the new genealogy research site. My bottom line is safety first and fancy later."

"There's a few people I know who would benefit from that advice," Gertie said with a smirk.

We all laughed.

Landry took one of the keys from his ring, the one that looked like the best candidate, and put it into the door lock of the adjoining room. The lock turned like butter and we were in. This time it was a similar-sized gargantuan room, however instead of shaded mirrors we had trompe l'oeil wallpaper. It was a swirl of ethereal clouds, cherubs and pastoral meadows. Chubby piglets, cows and sheep whiled away their days as angelic images floated in the skies above them. The image wrapped around the room a total of six repetitive times. It was almost like they'd run out of new wallpaper scenes before they ran out of walls.

This room had no furniture. One could see where the furniture once stood by the impressions in the carpet that had a repetitive gold Roycetonne House logo woven into the scarlet red. Upon closer inspection, I could pick out the lines of a few short bookcases, more sofas and a couple of small card tables ringed with chairs. A couple of light fixtures clung to the wall, their gilding flaking off under a heavy coat of dust. A fancy chandelier dangled from the ceiling, bagged up in a dusty cream-colored bedsheet.

"I heard stories but I didn't believe it," Bertie said. "So it's true." He stood in one place and turned in a small circle a few times, his head tilted back so he could take in the ceiling that was painted with the same cherubs extending up from the wallpaper.

"What do you mean?" I asked.

"That this was a world unto its own, a place where Lady Adelaide could truly lose herself and escape her father's wicked rule over her," Bertie said.

"Not much left of it now, hey?" Landry said. His strong voice broke the emotional understanding that Bertie was trying to share with us, but I knew that each person experienced the past in their own way. It was much the same when doing family history; some people wanted to know everything, whereas others only wanted the good bits to become public. To me, everything was fair game. In order to understand an ancestor, it was critical to know all facets of their lives. One could not understand how a person loved if nothing was known about what they disliked. It was key to understanding what warmed their heart when their feet were turned to lumps of ice in a brutal prairie winter, for example.

Never doubt the power of kindness overcoming an ancestor's dastardly ways. In the end, karma usually won out, regardless of the century. Many called it a guiding hand from above, the Almighty who ensured people escaped the worst scrapes so long as they were in his service. No matter what a family believed, history played a strong role in creating the future. The wisest families took the time to learn about their pasts.

Room number three was also accessed by an adjoining door from room number two. The decorator had cleverly covered the door in wallpaper, and then created a near invisible cut around the entrance, virtually unrecognizable to the casual observer.

Things were getting more interesting. This room looked like a female servant's sparse and clean bedroom. There was a small bed with threadbare sheets and eiderdown, a side table with an empty glass and a clock that had stopped ticking. An Edwardian wardrobe cabinet was in one corner and a dressing table sat against the opposite wall. The mirror over the small table was also covered in black crêpe. It was as if both women who lived here didn't want to see themselves or disturb any spirits that still lingered in the house.

"The Victorians covered up their mirrors so the recently deceased could leave for the other world and not be trapped here on earth by seeing their own reflection," I explained.

Everybody gave a solemn nod. Everybody except for Landry, of course. He'd missed Maude Livingstone's last lecture at the Greymore Genealogy Research Site. "I don't exactly follow all these ancient European traditions. I mean, what on earth does covering up a mirror with a piece of black cloth do for the here and now?"

We all sighed. Gertie decided to tackle this one. "Landry, I think the best thing for you to do is consider that it made your ancestors feel better knowing they were doing everything they could to help deceased spirits leave this world for the next."

Gertie spoke in terms that Mr. Texas could understand.

He nodded and that was that. Landry strode over to the dressing table and picked up a tiny crystal ornament of a hedgehog. Its eyes were made of pretty emeralds. "Well, I'll be schnookered. This is part of last year's Christmas gift I sent to Aunt Moyra. I'm glad to see she treasured it."

Chapter 10

"Always good to know we're in the right place," I said with a smile. "Do you recognize anything else?"

Landry looked around the room as we all watched. The tall man's eyes narrowed as he took in a display of fancy crystal and glass ornaments sitting on the windowsill that overlooked the front drive. He walked over and picked up a blown glass figurine of an elephant, its trunk raised high. The glass blower had put swirls of blue molten glass inside a crystal clear outer shell. It looked expensive. He held it up to show us. "I gave her an ornament twice a year. Once for her birthday, and once at Christmas. Aunt Moyra loved animals."

It was odd having modern, expensive ornaments in this austere room. I strode over to the wardrobe and opened both wooden doors. Each hinge creaked with the effort and one of them was a bit wonky as it opened wide. Inside were fourteen dresses, all the exact same style, all the exact same size. Seven different colors, for seven different days of the week, times two. Fourteen dresses were likely needed to economize on weekly washing needs.

I ran my hands over the cuffs of each dress, trailing over the history of a woman who was no longer with us here on earth. It was sad to see that Moyra lived her life in such a structured and unbendable way.

There were five more unopened rooms to visit.

Aunt Moyra's room had an obvious adjoining door to the last one at the end of the hall. Landry produced the requisite key, and as soon as we entered we knew that this was Lady Adelaide's bedroom. It was done in respectful tones of dusty pink, light gray and faded white. Vanilla yet luxurious velvet. Scrumptious and sumptuous. The furniture here was mahogany, albeit under a superfine sheen of dust. The bedding on the fourposter bed was exquisite; embroidered pillowcases with the Roycetonne family crest as well as satin sheets. The bed sat underneath an absolute monstrously-huge matching canopy, one with a real princess feel to it. Inside Lady Adelaide's wardrobe was a much more varied set of dresses, style-wise. The problem was, every single one of her garments was black.

"How odd," I murmured.

Gertie came to look over my shoulder. She frowned slightly. "Is there another wardrobe perhaps? Somewhere she stores clothes of a happier nature?"

Bertie came close. "Don't count on it. The rumor was Lady Adelaide never got over her lost love. Society never knew all of the details but said her father definitely stopped her from being happy. All he really cared about was the family name and tradition. Again, very strict Victorian." His phone vibrated and he looked down. His eyebrows raised and he got a huge grin on his face. "Score one for Scotford!" he murmured with restrained glee.

"Is a royal coming to visit?" Gertie teased.

Bertie looked up. "No, that's not until a few months later. Er ... it's rather the fact that I just sold twenty-five cases of mango chutney to a distributor in Asia! This is exciting. The estate's first big order for our new product."

Landry gave Bertie a bit of side eye. "Make sure you get your money before that product ships."

"Pardon? Well, I am chuffed." The large order made Bertie look as if he'd either just been elected prime minister or somebody was making him gold-leaf pastry for dessert.

"Over here, folks. We can't get this cabinet unlocked," Gertie said with a strained voice. She heaved on a drawer, yet it wouldn't budge. The drawer was part of a standalone cabinet recessed into the wall, almost like a safe. It had long lines of garnet inlaid in the marquetry and was covered in a thick layer of transparent gloss. Inlaid crystals twinkled at the corners. This was a woman's fancy cabinet, one where she undoubtedly kept a treasure or two.

Landry opened the lock on the front of the drawer. Gertie slid it open and our eyes feasted on a set of worn, tan-colored leather jewelry cases, seven in total. I lifted out the first one and handed it to Landry. "As the rightful heir, you need to do the honors."

"Let's see what we have here," he said. He lifted the lid of the case and we suddenly looked down upon a royal blue molded velvet surrounding a wonderful diamond tiara. We opened the other boxes in rapid succession and found diamond chandelier earrings, an assortment of rings with every type of precious stone one could imagine, necklaces with filigree gold plus a twisted gold necklace much like the ancient torcs found in hordes discovered by metal detectorists. There was also an elegant diamond choker with the large aquamarine stone in the center as well as gold and silver braided bracelets made in the most exquisite craftsmanship. It was quite the collection.

"One only has a tiara if attending functions with royalty." Gertie looked at us with a succinct glance in her eye. "I think this house holds a lot more secrets than it's letting on."

All eyes turned to Mrs. Neebles. She shook her head, slightly goggle-eyed. "I was well aware this was a fine family, but royalty? Not since I took over the running of this household."

Landry got a teasing grin at the side of his mouth. "Are you sure they weren't hosting the high society folks inside while you were outside doing your chainsaw carving, Mrs. Neebles?"

The housekeeper got awfully frosty at this comment. "Certainly not. My woodworking hobby–"

"Chainsaw carving hobby–" Landry added.

"Very well. Chainsaw carving hobby. It has never during my entire tenure interrupted or interfered with anything to do with the running of this household. It is merely how I spend time relaxing in my off-duty hours."

Landry broke out laughing. "You put on a pair of heavy duty safety glasses and pick up a power tool, causing woodchips to fly all over you, to relax? You're a woman after my own heart." The tall Texan guffawed.

"Come on, Mrs. Neebles. You must have found dealing with two ladies who hide themselves away in secret rooms just a bit stressful," Gertie goaded.

Mrs. Neebles shook her head. "I merely performed my duties. What the owner of this house wishes to do with her time and the premises is purely her own affair."

"Speaking of affairs ..." Gertie pulled out a tiny black leather box that we had somehow missed in our haste to look at all the jewelry inside the tan-colored boxes. She opened it and gasped at the sight of a one-carat diamond engagement ring with a wider band. "I think we just found more evidence of Lady Adelaide's true love's devotion."

"That's quite a sparkler," Landry said. "Go on, try it on, Mrs. Neebles." He plucked the ring out of the box and offered it to the housekeeper.

"No, no, thank you all the same," Mrs. Neebles said, backing away with rapid steps. She moved so fast that she bumped into an arm chair beside the bed.

"It won't bite, you know," Landry said.

"It is bad luck to try on a wedding ring that never made it to the altar. I would never, ever allow that on my finger," Mrs. Neebles said.

"Is that a local folklore?" I asked.

Mrs. Neebles' eyes were open wide and she looked worried. "It is this family's tradition. That ring needs to be handled with care."

"It proves there is something to the rumor that Bertie told us about," Gertie said, looking at Bertie who'd been silent through all this. She handed him the ring.

Bertie took it and carefully looked at the inscription on the inner band. "My father was right. Lady Adelaide's betrothed was banished and it broke her heart. Look at what her father did to the lovely inscription her banned fiancé put on the ring."

We all gathered close and Landry turned on the flashlight of his mobile phone so we could see with clarity. There, on the inside of the ring, we could just make out the inscription, 'Forever yours. All my love, S.' Someone, presumably Lady Adelaide's father, had taken a sharp object like a nail or file and had scratched out as much of the engraving as he could bear doing. He was a man on a mission, someone bent on splitting apart the couple. Lady Adelaide's father obviously didn't consider the man worthy of his daughter's affections or fortune. Although England was still very much a class-based society today, it wasn't half as vindictive as it was in Victorian or Edwardian times. Back then, upstairs simply didn't mix with downstairs. Society just didn't allow it.

"My father's friends said that Lady Adelaide was inconsolable. Heartbroken," Bertie said.

Landry took the ring back and fingered it in his big hands. "That's pretty sad, letting society dictate matters of the heart. If you find somebody you love, you should be with them."

"Not in the upper levels of aristocracy," Bertie said, "especially back in those days."

Landry carefully replaced the ring in its case. "Let's cross the hall."

Four more rooms to go. Landry's key opened the door opposite Lady Adelaide's room. It revealed itself to actually only be one more room to go, because door number five opened into a space that took up the entire right hand side of the top floor. We first set eyes upon an incredibly large hearth to our left. It was a colossal marble monstrosity, deep cream with prominent grey veins in the stone throughout. The carving on it was absolutely intricate and at each end had the Roycetonne family crest deeply etched into the expensive substrate. There were also lions, cherubs, and ostrich feathers dancing around the perimeter of the cold stone monstrosity.

"Tell me they had central heating, please?" Landry asked Mrs. Neebles.

"It was installed in the bedrooms but never ducted to this side of the house. I was always warm in the kitchen with the stoves going, but it was fireplaces with protective screens everywhere except for the bedrooms," Mrs. Neebles said.

"And what about your own home? I assume you live onsite?" I asked.

"Mr. Neebles and I live in a cottage on the opposite side of the maze. I insisted on central heating there." She stood up as if to protect herself from any questioning about that momentous decision.

"Good for you," Landry replied. "What the heck are those little creatures?" He pointed at an art collection depicting five life-sized young girls painted on boards of solid wood and placed around the hearth. They stood up like dolls in their crosshatched foot stands. The children were all dressed in ribbons and bows, their hair done perfectly, each with a toy hoop, stuffed animal or train at their feet.

"Dummy boards are meant to be companions for someone who is lonely," Mrs. Neebles explained. "Moyra once told me these specific characters were Lady Adelaide's young daughters and their friends."

All of a sudden, Landry looked incredibly sad. "I hope you're not telling me my aunt had no friends? She never mentioned being lonely to me." One got the obvious sense that he was worried about being a delinquent nephew, thousands of miles away and oblivious to a potential problem with the senior in his family.

Mrs. Neebles gave him a firm look. "She chose to cut herself off from the world. Lady Adelaide was her complete existence for so many years. When Lady Adelaide passed, your Aunt Moyra busied herself with paperwork. She got dozens of letters each week, the details of which I simply do not know."

Mrs. Neebles' words gave us all pause for thought.

"What's behind the calico curtain?" Gertie asked. Her words brought back memories of our recent trip when we learned more about the silk printing industry. Aunt Edwina had used a strip of calico for one of her clues in our riddle quest.

Today's calico was something quite different. It was a heavy, almost carpet-like curtain hung off forty brass curtain hooks strung from one side of the room to the next. The hearth and dummy boards were enclosed in a small sitting area with a couple of easy chairs, well-curtained off from whatever was behind them. We could see over the curtain, across the lengthy coffered and plastered ceiling taking up the full length of the floor, but could see nothing specifically of the room beyond the heavy curtain.

"Now ladies, I want to caution you. We could be walking in on an office, a pile of dead crows or something worse," Bertie warned. "I've been in old manor houses before when an elderly relative has died and sometimes the detritus isn't too pretty."

"Nonsense," Gertie said. "We're not going to pansy foot around just because our plumbing is different from yours. I want to see what's behind the curtain." And with that, she stepped forward with a flourish and yanked it to the side. It created another gasp-worthy moment.

The wooden floor creaked as we approached. There were more curtains firmly shut over what appeared to be two-story tall windows. It was an amazing sight: extra special for family history fans like Gertie and I. This section contained floor to ceiling stacks and shelves of yellowed letters, deeds, calling cards, land leases, business papers, mining company records, ledgers, diaries, and children's books. Dates on some rudimentary shelf labels showed they were mainly from Victorian and Edwardian times. The family bible had pride of place on a rolltop desk that was open to show its cubbyholes stuffed full of correspondence, all organized alphabetically. Glued to the front of the desk was a tiny strip of paper on which somebody had written in beautiful penmanship, 'Papa, I will never forgive you. A.'

"Well, I don't know about you folks, but I'd say it's high time to redecorate," Landry said, running a finger over the fine layer of dust that covered a pile of rolled parchment documents.

He didn't see it coming.

People outside the archival and family history worlds never did.

Gertie, Mrs. Neebles, Bertie and I all exclaimed together, "No!"

Landry staggered back, clutching his chest as if he'd been hit with a blast of hot, jumbo jet exhaust fumes. "Whoa. Now tell me how you really feel," he joked.

"It's about preserving history," I said.

"It's about doing things up for the future." He gave me a strong look. "My goodness, anyone would think that I was about to commit some major crime were I to bonfire all this old paperwork."

"You are. It goes against every single principle of archival preservation and family history standard," I said.

"But who the heck would want to read this old stuff?" he asked, dead serious. He really had no clue what he was looking at here.

"You've got items here likely going back 150 or so years. Every single invoice, photo, personal letter, newspaper clipping and so much more." I carefully fingered a few of the papers on top of one of the piles. It was a haphazard assortment, but in that pile alone I saw five different decades spanning two centuries and some official seals at the top of letters. "This all needs to be gone through, properly sorted and listed in an archival inventory called a fond."

"Do you think that's what Aunt Moyra would want me to do?" Landry asked.

"Unless there is something in the will preventing you from doing so, the executor has an unwritten duty to preserve this collection for local social history." Gertie nodded her head as she spoke the fact that we already knew. "Beyond that, you have one of the great industrial family's history here at your fingertips. Their contributions to this nation's records alone is worth preserving. Think of all the history that company files hold, ranging from workers to machinery to end products to customers ... The list is endless."

"She's right," Bertie said. "You simply cannot put a price on this type of record collection."

"Okay, so for a moment let's consider that perhaps I don't want to either have a large bonfire or sell it to the highest bidder. What the heck would I do with all this stuff?" Landry looked at us for help. We could tell he was extremely out of his depth.

"You'd set up a work team led by a professional archivist. They would use correct archival supplies to file everything, taking an inventory and cataloguing as they went. There are teams who specialize in this, and we certainly have volunteers at GGRS who could help," I said.

"And I'm sure that would cost me a pretty packet." Landry gave me a knowing look.

"Preserving history's not cheap. And those archival supplies? Let's just say acid-free materials and proper boxes are an investment. But think of how much you would contribute to society by saving all of this paperwork. You have a time capsule here. A wonderful opportunity to go through a century and a half of materials. It's a once-in-a-lifetime chance," Gertie said.

"Why this place?" I said, to no one in particular. It was just such an overwhelming sense of history and lack of filing that hit me all at once. Bits and pieces showed me that the documents were generally in good condition, but apart from being stacked in piles, there didn't appear to be much organization to them. Someone had made a good start, but then obviously got distracted with something else. It was as if some noble family had collected everything to do with their life on paper and just used this room as a random storage drop-off point.

"Amazing, truly amazing," Landry said, looking around at all the papers that surrounded us. There were more desks surrounding the perimeter of the room, and he ran a finger over the surface. It came away clean. "Not much dust over here," he said. "These two desks look well-used. Clean and organized as well."

"But why leave most of it like this? Was it too painful to sort?" Gertie held up what looked like a proclamation from a local town handing over the keys to Lady Adelaide's father for his benevolence and philanthropy. It was just stacked in the piles with what looked like family correspondence and invoices for turkeys and turnips at Christmas time.

"With all this wonderful history in front of us, why on earth wouldn't they put it into proper files and record boxes?" I wondered. "Obviously somebody knew their value in terms of social history being recorded."

"Perhaps they had other things to do with their time?" Bertie said, fingering a shiny locked desk and gesturing for Landry to come over and help him open it.

The desk now open, we soon had more answers to our question. Inside the desk was an old manual typewriter with one large, modern, manilla envelope, already stamped and addressed to a local post office box.

"What exact date did your Aunt Moyra pass?" Bertie asked.

"December 22, in the afternoon," Landry said.

"Seems to me that Moyra never got a chance to mail this before she passed. Do you know anything about this, Mrs. Neebles?" Bertie asked.

Mrs. Neebles took the envelope and nodded. "I took one of these to the post office every day for Moyra."

"For how long?" Landry asked.

"Since I started here. Just after Moyra came to nurse Lady Adelaide."

"One envelope a day, for multiple years? Who the heck was my aunt writing to?" Landry asked.

"I never asked. I considered it part of my daily duties after I had delivered breakfast up to the second floor and left it on the trolley for them."

"I'm amazed you never asked," Gertie said.

"I am not paid to be a curious person," Mrs. Neebles said.

"Ah, but that doesn't mean you avoid all curious wonderings, correct?" Bertie said with a teasing smile on his face. He put Mrs.

Neebles into a delicate quandary by asking her to break her composure on something her employers obviously kept very dear.

She answered him with all the diplomacy of a world leader. "Sir, I never bring my personal feelings to this job."

Bertie stepped back, impressed. Perhaps he was even considering making her a job offer over at Scotford Castle.

"So Landry, what do you plan on doing with this treasure trove?" I asked.

"Well, I certainly don't need it. Is it worth anything?" he asked.

All of us from the GGRS issued looks of shock at Landry.

"Sell it? It's your heritage? It's a social history from an entire village who worked for the owner of this grand estate either on the manor house grounds, at his other estates or in his mines. How can you can consider selling something like this? It's a treasure trove for any archivist on the planet!" By now my hands were on my hips, my voice was raised and I was speaking far quicker than normal.

Gertie backed me up with incredible vicissitude. "Landry, it is unthinkable that you want to put a price tag on something that is quite honestly, priceless. This is obviously a one-of-a-kind collection and it belongs in a climate-controlled, professionally-managed archives, not on the auction block."

The crunch of gravel outside made me stride over to one of the windows and seek daylight. Down below, I saw Severs arrive in one of Scotford Castle's SUVs and emerge with a large wicker hamper.

"Folks, lunch has arrived." I gestured for Bertie to look outside at his chauffeur's delivery.

"We didn't want to put you to any trouble, Mrs. Neebles," Bertie said. "There's plenty of food so you can join us if you wish."

"I don't think that would be appropriate, Your Grace," Mrs. Neebles said. "The aristocracy and the help do not comingle at the table."

"Nonsense. It's just lunch, not a royal investiture," Bertie said. "I insist."

"Plus, he wants to sell you a jar of mango chutney," I said.

"Never you mind about that," Bertie said. He slung an arm around my shoulder we headed for the door. "All of this can wait for an hour."

Chapter 11

—

Kitchen. Minutes Later.

"I'm a practical man. Before I make a decision on this printed material, I need to know what exactly is up there in those stacks of paper," Landry stated with emphasis.

"Don't forget all the albums on the bookshelves. There must be over a hundred of those," Gertie said.

Severs and Mrs. Neebles passed out the contents of the lunch basket the chauffeur had driven up from Scotford Castle. He was doing double duty in that Bertie needed a lift home again after the initial visit to Roycetonne House was completed.

Lunch was fabulous. There were three types of sandwiches—egg and cress, salmon, plus ham and cheese—accompanied by fresh fruit and small artisan cakes for dessert. Mrs. Neebles drew the line at using picnic basket cutlery and glasses; she had ample stock in the butler's pantry and quickly laid an impressive table with Severs' help.

We munched on our delicacies, reviewing in our minds what we'd just experienced. It was both curious and sad. A simultaneous treasure trove mixed with loneliness. A wondering about two senior ladies' mental states, yet also tempered by respect for the need to preserve the past.

"I have a feeling that there's some important discoveries to be made upstairs in that office," Gertie said.

"Is that what we're calling it? An office?" Landry chuckled. "How about the 'hoarding room'?"

Gertie shook her head. "Never accuse or doubt another's actions until the truth is clear." She turned to look at Mrs. Neebles who was cutting off a delicate piece of spice cake with her dessert fork. Somehow Severs had managed to make sure the cake's icing wasn't dinged en route. Spice cake was my absolute favorite and it was a real treat to have it here today with us. Bertie was like that, always thinking of how to make other people feel better. It was one of the reasons I liked him so much. At present, he had a little smile on his face, and a rather confident, self-assured expression. I knew what it was about.

"You're pretty chuffed about selling twenty-five cases of mango chutney overseas, aren't you?" I asked Bertie.

"Most assuredly," he answered. "All my life I've only managed what my father left me. This mango chutney venture is something I've done on my own, one-hundred percent, and success is quite a wonderful feeling."

"Where on earth did you get the idea for chutney sales?" Landry asked.

"A rather exuberant crop of tomatoes from our kitchen garden at Scotford Castle one year," Bertie said with a bit of a sheepish grin. "I was having a conversation with our cook about what to do with them all, and she told me there was only so much tomato sauce, tomato soup and tomato salad she could make. It's a fruit that needs to be dealt with on an immediate basis because it bruises and spoils rather easily."

"That's right, tomatoes are one of the odd vegetables that are actually fruits," Gertie said.

"I wouldn't call tomatoes odd. Just different," I said.

"Like the time Ozzie Boggs thought he could take over a multi-million pound confectionery company using suspect genealogy?" Gertie asked, reminding me about one of GGRS's more unusual visitors and his foray into a murky ancestral world.

"At the time, he didn't know the family lineage was suspect. He truly thought he'd accurately traced back all the generations," I said, defending the man who was now our solid friend.

"Where did your twenty-five cases of chutney ship to?" Landry asked.

"Germany," Bertie confirmed.

"Final destination?"

"No. It was a freight forwarder."

"Reputable?"

Bertie sat up a bit straighter. Landry definitely had his attention. "How so?"

"Lots of fake ones on the internet these days. They imperson-ate legitimate firms, give screaming deals and then scam the seller by disappearing with their freight." Landry spoke with the voice of authority.

Silence. Complete and utter silence around the table.

"Oh dear," Bertie said in a slightly strangled voice. "They've already shipped from my estate."

"How much did they get you for?" Landry asked in a low, casual tone.

"Twenty-five cases of specialty chutney, fifteen jars per box, wholesale price of £7 per jar."

Everyone around the table did some mental math.

"£2,625," Bertie whispered.

"I'm sure the lights won't go out at Scotford Castle just because you made a bad chutney deal," Gertie said with confidence.

Bertie shook his head, glum. "It's not so much the money. It's the first venture I've had that I've done all myself and I <u>so</u> wanted it to be a success. I need to prove to the world that I'm more than just a man with a fancy title and inheritance."

"Bertie, you are a good man, regardless of that silver spoon crowding your teeth. Frankly, I never thought of you any other way," I said. "Landry, you're in cybersecurity, can you help Bertie with this?"

"Sure. I'd need the complete file. Can you email it over?"

Bertie looked down at his phone, thumbs already busy. "As we speak. Just logging in ..."

Gertie and I looked at each other. Together we both said, "Chutneygate!"

Mrs. Neebles looked a bit confused so we explained how our good friend Lance Holgarth dealt with his brother Algy's escaped petting zoo animals that recently created vegetable mayhem via disappearing vegetables. Our private joke with Lance resulted in 'Lettucegate', 'Carrotgate' and 'Beetrootgate'.

Mrs. Neebles smiled. "Yes, we had those types of hijinks here at Roycetonne House as well. I remember one party shortly after I started work here where a policeman imbibed a little too much. He ended up finishing the night wearing a hula skirt over his trousers and a straw hat backwards on his head, prancing about like he owned the place. It was all we could do to prevent him from falling into the swimming pool."

"And here we were thinking this was all a stiff upper lip place," Bertie said.

"Not with Constable Snowdrop around," Mrs. Neebles replied.

"Did you say Constable Snowdrop? What was his first name?" I asked.

She thought on it for a moment. "I believe his first name was 'William'. That's right. But he went by 'Bill'."

I looked at Gertie. "Those two must be related. There can't be that many police families out there by the name of 'Snowdrop'.

"We'll have to ask Bud."

"Bud Snowdrop was at the Christmas dinner, wasn't he?" Landry asked. "The one who was dating the circus performer?"

"Although how long that relationship will last is a big question mark in my mind," I said. "Constable Snowdrop is one of the most inflexible people I know."

❊❊❊

After lunch, we headed back upstairs. It was like re-entering another world for the second time today. I knew old, great houses harbored many secrets, but the sheer volume of this paperwork gave one enormous pause for thought.

We reassembled in the room full of documents and the manual typewriter.

Landry took control of the situation after taking another long, visual survey of the room. "Well, no matter if it's auction or archives, we're still going to need some sort of inventory to figure out what we've got. Best place to start is by figuring out what they were doing. I'm looking at that one unsent envelope on the desk as a prime candidate to explain the secret world of Lady Adelaide and Aunt Moyra."

Landry headed for the envelope that sat like a beacon beside the manual typewriter. Manual typewriters were curious things in today's computer-driven world. Once hailed as revolutionary office technology, it was not uncommon in the 1950s to have secretarial pools full of women in one room, pounding away on their typewriters to produce an original copy and up to three carbon copies. High powered, multi-function photocopiers came later. Make a mistake? In the 1950s, one used an eraser, a pink circular one with a brush to sweep away the eraser detritus so it didn't jam the typewriter keys. Then one used the backspace key and typed over the erasure. In the 1970s and 1980s there was correction fluid or tape. Women who typed with perfect accuracy were prized employees. We'd come a long way, because male executives now did a lot of their own correspondence and women were slowly being represented in managerial ranks. It took us some time, but we got there. The key was to never, ever give up.

Landry held the envelope aloft. "There's quite a few sheets of paper in here," he said. He found an ornate silver letter opener in the top desk drawer and used it to slit the envelope open. He reached inside and pulled out a stack of eight sheets of paper. He furrowed his brow and read aloud:

December 22

Charlene Brinewaythe

Managing Editor

The Kind & Gentleperson's Reality Newspaper

London, England

Dear Charlene.

Attached are the six responses requested for this week's paper. I wish A.L.H.R. was still part of our team; we started this over two decades ago now.

There are days where I wish I knew more about the computer, but at my age I just like what I like. Routine means a lot to me. Thank goodness arthritis hasn't taken the use of my fingers so I'm still a pretty fast and nimble typist.

I do feel for the woman whose husband left her, as well as for the amateur chef who made a complete mess of his soufflé while entertaining his wife's largest client. Hopefully we can provide some help to them ... If anything, a little moral support and positivity, because that's what life is all about.

Yours, as ever,

T.M.

PS: We've recently been inundated with letters from Galfinches Farm in Yorkshire again. Could you please ensure the gentleman living there has all the home support he needs?

"Who on earth are 'A.L.H.R.' and 'T.M.'?" I wondered aloud.

Landry chuckled. "Well, this is fascinating. The pages behind this cover letter are responses to readers' letters. It looks like Lady Adelaide and my Aunt Moyra wrote a weekly column."

"Wait a minute. 'A.L.H.R.' is 'Roycetonne House', then 'Lady Adelaide' spelled backwards. 'T.M.' is 'Terry MacRood'," I said with glee. "Amazing!"

"Who is 'Terry MacRood'?" Landry asked.

He got a succinct response from me. "Only the pseudonym of a super popular advice columnist."

"You have <u>got</u> to be kidding," Gertie said. She read some of the responses behind the cover letter and clucked her tongue. "I don't believe it. These two seniors were the most famous agony aunt in the entire United Kingdom."

Mrs. Neebles looked like she was about to faint from the horror. "I just can't believe it. I did take their post every day but I didn't think anything of them sending a lot of correspondence. I just thought they were conducting private household business, as persons of great wealth do."

The envelope only had a post office box address, no newspaper name was shown.

"They obviously had to keep their identity quiet," Gertie said.

I chuckled. "Well, they most certainly did, and they were being paid quite handsomely for it." I held up a bunch of invoices that I'd found in one of the desk's cubbyholes. "£1,500 per response isn't bad."

"£1,500 for a few words of advice on marriage and cooking? Nice gig," Landry said.

"Terry MacRood is super popular. Tens of thousands of people read her column every week. It's been a full page feature in the paper forever," Gertie said.

"Her? Terry?"

"It's short for Antoinette," Bertie said.

"I forgot. Mr. Fancypants school," I said.

Bertie shrugged. "I am a storehouse of minutia concerning Latin wording, acronyms, abbreviations, and other esoteric paraphernalia."

"And one heck of a schnookered seller of mango chutney. Did you know your freight forwarder has nine lawsuits against them already? Fake damaged goods claims, unpaid invoices. Even the Feds stateside are poking around their balance sheet." Landry looked up from his phone. "Sorry, it's my wheelhouse. I checked earlier but didn't want to spoil your delicious lunch."

"Forget chutney. I want to know more about Aunt Moyra and Lady Adelaide," I said. "Did you know your Aunt Moyra worked after Lady Adelaide passed?"

"For all those years. How lonely." Landry drew in a big sigh. "That explains why she always said she was busy. I just assumed it was with her home care duties."

"Never underestimate a senior," Gertie said. "It's the quiet ones you have to watch out for the most." She grinned.

"So what's the plan, Stan?" I asked the group.

Mrs. Neebles started in a haltingly uncertain voice. "I'm quite uncomfortable taking apart my former employer's private life."

Landry gave her a reassuring look. "Mrs. Neebles. Look upon it as celebrating Aunt Moyra and her long-running column. You were part of keeping that engine running. As for me, I think her writing an advice column is a hoot," he said.

"What do you intend to do with all these historical documents?" Gertie demanded.

"Don't know yet," Landry said.

"So we still have ample time to lobby for them to be catalogued and donated to a proper archive?" I asked.

"You do. But what we see here doesn't leave this room, capiche? Until we know what's going on, then I don't want Terry's secret to get blabbed to the world," he said.

"You could set up shop here and continue the tradition," I joked.

Landry nodded. "I don't think I could do the ladies justice."

"Excellent, old chap," Bertie said. "Now, my drafty castle doesn't allow for offsite management. I need Severs to drive me back."

"It's been a real slice," Landry said, extending his hand.

As the two men shook, Bertie got a tiny smile at the side of his face. "Thank you for setting me straight with my chutney. Lesson learned."

Chapter 12

––––

After Bertie left, we did some more exploring in the house. Back upstairs in the 'office' or 'hoarding room' as Landry called it, we made another discovery. Against the far wall, perpendicular to the desks on either side of the room, were built in closets. We had to tug on them a bit to get them open, but the old, sticky paint finally gave way—it had expanded with time and presumably fossilized from lack of use—and we gazed upon a life forgotten.

"But there's dozens of them," I exclaimed as everyone crowded around me. We were looking at a long closet full of stylish Edwardian ladies' tea dresses and dinner gowns. Every color of pastel under the rainbow. Silk, satin and damask, floral lace and even some with trains that hooked to a lady's wrist for dancing. A plethora of hat boxes sat on a shelf up above the clothes rod, and elegant purses had their own shelf at the right end of the closet.

"A far cry from the completely black ensembles we saw in Lady Adelaide's room," Gertie observed. She turned to Mrs. Neebles. "Did they ever say anything to you about these clothes?"

Mrs. Neebles shook her head. "I only knew Lady Adelaide in her later years and all I ever saw her wear were black dresses."

"Like Queen Victoria. She mourned her husband Albert for decades," I said.

Landry ran a finger over a purse's shelf and it came away dusty. "There must be an air vent near here somewhere."

"Why on earth stash all these lovely clothes away? Why not wear them?" I murmured, finding the paper and cord tags hung over the top of each hanger. The one I currently held in my hand read: 'Doctor Parson's Ball, 1934'.

Gertie looked over my shoulder. "Either she was into costume balls or there's a collection we haven't found yet. People weren't wearing this type of dress in 1934. Try 1921."

"It's hard to say what happened here," I said.

"What are these fancy frocks worth in today's market?" Landry teased.

"Don't you dare even think that right now," I warned. "This is your heritage, something unique to enjoy and discover."

"I'm not a blood relative of Lady Adelaide," he said.

"Perhaps not. But you were related to her best friend, someone who thought highly enough of you to trust you with what she left behind."

"What, all this?" Landry asked, spreading his hands wide. "I can't imagine what I'm to do with it all."

"Preserve it," Gertie added.

Landry turned to look back at the room full of old documents. "Time to redecorate, I'd say. Out with the old, in with the new."

"But surely you must appreciate how your ancestors built your future."

Landry thought on it for a moment. "I appreciate those who built our nations. But I assure you, Aunt Moyra knew nothing of the cybersecurity business."

"You're missing the point. Her work with Lady Adelaide helped your family progress, put a roof over your head."

"It was my grandfather who started the retail catalog company."

"Yes. And didn't Moyra help select new product lines for the firm to carry in the 1960-70s?"

Landry looked shocked. "How on earth did you know that?"

"Gertie and I did some online newspaper archive research last night. It's amazing what old advertisements, grand openings and business organization meetings can teach you about the past," I said.

"And you got all that from newspapers?" Landry said, amazed.

"People were more open in the past. Didn't have so many sketchy people to worry about stealing your identity online. Take the 1950s picket fences versus today where we've got kids at schools with weapons and drugs, plus people stealing others' identities every minute of the day. It's scary," Gertie said.

"Hmm. I'm impressed." He rocked back on the heels of his boots.

"And, our point is, if someone didn't bother to save all the newspapers, then we wouldn't have them available to research, would we?" I said.

Landry broke out in a wide grin. "You've got me there, ladies. Show me some more and maybe this family history thing will start to grow on me."

"Wonderful!" Gertie said.

He held up a finger. "I said maybe, not guaranteed. I still need a lot more convincing than a few interesting facts about my grandaddy's business."

"Tough crowd," I observed.

We got on with more exploration of the closet and surrounds. All the purses were empty, save for one tortoiseshell hair comb and eight giant pennies from 1901. We'd reached the end of our quest inside this secret closet.

"Mrs. Neebles, have you ever looked inside any of these albums?" I asked, turning to the loaded shelves beside us.

"I'm afraid I've never laid eyes on them before."

"So they were never kept downstairs?"

"Never." She bristled at the mere thought.

"Fine. Landry, how about we look inside?"

"Go for it."

I pulled down the first tome. It was leather-bound and dated 1893. Inside were black and white photographs of an era gone by. At the front, photos of Lady Adelaide's parents in somber Victorian clothes. Her mother wore a masculine dress with leg-of-mutton sleeves, hat and coat that matched her skirt. Lady Adelaide's father stood rigid in his formal suit with tall top hat. It was followed by pictures of Roycetonne House under construction, completion and then with a full complement of household staff in a group photo out front. It then branched out into various chapters that showed the gardens, stables with carriage horses, fancy tea parties outside on the terrace, the beehive-busy kitchen, fancy bedrooms, the drawing room, portrait gallery, the dairy stacked high with aging cheeses and the laundry, complete with mangle.

"I recognize that man," Mrs. Neebles said, peering over my shoulder. "He was a Viscount from somewhere up north."

"Yorkshire?"

"No, I think it was farther than that. Perhaps Scotland. I remember Lady Adelaide speaking of him a few times. He was like an uncle to her. His portrait hangs in the long gallery downstairs."

"It's like an era frozen in time," I murmured as I placed the album down on a table at the side of the room. "Everything perfectly preserved, a living time capsule."

"It looks like they spent a packet on their house and staff," Landry observed. "And look at the carriage with four in hand. Horses are not cheap to keep."

"Do you have horses back home in Texas?" I asked.

"No ma'am. But a buddy of mine has a ranch and he keeps quarter horses for herding specialty longhorn cattle."

I turned the page in the album. "Look. The kitchen garden was absolutely massive back then. Check out the size of those vegetable marrows!" The gardens sprawled out with every kind of vegetable one could imagine, ample herbs, and fruit trees teased in the espalier gardening method to grow flat against the wall.

We moved onto an album containing photos from Lady Adelaide's childhood.

"Such a bonny baby," Mrs. Neebles said, putting a finger to the side of the page to hold it flat. "She only grew prettier as the years passed."

"Such as shame, the tragedy of the fire in 1941. Seems as though she paid for it dearly over the course of her life," I said.

"She paid dearly, indeed, what with the black dresses and locking herself away here at Roycetonne House. It appears the world was never quite sure if she set the fire or not," Gertie said.

Mrs. Neebles spoke in a quiet voice. "Her husband was a nasty man."

Gertie hauled out another album from the shelf. "Look, Lady Adelaide's wedding."

"What a beautiful bride." It was all white lace and demure smiles from Lady Adelaide as she was placed as center of attention, a vision of loveliness. Her dress was formal, high neckline, and long sleeved, making her look every bit the young, stunning aristocratic beauty. But Lady Adelaide's eyes looked haunted, lonely, as if something was missing on her special day.

"She looks deer-in-the-headlights, a bit," I said.

"She looks like she regrets doing her duty," Gertie replied. "One almost guesses that she's got her fingers crossed behind her back during her vows."

"I can relate," I said. Gertie and I exchanged a knowing glance.

In the photo, Lady Adelaide's father stood behind the just-married couple. Pleased as punch, yet stern and authoritative. It was clear to the viewer this was an arranged marriage that benefited the family bloodline and not amorous hearts.

"Why couldn't she just elope with the man she really loved?" I asked.

"It wasn't so easy back in those days. Father controlled the purse strings very tightly, and in a high society position, there wasn't much hope of a young girl getting away from his purvey, well, unless she joined a nunnery," Gertie said. "I could be here all day looking at these albums. What a lovely record of a family's history."

"I think we should broaden the search a bit more. Look into the active desk's cubbyholes. See if we can find out anything else about the work they were doing with the newspapers or the Yorkshire farm that letter mentions," I said.

"One more. Just one more," Gertie whispered. She pulled down a random album marked '1935'. Inside were photos of Lady Adelaide with her husband and their two lovely daughters. It was definitely a staged happy time. They were shown outside with ponies, inside with the harpsichord, outside again on a fancy carriage ride with two lovely matched dapple grey carriage horses. The family was there, watching Lady Adelaide's husband dedicate a new building. He wore an expensive suit with a fancy rose in his buttonhole for added good measure.

"Lady Adelaide's smile is frozen. Not real," I said. "If only pictures could talk."

Gertie nodded. We both looked up as Landry brought over a stack of Edwardian calling cards, business card sized items that were given to a grand house's butler who then in turn brought them to the lady of the house on a silver tray, as he issued an unobtrusive bow.

The stack of cards before us read like a who's who of the aristocracy in England during the early twentieth century. Each one was dated on the back, presumably by a member of household staff. It went up to 1939 and then abruptly stopped.

"1939. And then nothing?" Landry asked in all seriousness.

I shook my head. "A good family historian will put the date into context with social history at the time. Ask yourself what else was going on in 1939 on the bigger stage."

"Peace for our time," Landry said, referring to the misleading peace agreement signed to delay the outcome of World War Two.

"Exactly. It wasn't seen as very appropriate to deck oneself out in satin and pearls, fire up the motorcar and tootle along the countryside visiting friends on a whim," I said.

"Besides, petrol was on ration and many of the aristocratic men were serving as officers while their wives stayed behind to keep the home front fires burning. There were quite a few of the upper class women who donated countless hours of volunteer time to help with the war effort."

"I wonder what Lady Adelaide did?" Landry mused. "I wonder what Aunt Moyra did."

Gertie, Mrs. Neebles and I exchanged a knowing look.

I put another album into his hand. "Don't wonder. The answers are right in front of you. They just need discovering."

"That's what Bertie told me about Scotford Castle at Christmas dinner. He said that they're constantly learning new things about the past with all the restoration and preservation work that they do."

"So open the album." I already had taken a peek inside and knew what treasure lay within.

"Didn't we need to go through some more papers first? I thought you had to be back by tonight?" Landry asked.

"Yes, but I urge you to look inside this one."

"What's this?" he asked with a chuckle.

He stopped chuckling when he saw inside. Once Landry opened the album he understood why I'd been goading him. Inside the album was a hollowed out center—no surrounding pages—and in that hollowed space sat a floral-patterned diary. The nameplate on the front read 'Lady Adelaide Roycetonne – The Wrongs of My Life'.

"I'll bet there's some pretty poignant stuff in there," Gertie said.

Mrs. Neebles was interested. Not curious, never could she be curious. Of course not. But she did give us a solemn glance and said, "Moyra was indeed telling the truth about the diary's existence."

"She spoke of it?" I asked.

"Once. To me, following a New Year's Eve dinner after she had an uncharacteristic three glasses of champagne. She said there was a diary that set the record straight on Lady Adelaide's behalf, but never told me where it was. All I knew was that the truth was up in Yorkshire."

"What was that in the letter, 'P.S.' and something on a Galfinches Farm?" I asked.

"Something like that," Landry said.

"I'm due to go up to Yorkshire with Ewan soon for a house clearance evaluation. It's about a six-hour drive, so not a short commute. Maybe we could suss out the farm when we go," I offered.

"It's not as though we have a shortage of things to do here," Gertie said, looking at the mountain of historical paperwork surrounding us.

We all took another look around the room, full of towers of old family documents. Gertie was right. It would take a small army of volunteers to whip this chaos into some sort of order.

The question was, could we convert Landry over to our way of thinking about how precious this hoard of paperwork was? Only our best efforts and time would tell.

Chapter 13

———

GGRS. Next Day.

"I still love my commute," Maude said with a big smile on her face.

"All of your, what, forty-two steps from home threshold to entrance to the research site?" Ewan asked.

"Yes. And it's a fabulous way to spend my retirement. I'm so glad not to have to worry about leaky water pipes, plugged outdoor lake fountains and cracks in the walls." She raised her hands as if to push all those negative tasks out of her immediate sphere. "I am firmly convinced that I did the right thing by selling up."

"And Petmond Grange is destined as–" I started.

"An upscale bed and breakfast, you know, the kind that serves jams in individual jars? Some corporate group from Wales is taking over. Nice people."

I leaned back in my chair and appreciated the talented senior in front of me. She was truly a wealth of information when it came to genealogy and family history research. "Our world gets such a benefit from your time here spent helping people. Thank you."

Maude's eyes shone with delight. "I'm thrilled to be contributing at my age."

Ewan grinned as he fiddled with a stapler, trying to unjam it. "Maude, seventy is the new fifty. Never forget that. Eat healthy foods, don't smoke, do moderate exercise and keep your mind active. That combination will go a long way to keeping you 'around instead of in the ground'."

"Ewan!" I exclaimed.

Maude and Ewan smiled back at me.

"It's part of family history, Julie. Birth, marriage and death research. We all have to go sometime," she said.

I shook my head. "Well, I won't be ready for a long time yet. Especially when a certain someone here needs so much help."

A lone folded staple shot across the desk making me jump as it pinged off the computer printer. I rubbed the plastic, glad it hadn't made a mark. Ewan put the stapler back like a guilty child. "Sorry, but I did fix it." He looked like a little boy who'd been caught taking apart the family heirloom grandfather clock.

"Can you go and find something else to do besides loitering at our front desk?" I teased. "How about welcoming those two new visitors?"

Maude and I giggled as Ewan followed direction, sheepish, and strode over to the pair who'd just entered the site. One was a well-dressed woman in her forties, crisp designer dress and blazer. The other was a senior with white permed hair and a set of sparkling violet eyes. The senior used a walker and I silently thanked our construction team and planning committee for being so attuned to the needs of all visitors here at GGRS. The senior was able to enter without fuss, pushing the button at the side wall to open the entrance doors. To me, it didn't look like her walker slowed her down at all; in fact, she looked completely raring to go.

"Welcome, Ladies," I said as they approached the information desk. I noted how the younger of the pair took a big, obvious step forward to get ahead of the senior. I frowned, then put back on my happy face. "How can we help?"

"Good morning." The fortyish woman spoke with a firm Lake District accent and was all business. "My name is Hayleigh Grables-Muncton and this is my client Sherry Knox. We'd like to look at your heraldry library and do a few online searches using your genealogy programs."

Interesting. Someone who knew exactly what they were after and how the research site could serve them best.

"Of course, let me show you where you can hang your coats and then I'll take you to the stacks. I believe we have two computer carrells free right now; usually we ask visitors to prebook, but as it's the holiday season our numbers are a bit lower than regular," I said.

Hayleigh and Sherry turned for the locker area and got set up for their visit. They appeared to know all about protocol including no food, drink, pens, highlighters or large bags while using onsite resources. It looked to be a very promising start.

I felt a nudge at my elbow and turned to see Maude gesture me close, a worried look on her face. "Is there a problem?"

"I'm concerned," she said.

"About what?"

"Anytime I hear a professional genealogist ask to see heraldry references, I wonder if they are leading their client down a garden path."

"How so?"

"Oh, it's the classic scam, 'give me your money and I'll get you back to Alfred the Great in twelve easy steps'," Maude explained.

I was skeptical. "We don't know that's the case here. Besides, Hayleigh looks professional enough."

"Clothes aren't everything, Julie. I saw people taken advantage of an awful lot at the Family History Society when we had our library in Plumsden. We were constantly on the lookout."

"That's terrible."

"Just let's be cautious, alright?" Maude said. "Here they come now." Her face went from concerned to bright and happy. "Now then, you were interested in our heraldry collection? Is there a specific family crest you're seeking?"

I sat back down in the information desk chair, confident Maude would set things right. I saw Ewan over with them, helping Sherry transition over from her walker into a comfortable computer chair. The GGRS was warm, cozy and filled with the confident keyboard clicks of researchers busy finding more ancestors. Aunt Edwina had left me a wonderful legacy and I was honored to share it with the community. All truly looked calm and good in my little purvey. That was until I went over to the dedicated office to work on our newsletter. I looked left and was unexpectedly confronted with four large fluttering nostrils of two enormous Shire horses emitting clouds of breath on the windowpanes.

✳✳✳

Back Entrance. Milliseconds Later.

"What on earth are two Shire horses doing in Greymore's back yard?" I asked, giving an incredulous look at Gertie and three of the youth choir's young men.

"The brewery went bankrupt. Now Bingo and Jim have nowhere to go," a sixteen-year old explained.

I was astonished. "But they can't just turn two horses out onto the streets. Surely. I mean–"

Gertie approached with Harvey who was desperately wringing his flat cap like whey from white cheddar cheese. "Bingo and Jim are both in their twenties, not much value left on the open market. The bankruptcy advisor said there was only one option–"

A rousing hue and cry went up amongst all the youth standing in the vicinity. Different voices called out:

"We won't let that happen!"

"It's not right!"

"It can't be so!"

"Let's keep them somewhere safe!"

I had one initial question and looked at Harvey. "Please tell me you didn't steal Bingo and Jim."

"Not exactly," Harvey said.

"Not exactly?"

"Well, I paid for them. I gave them a generous amount more than what the abattoir quoted me for their estimated weight."

"So we're in the clear?"

Another unwelcome pause. A couple of 'Ahem's'.

"Well, the bankruptcy administrator said that he couldn't sell them until the paperwork was wrapped up."

"So Bingo and Jim are indeed stolen? On the lam, on the hoof?"

"Well, not really. I left my money with the bankruptcy administrator's secretary."

"Did she give you a receipt?"

"Well, no. I just left the money with her and included a note."

"So you did steal two horses?" I was getting concerned. At any moment surely Constable Snowdrop would race in, blue lights ablaze on his service vehicle.

"The abattoir's van was parked at the front entrance."

Well. That certainly changed things.

"And Bingo and Jim have worked at the brewery for how long?" I asked.

"Since they were three years old."

"And now that they're in their later years, the firm just wants to toss them out like used socks?"

A sea of sad faces surrounded me. Their wails started up again.

"It's not fair!"

"We need to do something!"

"Can't we keep them here, Julie?"

I held up my hands to quiet this rightly noisy crowd. By this point, I was sure it was louder than a mob attending an eighteenth century public hanging at Tyburn.

"Folks. Please. I'm not allowing these horses to be sold for meat."

I received a rousing cheer.

"Secondly, we need to ensure title of ownership is officially passed to Greymore."

Harvey looked pretty dejected. "I don't know how to convince them. The bankruptcy man is a pretty hardnosed person."

"There is one surefire way of getting him to sell you the Shire horses," a newly added voice said. We all turned to see none other than Fred Todling, smug solicitor, standing beside the horses and tentatively patting one. His fancy pinstriped navy suit and shiny black shoes were splendid. That was, until Bingo decided he liked the way Fred was patting his shoulder and started to bob his head up and down in time. Next, Jim reached out to see if he could get in on the action but as he did, he coughed.

Poor Fred was instantly splattered with horse saliva laden with small, bright green bits of hay. As a bonus, Fred's lapel now carried a rather interesting fern-like pattern of slobbery, munched up carrot, no doubt fed in abandon by the youth choir who'd ridden out with Harvey to save these magnificent animals.

"I say. Well, I do say …" Fred brushed himself off while small bits of chortling went around our group.

I shot everyone a serious glance to keep them quiet. Solicitors had a way of making an entrance and sometimes saving the day.

Or not.

One only had to recall Fred and his mistaken toga costume at Bertie's summer solstice party earlier this year. Fred had finished out the party in a tight Scottish kilt which, although more modest than the cartoon-bedsheet toga, still left too few things to the imagination.

It was wise to be a bit skeptical when Fred was in the immediate vicinity.

As the solicitor wiped the horse goo off his expensive suit, he harumphed and stood up straight. He'd need industrial cleaner for his glasses that were now filmed with green and orange smears. "I propose a rather ingenious solution to this indelicately unfortunate and horribly unfair situation, in every single aspect, motion and meaning of the word. It is not often that one walks the hallowed halls of the legal profession and so quickly stumbles upon such a brilliant, succinct, assured and well-defined plan. We have a veritable conundrum before this very talented group of people, the delightfully effervescent youth of this fine, upstanding community of Oakhurst."

Get to it today, not next year, Fred.

Fred continued. "And our youth will play an absolutely pinnacle, definitive role in the creative and slam-dunking, if I may be so colloquially bold, convincing act that we shall unleash, with your utmost permission, of course, on said bankruptcy trustees." He looked over the rims of his vegetable-filmed glasses at Harvey for confirmation.

Harvey shrugged. "I suppose the bankruptcy administrator works for a group of trustees."

"That is soundly typical. Right. Aforesaid group of trustees is the only body of authority able to approve expenditures and distribution of assets," Fred announced in a confident voice.

"But Bingo and Jim aren't assets. They're living creatures!" wailed a ten-year-old, rosy-cheeked boy in a puffer coat, bobble hat, scarf and mittens.

"After a lifetime of service pulling brewery wagons, they deserve better," Gertie said.

Fred cleared his throat again. He looked like he was talking though a manure-spreading tractor's windshield ... in the middle of a car wash.

"Ahem. So, as I was perambulating, the task at hand is to convince the trustees that Bingo and Jim belong in a suitable retirement abode such as the esteemed Greymore Hall estate. Correct, Julie?"

I was about to agree to housing two giant equines on my estate. And you know what? I didn't have to think twice. "Correct, Fred."

"So my undeniable, wholehearted and underlying prompt to this entire, categorically kind group here before me today, is to use our own assets in as wide a manner possible," Fred announced.

"How so?" I didn't quite get where Fred was going with this. Looking around the group, I didn't think anyone else did either.

For once, Fred decided that gestures spoke louder than words. He signaled over to Gertie who was quickly checking her phone.

Then the lightbulb went off in my head. "Social media. We'll shame the company into doing the right thing."

"Ah," Fred said, holding up a finger, "let's not corner our opponent just yet. Rather, let's tell the world we want to save these horses, are willing to pay a reasonable price and they will live the rest of their years in never ending comfort. Start positive, polite, and persuasive. That's always my first rule in any legal dispute."

"I think that might just work. I've snapped a few photos of the horses. Julie can you post these from the official Greymore account?" Gertie asked.

"It's as good as done."

A large cheer went up around the courtyard.

Fred beamed. "And how many followers do you currently have, Gertie?"

"Er, somewhere between eighteen and twenty million."

"Very well then. I think between you and the youth here today, the problem should be resolved by tomorrow morning, at three minutes after ten at the latest."

"Why then?"

"Because that's when I intend to take the call from the chairman of the trustee group. No sense in appearing too eager and answering at 9:00 a.m. sharp. Half of legal work is posturing." He beamed.

❊❊❊

162

"You have quite the goings-on here at GGRS," Hayleigh said in a dry voice as I re-entered from my foray outside concerning all things equine.

"Oh, it's all in good fun, really. We're animal lovers here too. Our new Shires will live in the old stables. Gertie and I both used to have ponies there as children."

"I hope they will fit into the ponies' old looseboxes," Sherry said, a twinkle in her eye.

"They already visited over Christmas and stayed in two of the larger looseboxes. My grandparents also had carriage horses and draft horses here at Greymore."

"Do you store a lot in your outbuildings, like old furniture and garden tools? That's what I do." Sherry was fascinated by our conversation and I sensed she was a good egg, someone who appreciated the past and cared to see it documented. The GGRS library's manor house book on the table beside her was a dead giveaway.

I smiled. "We do. Unused buildings tend to get a lot of old furniture, broken plant pots, plumbing accessories, farming implements. It's the 'do later' pile of stuff."

"Everything one can't bear to part with because it might come in handy one day," Sherry said.

"Exactly. Did you find what you need in our archives?" I asked, purely out of friendly interest.

I literally felt Hayleigh bristle beside me when I asked the question.

"We're doing very nicely, thank you. Come along, Sherry. I have found just the thing to add to your family tree." Hayleigh motioned for Sherry to follow her like an obedient sheep. It looked a bit off.

"Ooh. A new ancestor? How exciting!" I said in what I hoped was an encouraging voice.

Sherry nodded then dutifully went back under Hayleigh's so-called 'expert' guidance. I wasn't invited to come see.

Maude gestured for me to come into a break room. She shut the door behind us. "We have a problem."

"Worse than rehoming two stolen senior Shire horses?"

She nodded. "To put it bluntly, Hayleigh Grables-Muncton is a fraudster and taking Sherry for the ride of her wallet's life."

Chapter 14

———

Kilburn's Outstanding Antiques, Plumsden.
Next Morning. 8:00 a.m.

"Did you enjoy learning about the agony aunts?" Ewan asked me, completely bright and smiley.

My face fell about a mile. Ah, one of those not so fun ethical questions that arose when helping someone with their family history. Their secrets were supposed to stay that way until the family chose to disclose. I guessed that Landry trusted Ewan and let the information slip as a carrot to get some insights as to the value of the furniture, carpets, statues and collections on site. Roycetonne House's silver collection alone must be worth thousands of pounds. I would have to remind Gertie to check it for any of her favorite embossed swan design pieces; she was still trying to complete her coffee, tea and sugar bowl set.

Ewan soon put me out of my misery. "Don't worry. Landry swore me to secrecy as well. He called me yesterday about obtaining some antique furniture appraisals after he dropped you back at Greymore."

"I see. And yes, the agony aunt reveal was interesting. Fascinating, actually." I was at Ewan's shop to work the other side of Landry, i.e. ensure Ewan knew how Landry wasn't fully convinced of the importance of family history and its related paraphernalia. It wasn't unethical when one was desperate to save both a family's and a community's legacy … was it?

I decided yesterday to beg forgiveness later instead of asking permission first on this particular family history venture. My heart was in the right place, and thousands of archivists, genealogists and historians around the world would shudder at the thought of Landry's wonderful heritage collection being broken up and sold off in pieces to highest bidders around the globe. Our nation's heritage needed to be preserved, and great families' records fit squarely within that bracket.

"About Landry and–"

"Selling the proverbial kitchen sink?" Ewan asked with a grin. "Don't worry. It's like I've always said: the ethical conundrum in the antiques trade is preserving history versus letting some rich buyer purchase something to forever squirrel it away in a private home. There are so many treasures that the public will never see again."

"So how do you sleep at night?"

"Knowing that I have enough connections to alert the museums and national collection curators of a rare object first, before it goes into my store."

"I'm glad you've got that ethical balance."

"Yes." He gazed at me with kind eyes. "What else is bothering you?"

"Maude."

"Maude? How can that delightful woman bother you?" Ewan asked.

"No, not Maude herself. It's what she told me yesterday. She thinks a client of a professional genealogist using GGRS facilities is getting scammed out of her money."

"That's unfortunate. What's Maude doing about it?"

"She asked me to leave it with her. Maude will try to speak with the client at an opportune moment. She's apparently seen it before at the Plumsden Family History Society."

He grinned. "Is the client someone who's been encouraged to purchase a family tree that goes back to William the Conqueror in twelve easy steps? Photos included?"

I scoffed. "You and I both know that photography wasn't mainstream until at least 1860."

He smiled back. Then we shared a laugh.

"It's not funny, though. Maude didn't like what she was hearing about heraldry," I said.

"Good money being thrown after bad?" Ewan asked.

"Something like that. The client and the professional genealogist were only in for the first time this week. I don't know all the details."

"I'm sure Maude has things well in hand by now. Trust your team to handle it."

"Says the one-man-band of the antiques store."

He held up an index finger. "Ah, but that's where the gig economy and outsourcing comes in. I choose to bring in experts for the things I don't know how to do or cannot do well. Things like setting up accounting software, online marketing and heavy furniture moving."

"I'd still be careful with that arm of yours. Can't be wise to lift anything heavy with it for a while yet." Ewan broke his right arm not too long ago and although the cast was long gone, we still felt protective of him.

"Doctor says I'm fine, but I agreed to take it easy."

A thick horn and the hiss of airbrakes sounded outside his shop. I looked out the window and saw a 'Sammy B. Finchweather's Moving and Cartage' lorry pull up at the curb.

"Delivery?" I asked, curious. "More furniture to squirrel away in wealthy persons' private abodes?"

Ewan nodded. "I've been asked to help with a sympathetic restoration of an eighteenth century country house up in Yorkshire. Today they're here collecting two sideboards, a bedroom set, dining table and twelve chairs."

"And they're going to take all that today?" It was a lot of moving parts.

"Some of the pieces come apart and the craftspeople will reassemble on site. The rest go well-padded, as is."

The front door opened and the tiny shop bell trilled as two burly movers walked in. Both wore overalls and high visibility vests. "Ewan Kilburn?"

"Yes, hello gents," Ewan said.

"We have a work order to take a load of furniture to Yorkshire for you?" The older mover, about forty-five, looked unfamiliar with the place.

"Yes, and it's eighteenth century fragile, so we'll need to be careful."

The older of the movers spoke in a reassuring tone. "We've moved loads of fragile pieces before. All part of our firm's specialty training. The nose of the truck's got extra padding, too, in case of sudden stops.'

"I'm relieved to hear it. I have a local firm I usually employ, but this time the buyer arranged transport."

"A lot less hassle for you then," the younger mover, in his twenties, said. He was one of those people blessed with a baby face, someone who could pass for twelve when he was thirty. I surmised that if he ever wanted to pursue a change of occupation, he'd be a successful undercover youth crime policeman.

"Indeed," Ewan said. "I've tagged all the pieces with the house's name. If you park in the alley behind the shop then we can load through the double doors."

"Perfect. We'll move the lorry."

I looked at Ewan, watching the movers head out the front door back to their vehicle. "Hey, what happened to the house clearance up in Yorkshire?"

"It's off."

"Off?"

"Lady of the house changed her mind. And the carpets. Suddenly the old became new again."

"Oh dear."

"It happens." He gave me a grin. "Maybe next time."

✿✿✿

Two Hours Later.

Ewan and I were in the nose of the lorry, surrounded by furniture. He put his hand on the leather-padded, chair rail type protection that was an extra set of bumpering against damage. Large vehicles tended to lurch around corners, and up in Yorkshire there was always the risk of unexpected, wayward sheep loose on the road.

"This looks good to me." Ewan ran a caring hand over the straps holding his finely polished furniture pieces in place. "I'm just concerned the delivery gets there in one piece."

"I'd imagine some of these pieces are irreplaceable," I said.

"A couple of them are, yes. Much like a special lady I know." We stood facing each other and his compliment caught me off guard. Then, as we realized we were totally alone inside the lorry, Ewan Kilburn bent down and kissed me.

Right.

Then.

And.

There.

And it was wonderful.

170

I pulled back first and looked into his caring eyes. "I think I felt the earth move."

"Me too," Ewan said in his kind voice that I adored. His eyes looked dreamy.

I stepped back into the arms of a dining room chair stacked sideways in amongst the other furniture pieces. "Um, no, Ewan. The earth really is moving."

The lorry lurched forward. Then took a hard left. We were leaving the alley and heading out onto the high street of Plumsden. Kudos to whomever had designed the tailgate to close with such silence.

"There must be a mistake." Ewan banged on the nose of the lorry with his fist.

BANG!

BANG!

The noise was muffled at best.

"Didn't they say goodbye?"

"They checked that we were all done and I signed off on the paperwork. I called out that we were going into the lorry to check everything was secure."

I groaned. " And that's when I showed them where the toilets were. They headed out and assumed they could leave after both took time doing their, er, business."

His face fell. "We're trapped inside a moving lorry."

"En route to Yorkshire." I looked around at what would be our surroundings for the next six or so hours. "You really are keen on us going on a trip up north, aren't you?"

"Appears so." He looked downcast.

We looked at each other, panicked eyes. Then both of us started pounding on the walls of the lorry again.

No luck. We were locked in for the duration.

There was a small area in between securely-packed pieces of furniture. We slid down the wall, sitting next to each other, knees drawn up against our chests.

He looked at me, a concerned expression on his face. "I think it's going to get cold. We're in the middle of winter and just off a large snowstorm. North Yorkshire's even colder up on those remote moors."

"This furniture's going up there? That is a chilly spot in winter."

"The sheep are glad for their woolly coats." Ewan looked around us. He scrounged a couple of spare moving blankets and draped them over us. They were well-insulated so at least we wouldn't freeze.

"Six hours. Let's take stock of any sustenance we have."

"I didn't pack for a road trip," I said. I brought my satchel up on my lap and dug through. "One bottle of water, an energy bar, four dried apricots and a packet of sugar cubes."

"All I have is a packet of chewing gum and a highly preservative-laden, plastic-wrapped cake." He pulled the slightly mashed cake out of his shirt pocket.

"You just happened to have it in there?"

"I grabbed it from my emergency stash at the shop just before leaving. I was planning on getting an early start on paperwork today and skipped breakfast."

I picked up the sugary cake and examined it up close. "You do know that this could likely survive a nuclear blast? There's a reason they don't need expiry dates on these products."

He nodded, sorrowful. "The one day I go off my healthy diet–"

"One day?" I wasn't having any of it.

"Okay, the one day a week I go off my healthy diet and you notice."

We looked at the sorry mound of food before us.

"Definitely not a five star meal," I said.

"Let's forget food for a moment. Did you lock the antiques shop?"

He nodded. "Yes, once I signed the paperwork I was headed out to my car, parked right in front of yours. I was going to call Landry and–"

Our eyes met again. "Phone?" he asked. "We could call the moving company's dispatcher."

I held mine up. "Battery died last night because the pins in the charging port broke."

"Oh dear."

"What?"

"I left mine back at the shop when I put it down to examine the ageless cake," Ewan said, very woebegone.

We sat back against the wall and pondered our fate. It was quite unusual, this situation. It wasn't kidnapping by any means. But being driven six or more hours away from your plans and home village constituted a rather large upset in one's life.

"So we're stuck here, I suppose," I said.

"I'm afraid so."

"Too bad furniture doesn't do charades."

He smirked.

"Tell me about the house they're going to, all this lovely furniture." I had to admit I was a bit curious, seeing the lovely pieces with their gleaming wood burnished smooth from years of use.

"It's a manor house that was recently sold by a family which had owned it for centuries. The new owner is a business executive from Switzerland."

"More like business tycoon, no doubt, I said.

"Granted, those houses aren't cheap to run. But this man's on a mission to renovate the right way. He went down to bare framing in some rooms, fixed all the plumbing and heating properly, then redecorated in a manner sympathetic to the period."

"No sense in fixing dents in the ceiling if the trusses are cracked."

"Exactly."

I wrapped the blanket around me and because it was so huge, used part of it as a pillow for my head. Small mercies: the lorry had a good shock system. I looked around the pile of furniture and the hard floor slats we were sitting on. There was only one thing left to be said:

"Gosh Ewan, you really know how to show a girl a good time."

He grinned.

"So, what are we going to do when we get there?" I asked.

"Ask the drivers to ship us home. Pronto," he said.

"I doubt a train to Plumsden from Yorkshire will be running that time of night," I said.

"How so?"

"Six hours to Yorkshire. Then they have to get up onto the moors through snow. That's another hour or two. It won't be until this evening that we get there." I snuggled down more in my solo-blanket cocoon. "I expect you to find us two rooms, at a decent establishment, preceded by a healthy, hot meal. That's your job."

His face looked a little uncertain. And then he groaned.

"What now?"

"It's the Viking festival this weekend. All the hotels are sold out."

"But a manor house isn't going to be in a city center."

"No, but that particular manor house hosts parties and conferences. The Viking festival headquarters are at the house where the furniture's going. The owner told me a few weeks ago. I just remembered."

"Why would the owner schedule a furniture delivery in the midst of a festival?" It didn't make sense to me.

"He wants immediate revenue to make the house self-sufficient. He's also got family coming in six days for his daughter's winter wedding and the rooms have to be properly furnished." Ewan rested his head back against a folded-over piece of blanket and sighed. "This is going to be an awfully long day." He gave me a sideways glance. "This wipes the ceiling disaster slate clean for eternity."

Chapter 15

City of York, Yorkshire. Six Hours Later.

We stopped for petrol. At the station, we heard the drivers lower the ramp to check the cargo, talking animatedly between themselves about the latest rugby match on the telly. As soon as we saw daylight, Ewan and I were both up and scrambled to the end of the vehicle's cargo area.

The drivers both took huge steps backwards, the ramp clattering to the ground as they set eyes upon us, both still wrapped up in moving blankets and looking exceedingly worse for wear. I was dusty, hungry and bone-weary. I imagined Ewan felt the exact same.

"But ... but. Please tell me you haven't been with us all the way from Plumsden." The older driver spoke with a combination of amazement and embarrassment.

Ewan cleared his throat. "There appears to be some mix-up between my signing your shipment lading bill and Julie here showing you to the toilets."

"My boss will have my hide for this," the older man said, "Stowaway cats, I've had them twice. A marmalade tom plus a sneaky tortoiseshell kitten. Nearly transported a wayward calf once. But people? This marks a first."

The air rushing in was frigid. I saw a car loaded down with four hefty men dressed in Viking costumes. All exited the vehicle. Three went into the store, while the one with straggly grey hair, wool-lined tunic and leggings stayed to refuel. At this moment in time, I wished I had the hot blood of a Viking coursing through my veins. Six hours in a cargo bay of a moving vehicle wasn't the warmest idea of the century.

"Good grief. You must be frozen. Come with me into the cab," the older driver said. "Bryan, get some hot food and drinks for our, um, clients."

Ewan and I were escorted to the bench seat behind the two front club seats and immediately were cloaked in warmth.

The driver put his head in his hands over the steering wheel. "How on earth did we not see you? We couldn't hear you either."

"I will give you this, your vehicles are quite well-insulated," Ewan said. "We had the moving blankets around us and it only got really cold when you lowered the ramp and the winter air started to rush in."

"My absolutely, deepest apologies. I feel quite the fool now having been oblivious for six hours. Thank goodness you didn't have a pile of furniture topple on you."

"I checked all the rigging once we were on the road to no return. You did an extremely good job securing everything," Ewan said.

The second, younger driver returned with a bag of food and hot drinks. We gobbled down roast chicken, French fries, gravy and coffee. Not exactly fine dining and ambiance, but I no longer cared. The only thing Ewan and I had left between us was the crushed chocolate cake and I refused to eat something that might make me glow in the dark. The petrol station food was sustenance and not a minute too soon.

I used the driver's mobile phone to call Maude and let her know what happened.

The Vikings were all back in their refueled car and drove out, the car sagging under their weight.

"I'll bet they have a load of shields and spears in the back," Ewan said.

"Plus their helmets," I added. "Did you know it's a myth that the Vikings had horns on their helmets?"

The three men in the cab gave me sideways glances.

"Er, right," the older driver said. "Now, shall I drop you at a hotel here in York? My firm will pick up the tab plus, of course, cost of return transport."

Ewan shook his head. "Everything's sold out for the Viking festival."

"Well, we're heading on to Scotland after this drop. Have to be there for a pick up in the morning. That's why we have two drivers so we don't violate overtime safety regulations. But where can we take you two?"

Ewan looked at me. "To the destination manor house. Let's hope Anglo-Scandinavian relations are in top form tonight."

***

Torcwell Manor House. Yorkshire Moors. Later.

"You are <u>personally</u> delivering the furniture you sold? My architect said you were dedicated, but this? <u>Amazing</u>." The owner of the house was Clive Jakeman, a tall, toned, and gregarious man in his forties whose success in life allowed him to express himself in a crisp, tailor-made suit, complemented by the perfect pink and navy striped necktie plus matching handkerchief. He was a focused businessman, hospitable, tidy and above all, a decent human being.

"One could say that," Ewan offered.

"And this lovely lady is?" Clive asked.

I stepped forward and offered my hand. "Julie Fincher, Greymore Genealogy Research Site. I was helping Ewan with some family history plans when we got trapped inside the moving lorry."

"Dear oh dear. You two have had an adventure and a half."

On the trip from York City, we'd seen all sorts of vehicles dressed up in Viking fare, the best one being a long 1980s-vintage limousine covered in shields and with a fake warrior horse head affixed to the grill as if it was heading into battle. The second prize, in my mind, went to the car made to look like a long boat, complete with foldable sail that would no doubt be erected when they were at the festival itself.

We'd made quite the trolley tour, a moving van behind a long line of Viking vehicles slowly winding their way around the narrow roads of the dales, climbing up to the manor house itself.

"I'm afraid we must ask for the use of a phone. Ewan forgot his and my battery is dead."

"A telephone?" Our host loomed larger than life near us. "That is the <u>least</u> I can provide. You keenly shepherding my furniture up here in a freezing moving lorry? You <u>must</u> stay for a couple of hot meals, spend the night." His eyes roamed the sea of Vikings surrounding us. "Julie, we'll put you in my mother-in-law's suite. It's complete, right down to the diamanté-tasseled curtain ties. Ewan, you can take the tower room, used by the Lord of the Manor himself."

"Well, we–"

"Nonsense. You don't expect Julie to be up for a seven-hour train trip back again at this hour, do you?" Clive looked at Ewan and winked. "Stay put. I'll have dinner sent up to a private dining room. Your bedrooms each have telephones and most importantly, hot baths. We'll rustle up some clean clothes for you too."

I could only hope it wasn't a Viking costume.

I was escorted to a pastel-blue room with a four-poster canopy bed, an entire lady's bedroom set including toiletry and mirror table, full ensuite with the claw-footed tub and frosted glass-walled shower. It had a chandelier in the center of the room and a 60-inch television on the wall which one could actually watch while in bed. I sensed that Clive was trying to impress his mother-in-law and sometimes that was usually the best way to avoid arguments. It didn't quite make sense to have leopard-print sheets in the midst of all this pastel blue with ornate plaster ceiling work, but I suppose it was just her special request. I felt guilty as I looked around the room, realizing that this was a place meant for someone super important in the owner's life. Important enough that she be kept placated and happy at all times, regardless of her style. I resolved then and there not to knock the furniture or ding any of the wallpaper that covered the top half of the wall on one side of the room. Looking closer, I saw the wallpaper contained tiny pictures of a woman in modern day dress; could it be his mother-in-law replicated ad infinitum? Odd, but the bed looked comfortable and the bathroom was super clean, so I wasn't complaining.

I hoped the rest of the evening would be uneventful. After a hot bath and a change of clothes, Ewan and I met downstairs, wondering where our private dining room was located.

"He's got me up in the castle turret," Ewan said. "I must admit to feeling rather like the Lord of the Manor at this point."

"Don't go getting any ideas. The reality of Plumsden will hit us as soon enough when we get back home again tomorrow," I said.

"But I like Plumsden," he protested.

"I'm just warning you–"

"It's another world. I had to go up three flights of circular stairs and then I'm in a fourth story bedroom that's completely circular and has a commanding view of the 600 acres surrounding this estate," he said.

"I'm in the mother-in-law suite. It's, well–"

"Eclectic?" We heard Clive say behind us. "Please don't ask me about the leopard-print sheets and her darling face repeated a zillion times on the wallpaper."

"That's really her?" I said with a grin. "I wouldn't have believed it unless you told me."

"A happy mother-in-law means the world to me," he said with an overzealous wink.

Our host was affable and relaxed. He'd changed into a dinner smoking jacket ensemble, much like what Bertie wore at his club in London.

"The ladies of my family are all in London right now, enjoying shopping on my credit card," Clive said.

"No limit?"

"I'm afraid so. Fancy frocks cost a packet." He looked us up and down. "I'm glad to see our staff found you some fresh clothes to wear."

"The Viking underpants were a nice touch," Ewan added.

Clive chuckled. "I'm afraid that's all our gift shop sells. You know, for the Viking Festival here on site."

As if on cue, a large roar from a big crowd somewhere close to us suddenly permeated our existence. Clive looked around and beckoned for us to follow. "I'll show you why I didn't want to put you in with the rest of the visitors here this week."

Clive led us to a ballroom temporarily converted into a dining room hall from ancient Viking times. The entire room's wall was covered in thick canvas printed with a Viking village backdrop scene, presumably waterproof because the antics in here were getting quite rowdy. Long rows of tables and benches were filled with men and women dressed up as Vikings who had obviously already consumed much of the ale served by staff dressed as great house servants of the era. Cutlery was nonexistent and people were eating off wooden and pewter tableware. A variety of shields and spears sat off to the side of the room, currently at rest. We noticed a man and woman who were dressed more ornately than most; they each wore a golden crown and sat at the head of the table on a riser. They were presumably the king and queen of this Viking colony. Or was it a village? Or settlement? I didn't know enough about Viking history to be sure. I knew they were great raiders, traders and fierce people who dearly loved their families and their mythology. The room was loud, boisterous, and Ewan ducked as a turkey leg went flying past his ear. We saw it hit the canvas behind him, slithering down to the floor, leaving a streak of thick gravy as its mark.

"You should see some of the old ledger books for this place. It used to house parties of 500 locals to garner their favor for upcoming elections. Hundreds of platters of meat went through the kitchen doors and out into this great dining hall," Clive explained.

"I'm sure they must be fascinating reads," I said.

"Indeed they are. I donated them to the local archives in York to make sure that they were kept under proper conditions. It wasn't safe to keep those precious archives here on site when we had all the dust and damp from the renovations going on. Besides, the former owners aren't our bloodline, so the heritage of the long-standing family should be in archives for all to enjoy."

"Well said," I replied. "I have a new friend who could learn a lot from your wise words." My thoughts strayed to Landry and his choice between archives or auction. I shuddered because to me there was no contest: preserving history, keeping the entire collection together, was the right—and the only—thing to do.

More rowdiness and food fights continued amongst the Viking set. I wondered if it was authentic role-playing or the copious amounts of ale talking. Clive looked a bit embarrassed now that the volume had increased another notch or two. "I thought you'd find this interesting to see, but assumed you prefer something a little less rowdy after your long day on the road," he said, raising his voice above the crowd.

"I wouldn't even know where to start in this room," I said.

"I think you just pull up a chair and wait for food to come to you. They seem like a pretty friendly bunch," Ewan said.

We were already getting beckoned over to the group by five rough-looking Viking men sitting closest to us. One of them had huge feet with gnarled yellowed toenails sticking out of his sandals.

Clive intervened and shook his head, then quickly escorted us back out into the hall. "Dinner is set up for you both in the first floor turret tower private dining room. We use it for special occasions and when VIPs come to visit."

"Oh, please don't go to too much trouble," I started, "we feel awfully foolish about today's escapade."

"Nonsense. The room wasn't being used today anyways. Did you really think I'd let a herd of Vikings loose in there?"

We treated it like a rhetorical question and followed behind him at a brisk pace. Clive wasn't one to waste any time; self-made entrepreneurs usually didn't.

We walked into the unique room, one so fancy and exclusive it almost defied imagination. It followed the contours of the imposing castle turret, a structure that was comprised of thick, cold brick walls in a sandy color. Inside it had been completely renovated, shedding cold medieval and transforming into a warm sanctuary away from the overenthusiastic Viking feast. Royal blue carpet was edge to edge in the room and supported a beautiful circular mahogany table and chairs. On the wall was a collection of what looked like Roman swords and armor. In four separate places around the room, near the narrow windows, stood full suits of armor, helmets down to feet. The solitary, round table in the center of the room was covered with a vast white linen tablecloth that hung down a modest six-inches. A fire crackled in the hearth set within the curved wall opposite us.

A uniformed waiter entered the room, and it was penguin suit and formalities from here on out. We were sat down at the table and Clive wished us a pleasant evening. A fancy three-course meal was presented as the grandfather clock outside in the main passageway precisely gonged 8:00 p.m. It was absolutely perfect.

Ewan glanced at the opulent surroundings. "I think if that carpet got any plusher we would sink into it, never to be found again."

Was that a smirk on our patient waiter's face?

Perhaps this was some form of entertainment for him.

I nodded my head. "It's quite a change from sitting on the cold floor slats of the moving lorry."

"The look on those movers' faces when they set eyes upon us in their cargo space. I can't imagine what went through their minds."

"I know. Liability insurance. Social media disasters. Egg on face."

Ewan raised his glass of cranberry juice to me. "I'm glad this isn't anything stronger. I want to get to sleep the second my head hits the pillow tonight."

"Any idea when we'll get out of here tomorrow?" I asked.

"Julie, right now I'm so tired, I can't even remember my name."

"There is one silver lining here, you know," I said.

Ewan grimaced. "We're trapped in a Viking Festival after spending an entire day travelling inside the cargo space of a transport vehicle, ending up in a town we never wanted to go to. What possible silver lining can you see?" He just wasn't getting it.

"We could go to Galfinches Farm." I pulled out the loaner phone from Clive and accessed my cloud storage. I showed Ewan a picture of the letter Landry's Aunt Moyra had enclosed in the envelope being sent to the newspaper. "It is Yorkshire, you know."

"Did you search for the farm's location already?" he asked.

"I did. It's about half an hour from here. A working cattle farm. I have no idea how it links to Aunt Moyra or to Lady Adelaide, but we may as well investigate while we're here."

Chapter 16

———

Next Morning.

It was with a much lighter heart that I gazed out over the snow-laden moors of Yorkshire. This was a vast, harsh and unforgiving place in winter. A place where animals hunkered down inside barns and farmers kept warm inside insulated coveralls, hats with ear flaps, balaclavas and thick gloves. The Vikings were definitely warm and jolly last night inside their big dining hall ringed by two large fireplaces. They'd finally called it a night about two in the morning, according to the maid who delivered breakfast to my room. It was obvious that Clive decided to run this country house as it was in the eighteenth century, including the various roles of the household staff.

I was awakened at 8:30 a.m. sharp with the uniformed maid drawing my curtains, calmly announcing breakfast was delivered. If one was rich back in the eighteenth century, it wouldn't have been bad to live like this at all. From my previous history research, I knew that most of this was a façade. The engine, the workhorses of these great country houses, were the endless numbers of staff toiling away dusk through dawn, rubbing their knuckles and knees raw from manual labor. It got a bit better once one ascended the hierarchy of the downstairs staff, but even the butler and housekeeper worked long hours and couldn't once let down their shields of diplomacy.

I noted a curious thing. There were carved stone pineapples on the top of every corner of every row of balustrades that ringed the flat roof of the grand country house. I made a mental note to ask Clive about that; they were quite unusual yet defined the absolute joy of staying at country houses. Families that built and expanded country homes over the centuries had particular quirks, favorite possessions and design styles reflected in their homes. Many of them had histories as homes to senior government officials, hosted high society balls and community events, and some served as locations for famous military event signings. It was sad how so many of them were lost when death duties were introduced after World War One. Luckily, there was now a great rush to protect the remaining architectural wonders.

I met Ewan on the landing, trying to look nonchalant as a throng of Vikings clustered about, ready for the sporting events happening today out on the back lawn. I didn't want to get in the way of any clubs or swords, so it was our time to make a run for it. Ewan saw me and smiled, holding up a key fob. "Clive's let us borrow one of the estate's vehicles. You've had breakfast, correct?"

I nodded. "In bed. I <u>never</u> have breakfast in bed. Such luxury."

"Me too. It was decadent."

Ewan gestured for me to follow him. "It's apparently a navy blue SUV out back in garage number three."

***

Five Minutes Later.

We drove out of the front gates of Torcwell House like we owned the place. We felt awfully smug sitting there in the warm vehicle, the terrible journey we'd endured yesterday fast becoming a distant memory. I'd grown awfully fond of Yorkshire in the short time we'd been here. I think it had something to do with the vast ruggedness of the land, the unyielding landscape that still found enough nutrients to support large flocks of sheep scattered over hill and dale. There were misty valleys that appeared to have no bottom, the white clouds seemingly rising up from an endless cavern below. Little lanes with hedges on either side framed the countryside as sturdy, winterized vehicles wound their way around the county. It wasn't for the faint of heart. Neither was it for pansy city dwellers who wanted to rough it for a weekend. No, true North Yorkshire residency was for those hardy souls who decided to tackle a bit more in life than others. They were salt of the earth, kind, and above all else hard-working. This was the land of the dedicated Yorkshire farmer, men and women who dedicated their life to improving conditions for their livestock and ensuring they led contented lives on their farm. Cattle, sheep, pigs, llamas, alpacas and goats were all important parts of the landscape.

Galfinches Farm was no different. As we approached, we noted that the sprawling farm's interior yard was ringed by sturdy metal fencing. Tiny bits of straw littered the yard, inevitable as cattle ranged around bellowing and mooing at random. Two men were in the yard, wearing insulated coveralls, and surrounded by a couple of sheepdogs and twelve Limousin cattle they were herding into a barn. Both saw us drive up and park right outside the gate. Ewan and I got out, and the younger farmer came over to greet us. We noted the wind was picking up, and knew it was important to get the cattle inside on a nice bed of straw.

"Ewan Kilburn?" he asked. In his late twenties, the man had ruddy red cheeks and weather lines on his face from the harsh wind. He wore a sensible woolly hat with a bobble on the top and clompy black boots. "I'm Gerald Galfinch and this is my father Dougal Galfinch."

Ewan nodded. "Thank you for letting us visit."

The young man raised his hand and waved over at the older man. Cattle now inside and gate secured, the older man, a more vintage model of his son, came over to talk to us. "You're Moyra's nephew?"

"No, that's Landry Jackson from Texas. He's down in Kent. We had a rather unexpected trip up here to Yorkshire, and I appreciate you seeing us on short notice. We're friends of Landry and helping him with his family history project," I said.

The cattlemen welcomed us into their home. The farm was a complex of approximately eight different outbuildings, ranging from tiny chicken coops to large, long cattle sheds that each accommodated forty animals. The buildings were older but all well-maintained. One got the sense that this was a multigenerational family farm that had grown hodgepodge over the years as both family fortunes and livestock numbers grew. Every animal we saw look contented, happily eating, socializing or dozing. The house was a rectangular stone cottage with a corrugated tin roof, typical of the Yorkshire moors. There was green moss on the stones, remnants of summer growth that somehow managed to cling on to life during the recent colder months. When the front door opened, we were hit with a blast of heat from the inside hearth. We set eyes upon an arthritic senior working dog plus a plump tabby cat sharing space on the couch. They were asked to move, somewhat reluctantly, so the visitors could have somewhere to sit down.

The older man looked us up and down, then decided we could be trusted. "I thought Moyra's secret would stay with me to my own grave."

"She wrote something about a gentleman who lived here and needed home support?" I asked as a gentle question.

Dougal nodded. "That would've been my father, Keith. Moyra wrote him personally every week, bless her, trying to help with his troubles. He despised aging, you see, and found it troublesome. Moyra used to work for him when he had his saddlery shop in the village. People used to come from miles around to get him to fix their leather goods like bridles, harnesses and such. It's quite an art."

"So that's how they knew each other," I murmured. The tabby took a liking to me and wound himself in and out of my legs. Ewan had been similarly accepted and now had the kind face of a mixed-breed sheepdog firmly draped across his borrowed shoes.

"Moyra and Keith used to get along summat like a house on fire," Dougal said. He turned to Gerald. "You remember that, son, don't you?"

Gerald gave a dutiful nod of acknowledgement. "They became pen pals. Grandpa didn't use a computer. It was all old-fashioned writing."

"And do you know what he was seeking from Moyra?"

"Advice on love. The old gaffer spent his days writing to her."

Ewan and I didn't understand this.

I started again. "But why would he want to be pen pals with the shop girl he knew years ago? Moyra hadn't lived here for decades."

"Grandpa and Moyra used to be in love. She left for the big city and Grandpa never recovered," Gerald said.

That explained a few things. Moyra had left her beloved to go and help nurse Lady Adelaide.

Dougal sighed. "Moyra kept up a running correspondence. But her letters always came from a forwarding service and he only mailed to a post office box. She wouldn't tell him where she lived to prevent him coming to see her."

"Why would she be so secretive?" Ewan asked, removing his feet from underneath a heavy set of paws.

"She was protecting someone." Dougal got up and retrieved an inlaid mother-of-pearl box given pride of place on the sideboard's top shelf. He opened the box and took out a folded piece of paper.

"This is the secret my father said to guard with my life and I'm sure it will lead you to something else. I've never had the heart to follow it up."

I took the folded paper from him, gently teased it open and read: *Find the real fruit.*

I looked at. "That's it?"

Dougal and Gerald both nodded.

Dougal went first. "It's not as hard as it seems, if one's farming folk from around here."

"How so?" Ewan asked.

"Simple." He reached into one of the sideboard's drawers and pulled out a genuine gold bar. He turned it over and there, professionally debossed into the metal, were three duplicate images I recognized well: pineapples. I turned it over my fingers and then handed it back to him. It wasn't our place to take it. However, I did snap a photo of it with my loaner phone.

Ewan and I exchanged a glance. Dougal looked back at us and shrugged. "Moyra left this for our family, then she upped stakes and moved away the next morning. Didn't tell us much, just left a note for Dad saying that she would always care for him, but caregiver duty called."

"And she left no other information?"

"Just the gold bar. You'll recognize the three pineapples from Torcwell House."

"Indeed, I do," I said.

"She used to talk of a man, an expert horseman from Yorkshire, visiting a fine lady in Newmarket to discuss racehorse bloodlines. We figured it must be the root of the Roycetonne House scandal."

I nodded. "Where Lady Adelaide's father forbade the match. How did you connect Moyra, Lady Adelaide and the horseman?"

"The pineapples."

"Come again?" Ewan said.

"The family that used to own Torcwell House once had a fine stable of racehorses. Their saddle pads and jockey silks all bore the three pineapple symbols. When they ran into financial troubles, the Torcwell family announced that a mysterious Newmarket benefactor had swooped in, bought the horses, and continued to race them under the three pineapples symbol. There was only one woman in Newmarket rich enough to do that–"

"Lady Adelaide," I breathed.

"–And sentimental enough to insist on keeping the Torcwell pineapples instead of her own colors."

"What proof was there?"

Dougal leaned back in his chair and smiled. "It's on the horseman's tombstone. We sell to a butcher in Newmarket who told me it's rumored that the horseman is buried on the grounds of Roycetonne House. It's also rumored that a society lady who used to live at Torcwell was good friends with Lord Roycetonne and kept an eye on his daughter's 'inappropriate interests', shall we say, and dutifully reported back any news."

"My, oh my." I cleared my throat. "Quite a mystery."

Dougal and Gerald exchanged a sorrowful glance. "It is. And we never thought we'd get to the bottom of it. My father, Keith also passed away just before Christmas. Funeral was day before yesterday.

"Oh dear," I said.

"He did leave a final note that he didn't get mailed before he passed. Maybe he knew he was on his way out," Gerald said. He rummaged in the sideboard and produced an envelope that wasn't sealed on its flap. He pulled out a handwritten piece of paper and gave it to us to read:

> *Moyra, my light is fading to rest but I offer you one more*
> *solace for the friend you hold so dear. The embroiderer had*
> *hidden proof of Simon's innocence.*
> *I love you forever,*
> *Keith.*

Gerald and Dougal exchanged a glance. "You do know that Simon was the head groom at Torcwell House? Was, that is, before all his troubles."

"Do you know who this embroiderer friend of your father's was?" I asked Dougal.

"Steve Linham. Happy old codger. Spends his time down at the village archives as a volunteer nowadays. That is, when he is not gadding about in India learning new embroidery techniques from the locals."

Ewan groaned. "And let me guess, he'd rather be in India than Yorkshire during the winter time?"

"You got that right," Gerald replied.

"I think it's worth a trip to the local archives. Can you give us directions please?" I asked.

***

Clive's Loaner SUV. Five Minutes Later.

Ewan drove while I traced our movements on my phone screen. He gave me a look as we went out of the farmyard. The melting snow was really starting to take hold everywhere we looked, giving the signs of life after our massive winter storm. "Three pineapples, a gold bar, secret letters, Torcwell House, Simon the expert horseman. A banned love plus an embroiderer."

"I know, it's quite the list. There are pineapples on every roof corner at Torcwell House. I looked it up and found it's a symbol of man's prowess at horticulture. It's carved on the metal panels on their country house's front gates. The Torcwell family crest even has three pineapples on it."

"You know what I think?" Ewan started, "I think that Dougal and Gerald are pretty well connected for cattle farmers."

"Never doubt the power or knowledge of a farmer," I said.

"Do you think Keith knew about the agony aunt columns?"

"Perhaps. It sounds to me like he lost his great love with Moyra, yet didn't want to interfere with the new nursing life she considered so important," I said. "We need to ask Mrs. Neebles about the family graveyard at Roycetonne House."

"Agreed. First, let's get to the archives and see if the embroiderer has left any hints behind for us." Ewan gripped the wheel as we carefully navigated an icy patch of road.

✼✼✼

Village Archives. Ten Minutes Later.

We entered the generously-sized, converted stone walled barn with several degrees of apprehension. In order to get to the front desk we had to walk through a real rogues gallery. Prison inmate photos of thieves, gamblers, tramps and murderers lined the walls. Most of the criminals showed faces lined with various combinations of worry, fear, and cunning. All photos were in black and white, and the head shots were life-sized with their crimes listed underneath as if from a nineteenth century police mugshot book. Details of each case, along with often outrageous facts and accusations, were printed on the placards below. The poster line of scoundrels lasted sixteen full strides as we walked towards the front desk. Yorkshire had its own set of miscreants and criminals; this archives somehow seemed to take great delight in exposing them to the public. Some characters were extremely rough looking: greasy hair, long scars on cheeks, lazy eyes, missing teeth, unshaven and unkempt. Perhaps it was to encourage the interest of those people who appreciated sensationalism. Perhaps it was how the charity was able to get funding to keep the historical center open. It was an interesting read, albeit somewhat jarring. We were apparently looking for a clue supporting a lost love, someone who definitely did not belong on the criminal wall of shame outside.

There was a short, stout woman working the front desk. She was full of smiles and chuckles as we approached, and then we noticed she was wearing a slim headset and was on the telephone. She finished up a conversation about somebody's ill cow—perhaps it even had salmonella and needed a vet—then pressed the phone's 'end call' button. She looked up, resplendent with brown eyes, dark hair that was tucked back in a neat bun. "Welcome to the History Center. How can I help?"

"We need to know more about Keith from Galfinches Farm in the area. We understand he recently passed?"

"Yes," she said, "and it was a sad day when we lost the legend of the area. It's so sad when one of the true craftsmen passes away and nobody takes over his business."

"I hope at least his business records and some photos of his work are being donated to your archives?"

"We're looking for an embroiderer friend of his as well," Ewan added.

"Definitely. We already have Keith's diaries and work orders if you're interested. Steve Linham's embroiderer shop records are also here. Both sets of records were donated without any hold on them so they're accessible to the public immediately."

"That's wonderful. Could we see them, please?"

She nodded, and we noticed that her name tag said 'Gwyneth'. She certainly knew her way around the place, dodging in and out of slightly leaning book stacks and records boxes to lead us to the work desks. There were three desks set up in the back, in a little alcove that ensured peace and quiet from the front desk. Not that it was heaving with people, it wouldn't be out in a tiny village like this, but it was what their funding allowed to keep historical records pristine and accessible.

Gwyneth brought over two boxes of Keith's materials and placed them on the sturdy desk surface. The desk itself was rather battered and the chairs didn't match. There was no adjustable height button and I knew we couldn't sit there that long because the hard wooden chairs would put my bottom to sleep. After recently sitting for so many hours on the cold floor of the moving lorry, I couldn't take another day of that. My backside was about as flat as it could be at present.

We dug into the records with care and deference.

I looked over at Ewan. "I cannot believe those photos in the entrance gallery. They used to describe people as sly, slovenly, miserable and whiskered. How on earth is that fair to the accused?"

"Newsflash. It's not." He grinned. "Look at this." Ewan opened a battered-leather photo album, burnished shiny and dark brown at the corners from many years of use. It was easy to visualize Keith sitting by a warm hearth and flipping through the pages, one by one, as he relived the moments of his past. It was crammed full of photos, starting with the black and white pictures. They moved on to the early-color photos, ones from the 1950s that were now faded and turned into garish tones because of the lack of steadfastness of the ink. It showed a young man starting out in his craft, working through apprenticeship with the support of his father, to opening his own shop and hiring his first staff member. It was an entire history of the saddlery shop, a real treat to behold. So often these craftsman occupations were lost to time as technology outpaced them. One thought of the buggy whip manufacturer as a classic example. I felt like it was a true privilege to meet Keith's descendants back at the family's farm.

I leaned over Ewan's shoulder. "What a lovely memory. I'm so glad the family donated it to the archives so it can be preserved."

He nodded. "Indeed. Look at this here at the back," he said. There was an envelope half cut down to contain a few scraps of paper at the back. He gently pulled one out and I saw was an undated letter from another craftsman, this time the embroiderer named Steve Linham:

> *Dear Keith,*
> *You made an unusual request, however, as you fixed my double bridle in your off hours, I repay you with the same favor. Your secret is now hidden up at the big house.*
> *Cheers,*
> *Steve*

I put the letter down on the table and looked to Ewan. "I'm assuming he meant Roycetonne House. There must be a thousand embroidered items there."

"Who knows if it burned up in the fire or not?"

"Did you find what you're looking for?" We saw Gwyneth approach with a smile.

"Yes and no, I'm afraid," I said. "Do you happen to have any reference materials about embroidery craftsmanship?"

"You mean where they're doing cross stitches scenes, flowers and ships?"

"Um, perhaps more like on furniture. Fancy upholstery, carpet hangings, those sorts of pieces?"

"I have just the thing." She scuttled away like a beetle and returned about a minute and a half later carrying a heavy book from the facility's shelves. It was a tome that contained embroidery craftsmanship going back to the twelfth century. The medieval pictures, amazing drawings crafted by only the steadiest hand, included ladies' gowns, tapestries, table runners and leg-hose. The book also included embroidery patterns, a range of upholstered furniture, and fancy saddle pads for horses.

"It would take us ages to figure out where to look for the embroidered piece Steve refers to," I said.

"Have you thought of going back to Keith's original letter? Perhaps he left you a clue?" Gwyneth asked.

We showed her the letter from Keith to Moira. She read it over and then got a tiny smile at the side of her face. "He told you where it is, you just haven't seen it." She pointed at the second line quote *'my light is fading to rest'.* "Where I come from, 'rest' implies 'bed'," said Gwyneth.

All of our eyes met at the same time.

"Lady Adelaide's princess-style bed canopy. That's where he's hidden it," I said.

We spent another hour looking through Steve's plus Keith's donations to the archives but realized that with one sentence we'd already gotten our marching orders. We would find out what Keith had left to put dear Moyra's mind at ease, and possibly how it related to the elusive and heartbroken lady of the house herself.

❊❊❊

Private First Class Train Carriage. Next Morning.

A hot breakfast. Comfy seats. Oodles of leg room. Happy travelers. All courtesy of Clive's generosity.

Ewan and I were on our way back home.

"I've really enjoyed spending time with you. Even though the circumstances weren't ideal," Ewan said.

I gave him a grin. "It wasn't so bad. Clive was fun."

Ewan smiled back. "Next time I want to unleash my inner Viking, I'll know who to call."

Our eyes met and held. Distracted by the ticket taker. Back to focus again.

"Julie, when we finally do have some proper time together, I'll make this up to you," Ewan said.

"There's nothing to make up."

"But we got trapped inside a lorry and–"

"I'm still not sure if the lorry entrapment beats the waterlogged ceiling at the cottage."

"So we're on a points system now?" he asked.

"Maybe. And I think we should reset the clock and start over. Maybe next time dinner and the symphony. Or a movie. Just nothing about tidal waves or moving companies."

"Deal."

We settled back in our seats and enjoyed the stupendous comfort.

Chapter 17

Lunchroom, GGRS. Next Day.

"I'm ruined," Bertie moaned, head in his hands. "And I thought I was off to the races."

One couldn't help but feel sorry for the wealthy, titled aristocrat. He'd tried to make something of his own, not relying on the generosity of the family fortune, yet it appeared to have failed. In other words, his mango chutney was in the soup.

"You got schnookered, big time," Landry said. He gave Bertie a slap on the back, not exactly aristocratic protocol, but it was a friendly enough gesture. "Don't worry, we'll track down these nefarious beings. Just give me a bit more time to network with my contacts. They may be slippery as a dumpling in hot lard, but there are ways to track them down."

Maude, Gertie and I smiled at Landry's last odd, simile-prone sentence.

It even made Bertie stop whingeing and look up, slightly hopeful. "Twenty-five cases. My absolute, premium-level mango chutney product. Fully organic, custom designed jars and the label hand-signed by the Duke himself."

Gertie raised her eyebrows. "You hand-signed all the labels on twenty-five cases of mango chutney jars?"

Bertie nodded. "It's an added special touch. I sign the labels flat and then my staff put them on the jars, one by one."

We all sat around the table, commiserating with Bertie over his scammed luxury goods.

I gave Landry a telling glance. "I have every faith that you will find out who has done this and get Bertie's invoice paid."

Landry pretended to tip an invisible hat at me. "I'm like a dog with a bone on this one. Won't let it go until cash is in his hot aristocratic hand."

"I am much obliged," Bertie said. "And we've only just met. You are a decent chap."

Landry shrugged. "Just the way I was raised. You help friends, no matter how recent their acquaintance."

Maude cleared her throat. "Julie, we need to discuss that other matter?" She was being awfully diplomatic, but I could tell it was really bothering her.

The men took it as a signal to leave. Landry and Bertie headed out, beginning a conversation about collection agencies and currency exchange. Hopefully what Maude, Gertie and I were going to be discussing would be a bit simpler.

Perhaps not.

The manager of the facility leaned over and started in a serious tone. "This so-called professional genealogist Hayleigh Grables-Muncton? Well, I now know for certain she is scamming her eighty-three-year-old client out of good money."

"Sherry Knox is eighty-three? I don't believe it. I would've put her at about seventy-two."

"Oh, she'll be pleased. I'll be sure to tell her that," Maude said. "Hayleigh's leading Sherry down the garden path and is refusing all assistance because she knows I'll reveal her deception. I just don't think it's right to condone that nefarious behavior here on our premises. It sets a bad example and we have ethical standards to follow."

"I agree. Did you speak with Sherry yet?"

"I tried, but failed when Hayleigh showed up. I think the best thing to do, bringing you a solution with the problem, is to try and get Sherry on her own. I can give her a gentle warning backed up with evidence of proper methodology."

"And you're absolutely sure that this deception is going on? Beyond a shadow of a doubt?" The last thing we wanted to do was upset a business relationship and get a bad reputation for doing so. It was a delicate path to walk.

Maude nodded. "Absolutely positive. So far, Hayleigh has told Sherry about a false family crest that doesn't even exist plus explained away a 176-year gap on her family tree that eventually leads her back to royalty. Sherry is now absolutely convinced she's descended from King James the First."

"Oh dear."

"Oh dear is right. The research site's reputation is on the line here and we cannot allow a senior to be taken advantage of." Maude set her mouth in a firm line and I could tell she was quite adamant about what needed to happen.

Gertie finally piped up. "We can't police who our clients hire. We need to be careful here."

Maude shot her a look. "Understood. But what is the ethical boundary? We support correct research and provide a friendly environment. There's nothing friendly about a senior citizen getting, as Landry would say, schnookered."

We sat and contemplated Maude's last statement for a moment or two.

I spoke next. "I think you're dead on the money, Maude. We have to do something. Let's just try and make it as gentle as possible."

"How can you pry Sherry apart from Hayleigh?" Gertie asked. "Hayleigh keeps a pretty close watch."

Maude smiled. "I have Sherry's home telephone number. She extended an invitation to tea and now is the correct time to take her up on that generous offer," Maude said. "I just didn't want to overstep my bounds before speaking with you."

"And you'll be sure to let us know how it goes?" I asked.

"Of course. I'm glad we had this conversation. Now I can sleep at night." Maude finished her tea and then got up to put her mug in the dishwasher. All was to be set right in the world.

I hoped.

***

'Ballet en Fromage', Plumsden Theater. 8:00 p.m.

There was a buzz in the air, the kind that one always felt just before a live performance. Us genealogy diehards were all lined up in our seats: Ewan, Maude, Gertie, the Major, Bertie, and I.

I suppose being invited to a ballet done in a cheese theme was both intriguing and rather gooey-sounding. It made a bit more sense when I understood that Fred Todling helped compose this presentation. Knowing that he didn't play an instrument, I got the sense that he had meddled with the artistic side of things and as the ballet 'team' sponsor, likely the Artistic Director felt obligated to let him have his way. I did not, for one, understand the similarity of pointe shoes and Swiss cheese. Looking around the audience, many fingers excitedly pointing at the program, I could see that it was confusing quite a few others as well. Whatever we were supposed to be treated to once those red velvet curtains parted was turning out to be quite the mystery.

The curtains opened wide, gliding with an even clickety clack across the rails framing the stage overhead. Suddenly I understood the relationship to cheese. The backdrop was a swirl of gauzy oranges and creams. To the left and the right of the stage were long sheer curtains with perfectly circular holes cut in various places. A series of six metal fans blowing cool air made the material ripple. Cue the dancers. In they came, limbered up, lithe, and dressed in matching costumes, the lead ballerina and male dancer both standing out in mid-brown tones. I believe this was supposed to be a goat cheese representation. The others were various shades of white, cream and orange cheeses. They were surrounded by a small backdrop of trees—no, it was broccoli—and Fred Todling's influence was even more apparent. Yes, this was the man with the unbelievable acreage of broccoli in his back garden who proudly, unabashedly, turned the gassy vegetable into jam. Yes, this was the man who took broccoli, merged it with dairy, then bulldozed his way into a ballet performance. I couldn't help but smile as I saw one of the broccoli trees to the right break formation and head to the microphone set up in the center of the stage. This was presumably Fred's big moment.

Gertie jabbed me in the ribs. "I thought Fred said he didn't have any speaking parts?" she asked.

Maude leaned over to the both of us and whispered back, "The narrator was taken ill last minute, so Fred's now playing triple duty. A broccoli tree, narrator and a dead body."

"This is going to be good," Ewan said.

We watched as Fred leaned into the microphone and exhaled. He then straightened up and spoke:

"Tonight, it gives me absolute, immense pleasure to let you know that Miss Sympsonne's Ballet Company brings you an unusual modern and overwhelming interpretation of the classic ballet dance performance. We've taken a fairly pedantic yet robustly symphonic nineteenth century ballet and turned it into something far more contemporary, making the old modern whilst retaining its classical dance roots."

"Somebody needs to cut off that broccoli man's roots and get on with the show. We're not here to listen to him drone on," a salty senior quipped behind me in the next row back.

Hear. Hear.

The youngest dancer was four years old, and the rest of the troupe were preteens and teens, up to about twenty-one. Of course, the little children were very cute and fun to watch. How the older ones pulled off dancing like bits of cheese amongst broccoli was another question, but I had to admire their dignity.

Everybody laughed when the four-year-old girl in a pretty apricot tutu came over and dragged Fred away from the microphone. He pretended that she knocked him over and he lay like a withering piece of broccoli as they all danced around him, even jumped over him.

"It's a dual role," I whispered to Gertie. "Tree and dead body simultaneously."

"I don't know if that was scripted or not," she replied.

"Does it really matter?" Ewan added. "They could be reciting the dictionary for all I care. I'm just getting a kick out of watching our solicitor prance about in sparkly green tights."

We never did get to understand the plot. It was something about melting cheese onto broccoli and then saving Mother Nature, but it was all in good fun. Out in the hall where we had a post-performance reception, we saw Fred pose with his ballet company—all still in costume—for pictures in the local paper.

And that's when it hit me. This was what community was all about. That picture would be talked about for years to come. It was so unusual for a solicitor to perform like this. Fred got outside his comfort zone and put himself out there; he'd done something most solicitors—no, most people—wouldn't have the guts to do. In a way, it was akin to tracking down one's family history. One had to possess dogged determination to see it through, the perseverance to never take no for an answer and to persevere when brick walls appeared. We could all learn something from Fred here tonight.

But I would still never, ever, ever be tempted to try his broccoli jam.

Chapter 18

Hallway, Roycetonne House. Next Day.

"What is it with men wearing tights?" Ewan said those fateful words as he glanced at the row of aristocratic portraits lining the wall. Every single portrait from the seventeenth century in the collection showed men wearing silk hose.

"We cannot make fun of Fred about his costume. You know why he wore those?" I asked.

"To make a fool of himself?" Ewan joked back.

I gave him a serious stare. "Because the four-year-old who was dancing around him got stood up by her stepfather who apparently agreed to do it on a whim and then backed out. She was heartbroken, and so Fred stepped up. That's the type of man he really is."

"Okay, now I feel pretty lame," Ewan said. "I apologize."

"Hey, I joked about it before too. Just as guilty here," I said. "It just shows that we need to learn more about a person before judging them on appearance."

We examined some more portraits and noted one of Lady Adelaide in her early twenties. She was dressed in a summery light floral print dress, stood near the maze outside and looked back over her shoulder. Her left gloved hand was extended, her hair covered by an elegant hat with feathers. She looked secure, aristocratic and ready for the world. Lady Adelaide had lovely eyes, a slight flush on her cheeks and as she gazed off into the distance, one noted a tiny flock of birds clustering in a tree over a stream a field away. It was a portrait that cemented the Roycetonne Family's place in the upper echelons of the village, county and in fact, all of England.

"Well said, cousin," Gertie said, linking arms with me as she met up with us. "So what kind of damage are you here to do today, Ewan?" She looked at him suspiciously.

"Well ladies," he started rather sheepishly, "Landry's asked me to give him the valuation of the house contents. Harriet Tibbets, the auctioneer, is going to meet us here and we're going to do it together."

Landry walked in. "Now before everybody starts getting all rankled, let me just say that this is only one option for what I'm to do with my Aunt Moyra's estate," he said. "I didn't ever see this house and certainly didn't form any attachments to the belongings inside. Sure, I'll take a photo album or two, but I don't need a house full of furniture. I live in a two bedroom condo with a minimalist lifestyle. I'm great with that."

"Fine, get on with your valuations. Just know that we'll be watching you and telepathically willing you to go the museum and archives route instead," Gertie said with emphasis.

"Can we at least go up to Lady Adelaide's bedroom and figure out the embroidered bed canopy before you guys get down to pounds and pence?" I asked.

Landry held out his arm in a grand sweeping gesture. "After you, please."

✻✻✻

Lady Adelaide's bedroom was just as we left it. The heavily-embroidered upholstered bed canopy now took on greater significance and meaning. Mrs. Neebles had already placed a footstool at the side of the bed, and she stood there, holding a carpet knife at the ready.

"For you," she said handing it over to me. "I've already been around the entire canopy and pinpointed one side sewn with delicate pink thread as opposed to light cream thread. It's virtually unnoticeable unless you know what you are looking for."

"Well done, Mrs. Neebles. I'm only going to unpick a small part so we can preserve the artistry and craftsmanship. The last thing I want to do is tear it so the fabric can't be stitched up again to look as good as new."

I stepped up on the footstool, Landry firmly holding it so it wouldn't tip. I clutched onto the bedpost as I carefully ascended near the head of the bed. I gasped when I saw what was stitched onto the top of the canopy. I carefully turned my head and looked down at the people waiting for me below at the footstool floor height. "Does anyone know what's up here on the very top and facing the ceiling?"

"Presumably a lot of dust," Mrs. Neebles said. She winced a bit, likely horrified that she hadn't been allowed in here to properly clean and ensure that dust bunnies were banished like they were in the rest of the house she managed.

"There's a bit of dust, yes, but not too bad. Someone's been taking care of this piece. What I'm looking at, however, will take your breath away." I cast my eyes out over the top of the bed canopy again and it was a wonderful sight. Amongst the pink satin was a hand-embroidered depiction of Lady Adelaide Roycetonne, a groom and a beautiful racehorse. They were framed inside three pineapples. The initials 'A' and 'S' were intertwined in the rose garlands on the winning racehorse's neck. The horse was a tall chestnut thoroughbred, a star and stripe straight down the middle of his face and two white hind socks. His nostrils were flared and his flanks heaving as he stood at the end of a dirt track where presumably he'd come the victor. It was an amazing piece of embroidery craftsmanship.

"I had no idea she was so involved with horses," Landry said after I described it to them all.

"Involved with horses, or with the groom?" I asked. I stepped down off the footstool and people took turns stepping up to take a look. I'd also snapped a photo without flash to protect the colors and the fabrics, and showed it to those who didn't feel safe climbing on the footstool.

It was true. Lady Adelaide had a sweet smile aimed directly at the groom and he was smiling back at her. It was amazing how the embroiderer had captured this emotion so well with his needle and thread. Likely that was why he was in the embroidery trade; he was just that good.

"I think Dougal and Gerald were right. There was much more going on between her and the groom than just the racehorse," Gertie said.

"Mrs. Neebles, do you know anything about this?" Landry asked.

She appeared not to want to speak.

Landry tried again. "Mrs. Neebles, I sense you may know something that we don't?"

"I do not like to speak ill of the dead, nor spread unsubstantiated rumors." The housekeeper stood up ramrod straight.

"Mrs. Neebles, please," Landry continued. He gave her a look that meant she wasn't to avoid the question any longer.

"Very well then. As you insist. Your Aunt Moyra did tell me once that Lady Adelaide was due to be married to a horseman, a groom, who used to work here in the Roycetonne House stables. As the groom was much below her class, her father absolutely forbade it. There was something about her father forcing him off the estate to go work up in Yorkshire. Lady Adelaide was forever heartbroken. Her father then forced her to marry the Marquis and that was the end of it." She gave us all a winsome look. "But I think not."

"What do you mean?" Gertie asked.

"You can't leave us hanging like that, Mrs. Neebles," Ewan said.

She leaned in closer, as if the ghosts of Lady Adelaide and Aunt Moyra were both listening. "I said I think not, because there were whisperings that Lady Adelaide was still meeting her man long after she was married. They were planning to run away together and met at the races in Newmarket."

"And leave her two children behind?" I asked. "I thought she was close to her daughters?"

"And that's the big question. Love over duty. A true love over love for one's children. There is no easy answer."

"And presumably this is the groom she loved?" I said, enlarging the bed canopy's embroidery photo on my phone.

"Of course, although I'd never seen it prior," Mrs. Neebles said. "I never looked up top of the bed canopy until today."

"Everyone seems to have forgotten one thing," I said. "What's inside the canopy?"

Everybody murmured, realizing they'd just been completely distracted by the embroidered outside. It was now time to delve a little bit deeper and see what secret Keith from Galfinches Farm wanted revealed.

I went back up the footstool and carefully picked apart the outside edge of the bed canopy. It was tough to undo, because the stitches were small, neat and obviously created by an artisan. I kept at it and pretty soon I had some frayed edges of fabric showing once I had unpicked the stitches. I held the top piece of fabric apart from the bottom and looked inside. It was dark.

"Ewan, can you please turn on your phone's flashlight and hand it to me?"

Two seconds later his phone was in my hand, the bright beam of light ready to cast its glow inside the pieces of fabric. And it worked like a charm. For there in the center of the canopy, where I could just reach with my fingertips, was a faded brown envelope. I handed the phone back to Ewan and then set about retrieving the envelope. As I reached for it, stretching as far as I could without being dangerous, my fingers caught the edge of it and I slowly, agonizingly, pulled it towards me. It was like retrieving a precious fish at the end of the line. One false move and I'd lose it into the depths of the fabric again. Slowly, slowly it made its way to the side of the canopy and I could untense my body.

"Gotcha!" I handed the envelope to Gertie and then carefully stepped down from the stool. Mission accomplished. The next task was to look inside the envelope and learn what Keith had kept secret for all these years.

The gum on the envelope had dried out over time. Likely it was something to do with the dryness of the room with the bed being not too far away from the warm hearth. I looked out Lady Adelaide's window and saw the beautiful grounds that surrounded the house. The outbuildings, including stables, greenhouses, machine sheds and barns, were remnants of days past.

Above the fine copperplate script on the envelope were three pineapples drawn in brown ink and their leaves outlined in gold. The note read:

Dear Moyra.

Simon is innocent. He did not want to re-involve himself
in Lady Adelaide's life as she deserved more than he could
give her. Know that your mother didn't choose a bad man.
Love, Keith

We were all stunned.

"Lady Adelaide was Moyra's mother?" I asked in a stunned whisper. I looked over at the tall man with us. "Landry, it sounds like your heritage is part of this house. Aunt Moyra had more secrets than you ever could have guessed."

Chapter 19

Hoarding Room. Minutes Later.

"But we have to prove it first. Although Keith's letter is an original source, we can't go on his word alone about someone's family tree. We need official records to confirm it."

"Okay, you've got me hooked now," Landry said. "I want to know the real story behind my Aunt Moyra."

"I wonder if we'll find the full answers to Lady Adelaide's secret romance with her horseman Simon in here," I said.

"There's only one way to find out and that's to dive in." Gertie held up the nearest stack of papers and looked for a desk.

"Good morning," we heard behind us. The entire group turned to see Harriet Tibbets standing behind us, Mrs. Neebles in tow. "It looks like you've got half the family historians in England up here with you, Landry," Harriet teased. She was an elegant, smart antiques appraiser and auctioneer based in Medchester, Kent.

Harriet caught Landry off guard. Obviously, he'd forgotten she was coming and now his focus had changed 180 degrees. "Er, you're here to do the valuation of the house contents, correct?"

"Yes, Harriet Tibbets. You do look busy in here. I'm sure Ewan and Mrs. Neebles can show me around."

It was obvious Landry was torn. "That would be lovely. Mrs. Neebles, could you start in the guest wing? That should keep you busy for, say, two weeks?"

Harriet looked taken aback. "Two weeks?"

"I clean the rooms in the guest wing on a rotating basis," Mrs. Neebles advised. "I suggest we get started. Do you have a notepad and a camera?"

"I take photos with my phone and upload them to the cloud. I take notes on my tablet with a stylus." Harriet was one bundle of efficiency, that was for sure.

Ewan also looked torn but I shushed him, sending him away with Harriet and Mrs. Neebles to keep things moving. Landry had, after all, invited Harriet, not the other way around. The least we could do was be hospitable when she arrived.

Gertie brought out the hollow book and removed Lady Adelaide's diary. We carefully stacked some of the documents onto another desk and pulled up some mismatched chairs to listen. Gertie read aloud from some of the diary pages:

May 5, 1931
Dear Diary. The new groom here at Roycetonne House is a
darling. He has a way with horses that I'd never seen before
and was even able to calm father's rambunctious bay colt. I
sense he has a future here and I would do well to learn from

him. He is but two or three years older than myself and very handsome. I spoke with him today for the first time and although he was deferential, there was a sparkle in his eyes that made me think he aims for more in life than cleaning horse stables. I can see him as a trainer, a horse whisperer and a wonderful person in my life. This is why I hide my diary away from my father. I shall never reveal the secret. L.A.R.

May 6, 1931

Dear Diary. The new groom's name is Simon Chester. His father owns a bakery and his mother is a housewife. No aristocratic blood at all, but I am tired of that mattering in life. Simon is good, kind, and an expert with horses. We met out in the back fields today when I was riding through our little forest. He had our wildest horse well under control and it looked fabulous. The horse may win the stakes race come fall under Simon's expert horse management. When I am with him, I feel like time slips away. I am able to forget my father's overbearing attitude and directives. I long to be free of my life with him at Roycetonne House. I want to live life on my own terms and to be loved as a free woman without the shackles of my aristocratic shell. Simon says he can help me and I just need to find the courage to let him. L.A.R.

May 17, 1931

Dear Diary. Oh my, what a glorious few days. Simon and I

have fallen for each other and it didn't take long. I believe a lady's maid caught sight of us riding out in the fields together. Goodness only knows if she'll make something of it. At the very least I worry about our housekeeper who is my father's eyes and ears at Roycetonne House. Simon says I should become my own person and break free, but my father pulls all the purse strings. I have no control over my life. If my father wished to lock me up inside my room and never let me come out till he had found a suitable husband, that would be his choice. I am his charge. L.A.R.

"What a very sad set of circumstances," I said. "At least Lady Adelaide had Simon to help her through her difficulties."

Gertie was busy flipping through pages. And there were a lot of them. "I know I only have the day here so I'm not reading every page ... just scanning quickly ... it looks like they had a wonderful couple of months together and then the jig was up." She read some more aloud:

May 23, 1931
Dear Diary. What a glorious day at the races. Roycetonne House Stables brought home the silver cup at the stakes race today. My father was ever so pleased because it was the first stakes race he's ever won with a horse born and bred here at the manor house. I met Simon in the barns and nobody discerned the relationship between us. Simon is such a kind

man and I would be so happy with him for the rest of my
days, if only it were permitted. I have lost my heart to him.
L.A.R.

Gertie held the diary close to her chest and sighed. "Oh, how utterly romantic. Poor boy meets rich girl and they fall in love. I only wish they had a happy ending."

"I have the feeling that it's going to get darker from here on in," Landry said.

"Well that's being a positive person," I said in a disappointed tone. "You could leave us ladies here to enjoy the romance, then go to see Ewan and Harriet to talk cold hard cash."

"Just being realistic," Landry said, "remember the scratched engagement ring."

I looked over at Gertie. "Okay, let's burst the bubble. We already know it didn't work out, so let's just get the details and get it over with."

Gertie picked up the diary once more and read out loud to us:

September 9, 1931
Dear Diary. Roycetonne House is now my prison. Even
more so than it was before. My father, unbeknownst to me,
allowed the staff a day at the races and they wondered where
Simon was. The scullery maid caught a glimpse of me with
Simon in the hay shed. She told a housekeeper who told the
butler who then told my father. I was put on a carriage and

sent home in disgrace. Simon's been sent away to work at a manor house up in Yorkshire called Torcwell House. We know the people there and they are kind, they also breed good horses. At least Simon has a job. My heart is broken and I ache for his company. The dreams of our future together were attempted to be shattered by my father but I shall defy him. His Victorian rigidity doesn't work in this day and age. He is a dinosaur and I wish to live my own life and make my own decisions. L.A.R.

September 29, 1931

Dear Diary. The sundial in the maze is broken and a new workman came in to fix it today. I walked down the path near the sundial and saw that the workman had drawn some tiny letters and an arrow pointing at the sundial and the gravel path. He saw that I saw and then quickly raked them over. Four hours later after darkness had fallen, I went back outside wearing my cloak and examined the sundial. Affixed with a magnet underneath the sundial was an engagement ring from Simon for me. He's taken the trouble to get the inner band inscribed and his loving words took my breath away. I shall run to him as soon as I am able to escape. L.A.R.

"Oh the scandal," Gertie said. "This is where it actually really happens."

"Can I see the jewelry box for a moment?" I asked Landry. He retrieved it and handed it over so I could study the bottom of the case. "Look, you can see where the magnet's been affixed. It was attached upside down without worry of losing the ring because of the hinge on the front of the case."

"Well, I'll be darned," Landry said. "I just thought it was a result of normal wear and tear. But now matching the diary to the jewelry case it makes sense."

"All brought to you courtesy of your local Family History Society," I said with a grin. "We're more than just computers and gray-haired crowds, you know."

"So did Lady Adelaide run off with Simon?" Landry asked. "We knew it didn't last, but did they at least enjoy some time together?"

Gertie nodded. "She says here in the diary that Simon also left a clue on the sundial telling her where to meet him."

"Are you thinking what I'm thinking?" I asked them both. "Mini field trip, outside on the double!"

We tromped down the stairs as quickly as we could, then donned our coats that were in the front hall. We knew Ewan and Harriet would be tied up in guestroom furniture valuations forever, so we had lots of time before Landry was needed again.

We headed towards the maze.

Gertie spoke in reverent terms. "A perfectly clipped hedge represented everything her father stood for: barriers, cloistering and being locked away from the rest of the world. Lady Adelaide was like a doll in a glass house; society wanted to see her and photograph her, yet inside the façade she was miserable and ready to crack."

"The maze gave her a protective cocoon that she could go inside and get lost, reveling in the love she once had," I said.

"Exactly."

Landry trailed along behind us, not quite understanding everything we'd ascertained. "Ladies, wait up. How did you get all of that from a diary and ring box?"

"Because we're observant and have a lot of family history items to rely upon. The diaries are golden. So are the artefacts. It's not too difficult to figure out she was praying for Simon and desperate to escape with him."

"I'm sure glad I have you two here to help me. I'm a bit of a clod with this feelings stuff," Landry said.

"But wait until you help Ewan with his antiques shop website and fix Bertie's mango chutney scam. Then you'll come into your own and look like the hero of the day," I said. "Don't worry, we're here to help. We're enjoying this just as much as you are, right Gertie?"

"Of course. Look, there's the sundial," she said.

"I wonder if there are any traces left of their secret message," I said.

The sundial sat a bit wonky in the ground now, but it was still heavy enough not to completely topple. I crouched down beside it and looked underneath. "Look at this, guys. It's the other part of the magnet where she removed the box. Out here for so many years and we still find the evidence."

"And what about the clue to where they were to meet?" Landry asked.

"I think that's etched into the metal here," I said, pointing out something new. "It's a miner's pickaxe."

"He wanted to meet her in a mine?"

"Perhaps they had a special place, given that her father owned mining companies. She would've known the places to go so they could avoid prying eyes."

"I can't see a lady in fancy skirts going down into a dirty coal mine with all that damp and darkness," Landry said.

Gertie shook her head. "You'd be surprised at what some women will do for love."

"So we have a magnet and a pickaxe. Not a whole lot." I looked up and saw Ewan waving at us from a top floor window, somewhere in the middle of the guest wing. He was gesturing for us to come inside. "I think we'd better get back to the house. Ewan's signaling that we're needed."

"I just hope he hasn't sold the house from underneath me," Landry muttered. "This mystery is getting more and more intriguing."

Chapter 20

─────

Visitors' Wing. Roycetonne House. Ten Minutes Later.

We were all incredibly curious to see what Ewan wanted to show us inside the main house. I could tell by the expression on his face that it was something good, something unexpected. These words were music to an antiques dealer's ears. They also piqued the curiosity of any family historian on the planet. Manor houses built over a century ago undoubtedly held secrets that hadn't seen the light of day for decades. Many secrets were only revealed when renovations took place, either warranted or unwarranted, or worse yet, precipitated by a devastating fire. Fire had occurred at Roycetonne House here in 1941. All we knew was that workmen had repaired the home long ago and nothing further was ever done. The tragedy had come and gone, unfortunately affected people in countless ways, but now had faded into the history books.

Ewan and Harriet stood with Mrs. Neebles at the head of the corridor. Beyond them were dozens of similarly carved wooden doors, presumably each leading to a well-appointed guest suite. In these older houses one always wondered if there was an ensuite or not. Very few Victorian-era homes were built with indoor plumbing. I had to admit, I wasn't comfortable staying in a strange place that made me leave the security of my private room in the middle of the night in order to use to toilet. The people you would meet en route could be quite shocking. Gertie even met Fred Todling's potbellied pig Barnaby on one such nocturnal sojourn. It hadn't been a pretty sight.

"Go on then. Tell us. What did you find?" I asked Ewan.

"It's behind door number three," he said, leading us down the hallway. Harriet and Mrs. Neebles followed. A brass plaque over the door read 'The Reginald Barr-Smythe Suite'. We entered an opulently furnished room, surely fit for a prince. Red velvet was everywhere, sumptuous and plush. Ostrich feathers stood up tall on the corner of every post of the bed and the sheets were gold satin. It was a masculine room, complete with oversized desk, dresser, wardrobe and suit stand. There was an ensuite, including a huge marble bath that somehow fit inside the room.

"Who was Reginald Barr-Smythe?" Gertie asked aloud. She searched the name on her phone and then nodded. "Ah. Chairman of the bank and leader of the local Hunt Club. Someone Lady Adelaide's father wanted in his inner circle for numerous reasons."

The room named after this important banker looked over a vast acreage of rolling hills and forests. One could imagine the horses and hounds galloping over the turf, not a care in the world except enjoying themselves for the day. Thank goodness they didn't do live fox hunts anymore; drag hunts were just as good and far less cruel to animals.

"Imagine all the goings-on that must've happened when this house was filled with guests. I'm sure the wine flowed freely at dinner and then afterwards, well, it was anybody's guess," Gertie said.

Harriet nodded. "You'd be surprised at what you find doing house clearances. Would you believe I actually once found a complete set of zoo animal costumes that the lady of the house had commissioned in order to put on a pantomime for her party guests? Everyone was supposed to participate, although I don't think I'd be volunteering to do the back end of the elephant."

I shrugged. "Well, if our dear solicitor Fred Todling can play a tree, dead body and a narrator, perhaps the elephant isn't so bad."

We all laughed. My hat was still off to Fred for being so supportive of a little girl whose stepdad had let her down at the last minute for their ballet performance.

I looked to Ewan for some facts. "Well?"

Ewan looked at Harriet, then looked at Mrs. Neebles. They had obviously found something a little out of the ordinary and were deciding on who should tell the tale.

Landry was getting impatient. "If we can get to this before the moon comes out that would be great."

Ewan cleared his throat. "Well, it appears that there is a secret passageway in the house but no one was supposed to know about it."

"How do you figure?" Landry asked.

"It says so right over here." Harriet bent down and opened part of the walnut wainscoting. Behind the secret panel was drywall bearing a stenciled note that read 'no entry to secret passageway'.

"We thought that was pretty clear," Ewan said, smiling, "and that's when I started waving at you lot outside in the maze."

"Inside the maze we found remnants of the magnet that affixed the engagement ring's box Simon left for Lady Adelaide. We also found a symbol of the pickaxe showing where they were going to rendezvous and run away together."

Harriet frowned. "I don't understand. They were running away with a pickaxe?"

"Not with a pickaxe, but they were meeting at a location where a pickaxe would be used. Lady Adelaide's father owned mines, so I think Simon was telling her to meet near one of them. Perhaps they'd met there before, somewhere out-of-the-way where they could escape without being detected."

"I'm dying to go down the secret passageway. We could be entering a treasure room for all we know," Gertie said in an excited voice.

"We could also be crawling into the world of rusty plumbing," Landry said. "I don't know much about these old houses, but I've heard some pretty odd creaking and clanking in this one."

Mrs. Neebles stood up straight. "That is typical of older manor houses. We call them 'characters', not odd abodes with 'creaks and clanks', thank you very much."

"Pardon me," Landry said, tipping his imaginary cowboy hat. He'd taken it off when we arrived inside the house and where he'd set it down was anybody's guess at this point. With dozens of rooms to check, I didn't envy him trying to hunt it down.

"So what does this mean for us?" I asked.

"Well, I don't think we should break down a brick wall," Ewan said, "but I am intrigued about the note."

"One has to worry about loadbearing walls and all of that. Especially in manor houses," Harriet said with an air of authority. "I wouldn't start knocking anything down structurally until you consulted the plans."

"Do you have house plans?" I asked Landry.

He shook his head. "Nothing. All the solicitor sent me was this huge set of keys." He held them up and they jangled, a cacophony of metal trinkets.

"I know one place that would have historical building plans," Gertie said.

All eyes went to her.

"The village archives. This manor house would've been a huge boon to the area when it was built. I bet you dollars to donuts, sorry Julie, that there is some form of document with house plans or construction details lodged in those archives."

"What about all the piles of paper in the hoarding room back where the ladies were living?" Landry asked.

"It would take weeks at minimum to sort through and catalog all of that. I think the archives is the best place to start for something specific. We can always come back and look at the paperwork if the archives don't come through for us." Gertie said, distinctly and logically.

"Do I hear field trip?" I asked.

Gertie laughed because that had become our trade phrase back at GGRS when wayward family historians came in looking for help off-site. She and I were never ones to turn down a good genealogy adventure, and once again we had stumbled onto a deep, dark secret that was too intriguing to pass up.

❊❊❊

Denslough Archives.

I always enjoyed going to the smaller archives; their quaintness was fun and their incredibly dedicated volunteers were impressive. A larger archive would no doubt have paid staff and fancier surroundings, and that was fine, there was certainly a need for those. However, it was the smaller village archives where people tried extra hard and stretched their meager budgets to the absolute limit. It was here that they preserved the social history of the local area and literally brought it back to life.

The Denslough Archives were no different. They were housed on the high street in a former shoe cobbler's shop. They kept the authenticity of the place by hanging old shoe forms and shoes themselves high up on the walls, arranged in a walking pattern which overlaid a map of the village. It was both clever and eye-catching. There was only one volunteer on duty today, Tricia Belvedere. Her companion was a rather fierce looking German shepherd whose dog bed was embroidered with 'Rex'. Rex was no doubt there to protect her in case of any sketchy visitors on site. I hoped us tromping in with our entourage didn't upset him, especially if we got worked up about a new family history find.

Tricia was thrilled to see us walk through her doors. No one else was on site at the moment and it appeared that she was doing some rather repetitive indexing work of a seventeenth century parish register. She was having to read incredibly convoluted Olde English handwriting that was complicated by brown foxing of the paper and random blobs of ink across the page. Tricia grinned up at us with wonderful bright eyes underneath frizzy blond hair stuffed back into a claw clip.

"Good afternoon, how can I help?" Tricia asked.

I stepped forward. "Hello, my name is Julie Fincher and we're from the–"

"Greymore Genealogy Research Site. I know," she said excitedly. "We're thrilled to have you in Denslough. We've heard wonderful things about your site. I must get down there myself one day to see it."

I had to admit I was rather taken aback. I always forgot how quickly word spread when strangers arrived in small villages. Thank you's owed to the pub grapevine as well as to social media. "You'll be most welcome at Greymore. This is Landry Jackson, the new owner of Roycetonne House." I also introduced Gertie. Mrs. Neebles had stayed behind to rustle up some snacks while Ewan and Harriet continued their lengthy appraisal work. Harriet was pressed for time because she was due back by end of day in Medchester to prepare for an auction tomorrow.

"Do you happen to have any records of Roycetonne House's construction?" I asked.

"Do you mean newspaper articles?" Tricia asked.

Landry shook his head. "No, actual house plans that would show the various layers of the house, basement, oh sorry cellar, construction. Things a builder would've used."

"We probably do. I know the family was quite private, but a multigeneration local builder donated all of their records in 1980 when they went out of business. There was a hold on the records, however it expired upon Moyra's death so they're now open to the public. I can check on those for you if you'd like?" She looked at us expectantly.

"That would be lovely," Gertie said.

"Come over to the map cabinet and I'll show you what we have here. If it's not here then it's still likely back at Roycetonne House."

"I was afraid you'd say that," Landry said. "We are faced with the huge task of sorting through over a 150 years' worth of records in a big old room. It appears they saved everything, right down to receipts for balls of twine. It's a mishmash of photo albums, land leases, mining business contracts, personal letters ..." He trailed off when he saw how fascinated Tricia was. He didn't quite get it.

Tricia's cheeks flushed with excitement. "Oh really. Oh my, my, that really is fascinating to hear. Imagine being let loose in that

room and cataloguing over 150 years' worth of continuous archives."
Her eyes got misty and she had a faraway look in her eyes as if she
was gazing upon a princess and a unicorn frolicking in a pristine
meadow.

She refocused. "This way. Please." Tricia led us over to a large,
wide cabinet at the side of the room. It had deep drawers specifically built to accommodate oversized paperwork such as maps
and large photos. Tricia bent down and read the labels on each of
the drawers and then smiled as she put her fingers to the handles
on the fourth one from the top. "Here we are. Roycetonne House.
I wasn't the one who catalogued this particular collection but I'm
glad to see that it's relatively easy to find."

As she pulled open the drawer, we set eyes upon a tidy pile of
architectural drawings. It was like Christmas and New Year's all
rolled up into one. Perhaps we'd easily find the answer to the secret
passageway underneath the manor house. It would be unusual for
an historical mystery to be solved so quickly, however, it wasn't
unheard of. The elusive Lady Adelaide's past had already come
to light through some of our efforts. Even a minute hint of what
happened to Simon would be a welcome bonus.

It appeared we were in luck. Each of the layers of the house, as I
liked to call them, stared back up at us in glorious detail. These were
the actual architectural drawings the builders had used to create the
manor house and its outbuildings. We even saw the initials of Lord
Roycetonne himself on every single page, proving that this was in
fact the correct set of plans. When we got down to the cellar layer,

it was clear that this was where the kitchen supplies and coal were stored, along with spare furniture, travel trunks, servant offices and a couple of larger living quarters.

Tricia had left us to it. By now, Landry, Gertie and I had spread out the plans on a vacant table and poured over them, looking for the secret passageway.

"I don't see anything secret," Landry said.

"Do you really think a building plan would have 'secret passageway' written on it?" I asked.

"It would have to in order to meet building code. They couldn't just willy-nilly put one in after the house was designed," Gertie said.

"Maybe that's why it was so secret," Landry joked. He caught disdainful looks from Gertie and I, then rapidly stopped laughing. "Sorry ladies."

"Well, look at this," I said. "Mrs. Neebles didn't mention anything about the servants' passageway." I used my finger to track a narrow hallway running behind multiple rooms on the second floor, down a circular staircase hidden behind the mechanical room and then down into the basement. It wasn't clear where it went after that.

"I think you're right," Landry said.

"Maybe she didn't know it was there," Gertie said.

"How can a housekeeper who's been there for decades not know about all the secret passageways?" I said. "It seems highly unlikely."

"You know what Bertie says about secrets and big houses," Gertie said, "Five-percent of the information and rooms stay private, away from staff."

"He meant private rooms, not private passageways," I said.

"A passageway could be a sort of room. And what if that's the case in this instance? We should go back to the house and see if we can get into the secret passageway, hopefully finding something more about Lady Adelaide and Simon's tragic romance."

"For all we know, he found someone else and lived happily ever after," Landry said.

We both gave him incredibly disgusted stares.

I wasn't going to let him get away with that comment. "Landry, please don't burst the bubble of an elusive romance before you even know the facts. I'm going with the premise that they were madly in love yet denied the opportunity to be together. It's a classic, tragic love story, one that will defy the ages and be remembered for all time."

"I agree. Let's think positively," Gertie said, with all her usual jolliness.

"It appears I'm outnumbered. Again. Perhaps I should just keep quiet." The tall man with broad shoulders knew when he was beaten.

"Is there anything else we need to find before we go back to Roycetonne House?" I asked Gertie.

"There were a few other files about the family mining businesses. Construction of outbuildings etc. on various sites. I think we should look through those files before we leave. We might find the secret location where Simon wanted to meet Lady Adelaide before they made their escape."

And so we looked. After an hour of all three of us going through various bits of corporate paperwork, we realized we were at a dead end. The only pieces of information that yielded enough insight into our mystery were the actual housebuilding plans. Construction drawings of Roycetonne House showed the beginning of Lady Adelaide's journey away from her oppressive father. We hoped it would be enough to explain what had gone so terribly wrong in her quest for true love.

Chapter 21

––––

Roycetonne House. Evening.

We had completely given up on any notion of getting home to Oakhurst at a reasonable hour. The concept of finding a secret passageway in a great old manor house was simply too good to leave for another day. I'd taken photographs of the plans, layer by layer, and we'd put them on Gertie's laptop. Harriet had left us to it and so it was just Landry, Ewan, Gertie, Mrs. Neebles and I.

"I can't believe Harriet left with this mystery unsolved," I said.

Ewan shrugged. "She's got an auction tomorrow and had to go home to get ready."

"So, what are the house contents worth?" Landry asked. He ducked to avoid the shards of icy glances that were being thrown his way at that particular moment.

"We reckon you've got at least a couple of million here. Two of your guest suites have quite fancy furniture," Ewan said.

"I'm certainly no expert but I'm not surprised this house contains some swanky things," Landry said.

"All that luxury, yet they chose to exist in an office piled high with dusty old papers, holed up at a couple of desks to crank out their agony aunt columns." Gertie looked at us with a quizzical expression. "Why?"

We all struggled, at a loss for words.

Landry sighed. "Moyra came home to nurse her mother. That makes Lady Adelaide my grandmother, right?"

"Possibly. We'd need more official records to confirm who your grandparents were," I said. "You said your paternal grandfather's name was Sheridan?"

Landry nodded. "I'm going to need some time to process this. I had no idea my grandfather had a romance in England before he married my grandmother."

Gertie smiled. "Remember, assume nothing. Prove each linkage multiple ways before considering it fact."

"All I was ever told was that my paternal grandmother died. I never met her," Landry said.

"Regardless guys, we need to figure this out. I'm now totally intrigued." I peered down at Gertie's screen. "Can you enlarge that row of rooms on the house plans so we can try and figure out where the entrances are?"

She did as asked and we soon discovered that the secret entrance was at the end of a long hallway on the upper floor. It went from a linen room, down around a winding staircase behind the kitchen walls and the servants' quarters, then down a few more stairs into a second coal cellar.

"Maybe that's what the pickaxe on the sundial meant," Landry said.

"Could be. Have you ever seen that coal cellar?" I asked. "I only knew of the first one."

He shook his head then got out of his chair. "I think it's high time we figured this out."

We found the linen room because, quite frankly, it was marked 'Linen Room'. It was at the end of a long row of guest rooms in the visitors' wing and Mrs. Neebles was very familiar with it. What she didn't know was that the wainscoting at the back of the room swung open on a concealed hinge. The wainscoting was usually hidden behind a laundry cart filled with used bedding and towels. Ewan pulled the wheeled cart aside and that gave us access to a tiny knob hidden at the baseboards. Pull on that and the wainscoting swung open. A dark cavernous gap was before us.

Once again, Ewan came to the rescue with the flashlight on his phone. He went first to check it out, then called out to us. "It's pretty narrow back here, and Landry you might have to duck. Just watch yourself on these overhead crossbeams."

I smiled to myself, recalling the multitude of times Ewan had clonked his head on the sloped ceiling at his antiques shop.

Once we were inside the narrow passageway, our eyes became somewhat adjusted. We went down the circular stairs, much like a line of fireflies, each one of us using our phones to light the way as we slowly put one careful foot in front of another. There were a couple of rolls of old rose print wallpaper tucked inside one of the framing areas left open without drywall or brick. We also found old receipts for some pots and pans plus a delivery of whiskey. It was almost like the builders had purposely walled up remnants of the past workings of this great place. We then walked for what seemed like forever behind the kitchen, a vast, wide room filled with old ranges, refrigerators plus copper pots and pans hanging from the ceiling. A great wooden worktable stood in the middle and there were various sinks and vegetable cleaning areas around the perimeter of the room. One could imagine the head cook barking out orders at scullery maids and undercooks to get the family's fancy meal up to the dining room at precisely the correct time. We saw all this through a peephole we found inside the corridor. Was it installed so the mistress of the house could observe her servants at work? Was it a place to hide precious commodities and valuables in case of war? Perhaps an escape route in case of danger? It appeared that Roycetonne House concealed an important secret.

More walking. More overhead beams. Landry clonked himself once on his forehead—ouch. We were now behind the servants' rooms; we could tell because there were a few little cracks in the walls from the building settling that showed us the plain cots and dressers that the servants were assigned. We then ran into a thick metal door. It was covered in coal dust. I raised a hand up to the door handle and as I pulled my fingers away, they got covered in black.

"Looks like we found the entrance to the second coal cellar," I said.

"Well, look at this," Gertie said. She shone her phone up higher on the wall and there was an exact replica of the pickaxe we had seen on the sundial. Underneath the pickaxe were two initials 'S' and 'A'.

"It's like retracing their steps on that fateful day," I said. "The door's locked. Landry, try one of those keys on your mega keychain. We need to get inside."

"How do we know that when I open this door there's not going to be a mountain of coal that rushes out to bury us?" he teased.

"You don't. That's why you're at the head of the line," I lobbed back.

"Very funny. Back home in Texas we'd put you on a rogue horse, slap his hindquarters and send you out to ride fences for a few hours."

"Oh really?" I smiled back.

"In your case, in a blizzard. For days," he said.

"Just get on with opening the door. We can't stand the suspense," Gertie said.

"Very well. Here we go." Landry had to fumble with the keys for a few tries and on the fifth one he actually got it. It was one of those old brass keys, the ones that looked like they belonged in a tool museum with all the fancy filigree work inside the handle of the key. It looked too fancy to use for a coal cellar door, but then again back in the Victorian days, craftsmanship counted and people invested in quality. I often lamented today's throwaway society. As my father often said, 'they just don't make things like they used to'.

Landry leaned on the door. It wouldn't budge. He tried again, this time with a bit more effort. Still nothing. Ewan got in on the action as well, putting a shoulder to it and both men pushed hard against the door, trying to open it. Gertie and I stood well back, taking in the scene.

"Gentlemen," I said, "sorry to interrupt your stellar efforts. But you may want to look at the sign above the door." I pointed up and everybody's eyes went to the little sign that said 'Pull Door To Open'.

The men shook their heads, Ewan stepped aside and then Landry did the honors. The door opened on well-oiled hinges without complaint. Inside was a fifty-foot square room that had a few chunks of coal left in various corners. It was most likely a place for emergency coal storage, a hidden room away from those who shouldn't have access. Coal was precious in times of war and it made sense for a family to have a backup supply if things went wrong. There was one small wheelbarrow and two brooms, along with some workmen's tools on the walls, but there wasn't much here at all to speak of. The room was basically bare. But I did see a lump hidden under some burlap sacking, way over in a dark corner. It had the shape of a suitcase, and it lay beside a sturdy ladder.

I went over to look at the suitcase and knew instantly what we'd found. In brass lettering on the top of the handle was printed 'Lady Adelaide Roycetonne'. The suitcase looked packed and ready to go, yet very out of place in a dusty old coal cellar. It also looked forgotten, like a trip interrupted. Very out of place.

"Do you need another key?" Landry asked, standing over my shoulder.

"I don't know. Maybe I can try to open it without one first." I lay the suitcase down on its side, trying to set it on the most dust-free place possible I could find. It was a beautiful leather case, hand tooled with images of roses on all sides. It was obviously a valued possession of an upper class lady.

"This could be the answer to the mystery," Gertie whispered, kneeling down beside me. To heck with the coal dust all over her knees.

"Or the start of another one," Ewan said in a calm voice. "Just think about this for a minute. The lady of the house has a suitcase in the coal cellar, obviously ready to make a getaway with the love of her life who is completely uninvited by the woman's father."

"Simon came back for Lady Adelaide, all the way from Torcwell House in Yorkshire," Gertie said.

"What a wonderful find," I said. The suitcase's clasps easily sprang apart and I opened the suitcase. Inside was a thick layer of tissue paper, now yellowed with age. I lifted the paper up and we looked down upon a set of four folded dresses, a money purse embroidered with the same roses on the outside of the suitcase as well as another diary. Deeper down in the suitcase, we found elegantly folded woman's undergarments, a toiletries set made out of silver, handkerchiefs embroidered with Lady Adelaide's initials, two more pairs of lace-up shoes plus an envelope containing some family photos. One was of her father, and I recognized it from a newspaper clipping I'd seen at the archives. He was dressed in a top hat and tails, ready for the day at the races. He had a thick grey moustache, and incredibly piercing grey eyes. Everything about him said stern and unyielding. A big 'X' in blue ink was drawn across his face. Another envelope contained one first class ticket on a sailing ship to America.

"Run, Adelaide run," Ewan breathed over my shoulder. "This is her getaway case, but what happened to the getaway?"

"It doesn't make sense. She made it this far, Simon likely had a horse waiting outside. The coal merchant delivered directly to this coal cellar, tipping down the chute. She'd be dressed in old clothes to scramble up the ladder to outside. It's an easy way to escape down the back road, the one near the servants' entrance."

We all stood and pondered this for a moment. Then something caught my eye. It was hard to see but the reflection off my phone's flashlight made me go over to investigate further. There, in the roughhewn wall, was a message quickly scratched below another image of a pickaxe. It read:

We are discovered.
I will love you forever.
You must marry your destiny.
Forget me.
Love from Simon

"How terribly sad. One can just picture Lord Roycetonne storming down these hallways, opening the door and spoiling their getaway. Their love ended right here, so many decades ago now." I could easily see it in my mind.

"Simon likely had to give up and run away from the lady that he loved, else likely risk his life under Lord Roycetonne's fury."

You don't think it would've gotten that dangerous, do you?" Gertie asked.

"My sense is that Simon would've hightailed it out of here, maybe even at Lady Adelaide's request. She wouldn't want anything to happen to him," I said.

"So we found their rendezvous and the fact that it was halted at the last minute. That doesn't tell us what happened to them. It doesn't explain Lady Adelaide's reclusiveness," Landry said.

"No it doesn't. We need more information to figure that out."

"So how does one track a person who deliberately goes missing?" Landry asked.

"Your local family history society," Ewan said. "We're dealing with people from a completely different era."

"Simon likely took off, never to be seen again. It would've been incredibly difficult for Lady Adelaide to escape and see him ever again. Her father would've had everyone in the house, all the servants, plus all his friends up at Torcwell House, making sure that Lady Adelaide had no chance to set eyes on Simon."

"She did as Simon told her to and married the Marquis."

"And broke her heart in the process." I looked around the room and saw nothing else that could help us, apart from noting a broken rung on the ladder. "We need to go back to the office upstairs and read some more of her diary."

"You think Simon made a clean getaway?" Ewan asked.

"Only the ship's passenger lists will tell us," I said. "I see a lady who became a recluse because of what happened to the love of her life, but without knowing the exact specifics the story will always be unfinished."

"And if there's more archival evidence to look through, then that's what us family historians always check," Gertie said.

"After you, ladies," Landry said, gallantly holding the door.

We all trooped back upstairs.

✻✻✻

The Hoarding Room.

The suitcase had pride of place on a nearby table. Ewan busied himself gently wiping off the dust from its many crevices.

I read an entry in Lady Adelaide's diary, the one we'd just found in her abandoned suitcase:

> *October 3, 1931*
> *Dear Diary. Father has found my engagement ring and ruined it. He scratched the lovely inscription Simon commissioned. Father's fervent anger frightens me and angers me at the same time. I was raised to be a lady with all the social graces, dancing and musical talents and speaking*

niceties. None of those help me now. I am so desperately in love with Simon. My life seems hopelessly vain and shallow compared to his hard work with the horses in the stables. I would be very happy as his wife on some farm, left to our own devices.

This gilded palace that I live in is cold and lonely. I am but an object for my father to put on display in front of his high-ranking society friends. Father just informed me that I shall be married to John Cantonleigh, the Marquis of Estonburgh. My heart breaks and I feel it shrivel up like a little prune inside my chest. I know nothing of this man, this Cantonleigh, other than he is wealthy and well-connected. Those two traits, according to my father, are sufficient to qualify as my fiancé. I disagree. I long to be with the man I love. Simon.

Will I ever see you again, my dear, sweet and only love?

L.A.R.

"It's all so sad," I said, handing the diary to Gertie. "Imagine being a mere pawn as someone else decided your future."

"It's a clash of two eras. At least she had two daughters to love for a brief time."

"Likely why she became a recluse," Landry added. "Maybe she gave up on her own happiness and decided to help others instead as their secret agony aunt."

"We know Lady Adelaide lived out her days here at Roycetonne House. However, I think we all need to know what happened to Simon," Ewan said.

"Ships' passenger lists. That sounds like a job for Maude back at GGRS," I said. "Everyone agree?"

Chapter 22

—

GGRS. Next Morning.

Our team eagerly started on fact finding as soon as GGRS opened. We needed the resources at the GGRS and that included my desk, computer stations and above all else, Maude and Gertie. We had secret house plans, a lost love, one unused passenger ship's ticket, an unwanted aristocratic marriage plus a room crammed full of unsorted archival documents. It was at the point where we needed to stop rummaging about and come up with some solid facts before proceeding. Goodness knows where we'd be if all we did was rely upon a diary and high society rumors.

Landry grinned. "It was tough to pull away from the thrill of the chase yesterday."

Gertie and Maude nodded. "Of course," Maude said. "But if one's constantly diving down family history rabbit holes, then all you end up with is a deep, complicated warren. The purpose here is to figure out what really happened. The only way to do that is via facts."

"Old houses don't lie," Landry said.

"No, but they can deceive. And we need to keep in mind that many times people fudged the truth when working on their private correspondence or responding to a census survey." Gertie looked at all of us. "It wasn't that long ago that some people literally didn't know when their own birthday was."

Landry had brought the last box of the letters here and asked us to go through the box to see if we could figure out Aunt Moyra's final correspondence.

"Look at this." I showed them the first letter on the stack and read:

Dear Terry:

I write to you with a heavy cattleman's heart. The lady I love left me for family duty years ago. I have my own family (my first wife died after giving birth to our son and he now runs the farm with my grandson while I provide advice from the peanut gallery). May I ask you this: what is a man to do in his twilight years when he still carries a torch for an old flame? My hands might be a bit shakier but the flame burns strong. I wish it was her with me here by the fire. Is it selfish for me to want her back after all this time? When she left she said she couldn't come back.

Signed: Lonely Lad up North

The reply from the agony aunt was succinct, tough love and to the point:

Dear Lonely Lad:

Firstly, there is nothing selfish about wanting to pursue a true love. You are commended for staying true to the one you adore. Second, consider, perhaps, that her heart pines for a true love that can never be. Sometimes life circumstances make romance impossible. Be steadfast with the memories in your heart. Take up a hobby and try to distract yourself because she may very well be unable to change the path of her life's course. It is sad, but don't let it become a bitter mantle for you to wear.

As Always, Terry

"It's Keith writing to Moyra," I said in a whisper, pointing at the return address on the envelope stapled to the letter.

"Indeed," Gertie replied.

"And here's another one," I said, holding up the next letter. "It's in Lady Adelaide's handwriting."

Dear Terry:

I have a delicate conundrum. My father banished my fiancé because he was 'beneath the family'. I was in my early 20s and it broke my heart. He left the country and now I wonder if I should run to him? Shall I abandon my old life forever? I am well into my golden years.

Signed: Restless Inside

Dear Restless Inside:

A grown woman, and one in her senior years, likely has more than a whim to consider acting upon. If you say run, I ask how far? If there is already a great distance between you both, such as an ocean, ask yourself about the physical demands of making such a huge change at this point in your life. Have you kept in touch with him? Is he still waiting for you too? If he's moved on, I suggest you do the same. As always, Terry

Gertie and I both held back tears at the thought of both seniors agonizing over their lost love.

I shook my head. "How sad. How very, very sad."

"I agree. To attain a fancy family image, Lady Adelaide's father made the rest of her life miserable."

"Parents shouldn't be allowed to meddle so much," Gertie said.

I sighed. "I wish my family had kept me apart from my ex. He was a bad decision through and through."

Gertie patted my hand. "Well, Chris is out of your life forever now, so let's not dredge up the past."

"That's really rich, coming from a genealogist," I shot back.

We laughed.

"How, exactly, will my ex be listed on our family tree? I know I can't exclude him, that would be like changing history."

Gertie thought on it for like a millisecond. "Well, technically you can leave him off because we proved your wedding ceremony wasn't valid. However, if you do feel the need, may I suggest a small type-face, in fact the smallest one you can possibly find?" She gave me a hug. "How about six point font?"

✳✳✳

Five Minutes Later.

Fred Todling walked into the research site, looking highly officious and smug. He gripped his briefcase in his left hand. "Ladies, the pleasure of your company, please? A meeting room?"

"Fred, you have a knack for appearing every time the café bakes a new date loaf," I said with a grin.

"Ah, I thought I could detect a delectable scent wafting through these hallowed halls." He stopped in his tracks and took an extra deep breath, likely imagining a piece of date loaf sandwiched between his teeth.

"It's almost like you have date loaf radar," Gertie said.

"Never underestimate the power of the esteemed legal profession," Fred replied, setting his briefcase down. It looked heavy.

He waited.

We waited.

"Perhaps if we could find our meeting room?" he gently probed.

I stood up. "Right. Follow me, please." I led the way, Gertie and Fred traipsing along behind me. Once settled in a meeting room, Fred put his fancy briefcase on the coffee table. With two satisfy-ing clicks of the brass locks, the lid to legal paradise opened and we were faced with a sea of excessively tidy manila folders. The files even had laser-printed, color-coded labels. I wasn't sure if that was meant to impress us or simply to keep Fred in order; either way, it was reassuring to see.

"My esteemed colleagues, you are no doubt in breathless anticipation of what prompted my impromptu visit here today," he said with both a kind look and a cheeky grin.

Gertie put a hand to her collarbone, breathless. "Oh, I couldn't sleep last night what with all the anticipation."

Fred's face fell. "But you were not aware I was coming. How could you anticipate my announced arrival on said premises when–"

"Fred. What can we help you with today?" I interrupted.

"Cozying up to the very heart of the matter," he said in a smooth tone.

In my mind, I still visualized him in his broccoli ballet costume. *Focus, Julie, focus.*

Fred took the file out from his briefcase. "I'm here to report on recently received correspondence from Jacobs, Jacobs and Jacobson."

"Rather an odd name for a company," I mused.

"Why the 'son' on the third moniker? They could've coordinated that a bit better," Gertie said.

"I am not certain of that peculiarity," he admitted, "however if you would care to draw your attention to the letter on top of the contents of this file–"

"Oh, they're the bankruptcy trustees for the brewery," Gertie said, quickly scanning the document.

He nodded. "Indeed they are the miserly bunch whose penny-pinching is fraught with malevolence and coldhearted demeanor towards our maned and tailed friends."

"Did we win?" I asked, ever so eager.

Fred looked at me. Then he looked over Gertie. He nodded. "The opponent has in every delectable sense of the word, now and forever more, caved."

Gertie whooped. "That's wonderful! The youth group will be ever so pleased. They've already established a feeding, grooming and exercise rota."

"Now Bingo and Jim will no longer be considered equines-on-the-lam, so to speak," Fred said.

The solicitor could not have looked more serious if we'd just unearthed the bones of Oliver Cromwell in our miniature goats meadow.

"Julie, I just need you to sign here please." Fred gestured at a blank line on a multi-page sales contract. It sat right underneath a relatively simple-looking sentence:

Sold to the Greymore Hall estate charity for the sum of £3,800.

It was already countersigned by a principal of the firm. I signed it as well. Then I looked up at Fred for direction. The solicitor was fully engaged in the purchase contract. "Please sign here again. And here. And here. And initial here. And here." He pointed out the spots on pages faster than I could put ink to paper.

I started to protest. "Fred, I'm buying two retired Shire horses, not a skyscraper in New York."

"One must protect Greymore at all costs," he advised in a somber tone. "Genealogists always prefer a strong paper trail, am I not correct?"

"He's got us there," Gertie said, a defeated look on her face.

I sighed. "I'm going to run out of ink in this pen, Fred."

"Ah, never fear, I have just the solution for that." He unsnapped a divider in his briefcase and showed us a forty-strong pen collection, all lined up like soldiers in their individual elasticized loops.

"Fred, you could open up a pen store," Gertie said.

He smiled. "Stationery is a sideline in my uncle's bookshop. Do you remember him, the bookshop owner in Pixleton?"

"And you're promoting it on your lawyerly travels?" I asked.

"Indeed I am." He pulled out a pen and gave it to me. I saw it was engraved: *'Todling Law: Enthusiastic Intellectual Property Protection.'*

"What was your old slogan? Minding IP? No period between the 'I' and 'P', right?" Gertie asked.

Fred's face turned a bit red. "I rebranded."

"Wise move. So are the horses now officially ours?" Gertie asked.

"Indeed they are, and not a moment too soon on this glorious, sunshiny day. I have to admit that on the drive over here my thoughts turned to green pastures and those brown and white lambs frolicking–"

"Goats, Fred. They're miniature goats," I corrected.

Fred didn't break stride. "Miniature goats frolicking with wild abandon in your back meadow as wise old Bingo and Jim gaze out across the field with carefree hearts."

"Er, Fred, we're not paying you by the word like the solicitors did back in the eighteenth century when they composed people's wills, right?" I asked.

"Good gracious, no." Fred looked rather offended at my question.

"Thank goodness. I was worried we'd need to mortgage the place," Gertie whispered to me.

I cleared my throat. Fred was a kind man, just rather overly verbose. "So, the power of social media really came through for us? It convinced those nasty trustees to sell the horses to us instead of to the abattoir?"

"Yes. That plus the tiniest other thing," he added.

"What's that?" I asked.

"Well, it just so happens that the second Jacobs at the firm is the man who refused to dance at his stepdaughter's ballet performance."

Gertie and I looked shocked.

I had to ask. "The one where you stepped in at the last minute?"

"The very same. Once I showed him the video of my performance, he agreed that the horses were a small price to pay for him not having to wear tights in public."

"Sure, that plus the fact that he'd be shamed online for filching out on a four-year-old," Gertie added.

Fred got a look on his face, one that implied insider knowledge rolled up with a bit of craftiness. "Indeed. It actually made all the difference in the world."

Chapter 23

—

Next Day.

"I'm seeking some information about cat fanciers in Suffolk," the gruff voice in front of me said. I looked up to see a tall, skinny man with thick glasses, a fringe of grey hair and a long, narrow face. His clothes hung off him like an underfed scarecrow, and there was a hole in the elbow of his already-patched denim shirt. What made his appearance all the more intriguing were the eight gold rings he wore, one on each finger except for his thumbs.

Are thumbs considered fingers?

"Miss? Cat fanciers? Can you help me?" he asked. He had the voice of a sports announcer; deep, rich and smooth ... kind of like a perfect afternoon cappuccino.

"Oh, right. I'd recommend an internet search to start," I suggested.

"Right. Cats don't usually get listed in a church parish register," he said in a teasing tone. His voice was still gruff but it was clear he had a sense of humor. He stuck his right hand across the desk. "Wally Dunstable? It's a pleasure to meet you."

"Welcome Wally. How did you hear about us? We keep statistics, you see," I said.

"Right. I heard about your research site from a friend: Ozzie Boggs. I believe you recently assisted him with a genealogical endeavor?" His eyes looked at me with a steady gaze.

Did I detect a hint of a smile?

I replied, "Of course. Ozzie provided us with–"

"Stale scones, smoked mackerel sandwiches and a dent in your collective sanity?" he offered.

"I wouldn't quite put it like that ..."

"You don't have to. He's been a good mate of mine for fifty-one years now. We're still getting up to mischief together."

So Ozzie did have at least one friend outside GGRS. Good for him.

"Just not at our research site, please." Wally was all right. A little—no, a lot—on the eccentric side, but that was fine. Family history, like all pursuits, had its fair share of extreme and exuberant personalities.

He smiled. "Right. I found a note in our family bible proving ownership of a prize-winning Maine Coon cat. The cat took Best of Show at the Suffolk County Fair years ago."

"Ah Maude, perhaps you can help this gentleman?" I gestured for her to intervene with this feline-related query as I heard the telephone ring. I answered. "Greymore Genealogy Research Site?" I stopped talking as I saw Wally bend down to pick up a pet carrier from the side of the desk on the floor and talk to what was inside. The resultant purring sounded like an engine. I'm sure that Wally's cat was lovely, but we certainly couldn't have animals running amok in the research site. Partly it was due to other patrons' allergies and partly it was due to records' protection needs. No doubt, Maude would elegantly handle the situation. I had to smile; it wasn't often that a visitor brought in live animal evidence of the family history they were researching.

Squawking on the other end of the telephone line brought me back to stark reality. "Hello?" I asked again, "you've reached the Greymore Genealogy Research Site. Can I help you?"

"Yes," the likely-female caller said in a tentative, high-pitched voice. "My sister and I are looking for information on oast houses from 1902."

"Oh, do you have hop pickers in your background?" I asked.

"Yes, our ancestors earned money picking hops for a brewery every summer for years. The problem is, all the photos were lost in World War One, and all we have is an old address. Are you able to help?"

"Of course. We have access to multiple Kent County history magazines as well as online resources."

"Do we need to pre-book a computer?" the caller asked.

Music to my ears. A researcher who actually understood.

"It is preferable," I replied. "Just visit our website and you can do it there."

"Right. We'll be in as soon as we can. I'm Anne by the way, and my sister is Gloria. We read all about your new research site and look forward to meeting you."

"Until then. Thank you and good-bye."

I hung up then leaned back in my chair, satisfied with the hive of activity the research site had become. Aunt Edwina would be so pleased. I got a super warm and cozy feeling side.

Maude came into my line of view, carrying the cat inside its carrier. "Wally is returning tomorrow, sans feline, so we can have a proper session. I gave him a couple of quick website references he can start with back at home today."

Wally caught up to Maude and waved on his way out.

"That man should definitely be on the radio," Maude said, "but his voice certainly doesn't match his demeanor. Rather uncertain with himself, until he gets going on the topic of cats. I have never learned so much about Maine Coons in such a compressed timeframe."

We shared a pained smile.

"I was once cornered in a family history society office, years ago. A man in his thirties wanted to tell me all about llama breeding," I admitted.

"At a family history society office?" Maude was taken aback.

"Turns out, his grandfather was the pioneer of the industry here in England decades ago and his grandson was now trying to piece together every single farm show his grandfather ever went to where he earned a championship ribbon."

"How did you extricate yourself?" Maude asked.

"With a crowbar ... and a timely rescue buddy. A friend noticed my dilemma and called me from an office two doors down. She said there was an urgent meeting I was needed at immediately."

"Well done."

"Sherry!" We both focused on the main entrance doors and saw Sherry Knox walk-in. Sherry looked super happy to see us, Maude in particular. The ladies embraced.

"Thank you again for a lovely tea," Maude said to Sherry.

Ah, so Maude had met with our visitor being led astray by her contracted genealogist.

"We must do it again soon." Sherry stepped back, her eyes sparkling. "I found the treasure," she said in a somewhat gleeful manner.

"Really?" Maude replied.

"What treasure?" I asked.

"These," Sherry said in a definitive voice. She held up a bulging canvas bag, the kind they hand out to full registrants at trade shows and conferences. Hers was emblazoned with a logo for an historic greengrocers association in a neighboring county. I surmised that a relative of hers was in the trade many years ago. We followed Maude to our aptly named 'chat room', a room where researchers could meet and discuss their work without disturbing others. I noticed that Sherry's bag was stuffed full of bubble-wrap, the kind that was addictively fun to pop when enjoying a few idle moments. We sat down on comfortable chairs and peered excitedly at Sherry's bag.

She spoke. "During our tea, I mentioned to Maude that I have an heirloom collection of greeting cards. I keep them in a storage room, but couldn't find them at the time because I'd misplaced the index sheet to my storage tote collection. I had to rummage in my hard drive for a bit and finally found it. I'm now proud to show you the contents of tote number 16-B."

Sherry laid out a series of bubble-wrapped, vintage greeting cards from her canvas bag. There were six in total and all were incredibly fancy.

I looked at them up close. "They all appear to be handmade. Lace, embroidery, velvet heart stitching. What incredible craftsmanship," I said.

Maude nodded. "When Sherry described them to me, I said they sounded one-of-a-kind, likely TNA-worthy."

I sat up straight. "TNA-worthy?" That really meant something tumbling from someone like Maude's lips. 'TNA' stood for 'The National Archives' and was one of my most absolute favorite places in the world. It held England's centuries of history, with some of the rarest documents in the world carefully housed in its collection. GGRS team members had taken a daytrip there not too long ago, helping two researchers—Ozzie Boggs and Pamela Fulham—with their own family history.

"I'm quite sure," Maude continued. "I went online to look at TNA's greeting card collection—they have many of the samples used for original copyright registration—and didn't see anything matching Sherry's cards."

"How old are they?" I asked, leaning forward again to look at a St. Patrick's Day card decked out in green velvet and silvery ribbon.

"I'd say late nineteenth century," Sherry guessed. "Victorian times, likely."

"And they're just kept in a plastic storage tote?" I asked.

"Yes. Seems a bit of a waste, doesn't it?" Sherry said. "I'm sure it's not the proper archival storage container. Plus, I don't even know how they came into our family's possession."

"That's the case with so many family heirlooms. And thus proving why it's important to document what one does actually know." I looked at the cards, pure eye candy for any historian. Then I looked up. "What does Hayleigh think?"

Sherry cleared her throat, uncomfortable. "She advised me that I should sell them," she said in a tightlipped tone. I noticed how her fingers clenched together after that statement.

Maude and I both shook our heads.

"I know, bad advice. I'm starting to think that Hayleigh is just about the money. When Maude explained how dangerous Hayleigh's gap was on my family tree, I did take a significant step back," Sherry said.

"Did you sign a contract with Hayleigh?" I asked.

Sherry nodded, chagrined. "I'm afraid I did, yes. A thirty-percent deposit and guaranteed fifty hours of work."

I whistled low, almost under my breath.

"But Sherry does have an escape clause," Maude said.

"Really? Is Fred Todling involved?" I joked.

Maude smiled. "The contract states that it automatically terminates if the researcher is unable to continue work."

Sherry gave us a stare. It was clear that she was not altogether helpless. "So apart from slipping a rotten egg into Hayleigh's oatmeal, I need a really good opportunity to wiggle away from this shyster I've hired."

"Well," I said, "I'm glad that Maude has at least steered you onto the right course. First things first. We need to properly preserve these fabulous vintage cards. Acid-free containers, proper indexing, research their provenance."

"There's only one place I know that already has a substantial collection with wonderful curation," Maude said.

My eyes shone with delight. "Do I hear field trip?"

❊❊❊

GGRS Electric Bus. Next Morning.

It would be tackling two problems at once. The trip to TNA would not only help us decide what to do with Sherry's greeting cards; it would also provide an opportunity for us to look up more about Roycetonne House plus Lady Adelaide's missing fiancé. We decided not to tell Hayleigh that we were going to TNA; Sherry had divulged to us on the bus that Hayleigh had already discouraged her from going there. It made absolutely no sense at all, and Hayleigh was looking more and more like a very untruthful businesswoman. We were determined to put things right and also solve the mysteries of the past.

❊❊❊

The National Archives, London.

"It sounds like you've been here before." The experienced TNA archivist made the comment with an air of kind authority as she smiled at Maude, Sherry and I. Her nametag read 'Peggy' and she was super friendly, clearly knowledgeable and in control of all in her purvey. I'd requested a meeting with her in advance of our visit so we could get her insights on Sherry's greeting card collection. When one did any form of family history research, it always paid to be organized well in advance. Luckily Peggy had a fortuitous cancellation that created an appointment opening; it helped that the organization was likely keen to ensure donations it wanted were acquired before the donor changed his or her mind.

"Indeed, Maude and I both have," I said. "The last time we were looking at records from a few royals plus a matrimonial bureau."

"How interesting," Peggy said.

"I adore coming to your facility. And I've only been here once, today!" Sherry added.

Peggy smiled. "So many records, so little time, is what I always say. TNA has many miles of records, and I'll only ever see a tiny fraction of them in my entire lifetime." One sensed that Peggy would gladly spend every single waking minute in the facility if she could.

"Last time we were here, I learned why it's smart to wear dark clothes. One of our requested boxes was quite dusty," I said.

"It happens. We do try our absolute best, but with such a high volume of records, we haven't been able to go through them all to catalogue and clean them."

"It must be an overwhelming task," Maude said.

"It is. But not so daunting that one gives up," Peggy replied. "History never ceases being made. Now, I understand you have a possible donation to our greeting card collection?"

"Yes, these fancy Victorian cards have been in our family for generations, but I honestly don't know why," Sherry offered.

"They are unique, truly," Peggy said. "I've helped curate some of the existing greeting card collection here and I've not seen anything as fancy as these before." She peered closer at the six cards we had laid out on the table. "This one even has tiny gold horseshoes tied onto the lace for this wedding card. What an incredibly detailed piece of craftsmanship."

"Yet they are blank. No names," Sherry said, "which is why I am wondering what they're doing in my family's artefact collection."

"Trade sales samples perhaps? From an artist's portfolio? An apprentice's glass bowl?" Peggy suggested.

"Sorry?" I asked. "Glass bowl?"

Peggy smiled. "It's a general reference made to a sample piece an apprentice would create for his master before being allowed to become an approved tradesperson himself. The famous cut crystal bowls at glassworks factories are the epitome of earning a final stamp of approval. They even have them in their visitor display cases up front."

"How fascinating," Sherry said.

"We could use a lot more expert craftspeople in today's world. Sadly, we've lost a lot through retirement and industrialization," Peggy said.

"The unique has been replaced with the thousands of plastic clones turned out by factories," I said, "but I do think we're in the midst of a handcrafted products' resurgence."

"And this is why I want to do the right thing and preserve my cards. No one handcrafts cards like these anymore, at least that I'm aware of." Sherry gave us all a firm glance.

"Can't argue with you on that point," Peggy said.

"There was a woman I knew who handcrafted lace in Devon, but that was a long time ago," Maude said. "Sherry's cards really do belong in a professional archive facility."

Peggy looked over the six cards once more. "They really are stunning, one-of-a-kind." She looked up at us. "I can promise climate control, proper cataloguing, professional management and your name on both the official donation form and public record."

"And they'll be protected from ultraviolet light?" Sherry asked.

"Of course. If they ever do go on display, we have special cases that prevent their being affected by light. Plus we never allow flash photography in our exhibits."

"Right. Where do I sign?" Sherry asked.

Maude and I share a warm smile of satisfaction. Another wayward artefact had found its way home.

"Let me go and fetch a donation form. I'll be right back," Peggy said.

I leaned back in my chair. "This is a job well done, ladies."

"At some point today, I'll treat us all to tea and a gooey scone in the café," Sherry offered.

"Sounds wonderful. And this is very generous of you, Sherry," Maude said.

"Well, what was I doing with these lovely cards all tucked away in a non-archival friendly container at home? I'm not helping history much by squirreling them away inside my house," Sherry said.

"You're doing your bit," Maude said, "just like all ordinary British citizens did during both World Wars."

"I wonder what Hayleigh would say to all this goodness," I mused aloud.

"Hayleigh didn't want me to come here," Sherry said. "She was quite adamant about that."

Maude looked shocked. "Why on earth would a professional genealogist not want to visit TNA? I'm all for bringing a sleeping bag to maximize my time here on site." Maude was quite indignant. She positively bristled at the bad advice Hayleigh gave to Sherry.

Sherry continued. "It was rather odd. Hayleigh told me that there was no need to visit TNA, that I'd be wasting my money and she'd find everything she needed online."

"But not everything is online. She should know that," Maude said.

"There's lots of records here that haven't been digitized yet," I said. "And I know that even though I'm just a beginner in genealogy research."

"Well, Hayleigh's an odd duck. You stick with us and we'll keep you on the straight and narrow," Maude said to Sherry.

"Just don't ask Maude to help you with any lip balm storage while we're here," I said giving Maude a teasing side eye.

"Oh, I'm never going to live that down." Maude shook her head yet couldn't help but smile.

"Lip balm? What's this about?" Sherry asked.

"Alright, I'll admit what I did. On one of my greenhorn trips to TNA, I had forgotten a lip balm in my pocket. I ended up having to store it all by itself in a locker before I was allowed access to the records. I took up an entire locker with one little tube of lip balm. It looked so forlorn and lonely in there. I was highly embarrassed to take it out again. I felt like I wore a big neon sign with an arrow pointing to the top of my head saying 'Archive Newbie'."

"Oh, that's just priceless," Sherry said. Then she got a scattered look in her eyes. "I tend to keep one of those tubes in my pocket as well, but I think I left it in the locker." She patted herself down and then breathed a sigh of relief. "No newbie sign needed over my head."

"Ladies, I think it's time we took a break down in the cafeteria. Sherry, let's get this form signed and then go rustle up tea and scones," I said. My stomach rumbled.

❊❊❊

Chapter 24

One Hour Later.

We were all deep into a box of records from Lady Adelaide's passenger ship. It was fortunate that someone at the ocean liner's office had the presence of mind to donate these records when the company disbanded in 1973. As it turned out, the glorious person was none other than the grandson of the company founder. It didn't matter whether he donated this box of records out of family pride or completing his archival duty to the nation. Either reason gave us a box to delve inside and look for Lady Adelaide's elusive fiancé.

Landry had now given us full rein to talk about Lady Adelaide's tragic past, so long as we didn't veer into any conversation about the agony aunts. That topic, well, he was still deciding what to do and had a meeting with the newspaper about the column later this week.

"This could take a few hours," Maude said.

"No worries. Harvey's bringing sandwiches and tea on the bus for the trip back so we can stay until late closing if we like." TNA had a couple of days per week when it was open super late and us researchers leapt at the chance to spend a full day here. Heck, we would spent 24/7 here if allowed, sleeping bags and thermoses on standby.

I wonder if anyone really ever had slept amongst the shelves and record stacks?

"Look at this," Sherry said. "Old menus."

We continued our conversation in a whisper, out of earshot of the nearest researcher two tables away.

"Oh, how fascinating," Maude said. She held the deckle-edged paper in her hand and read through the cornucopia of first-class dishes. Half of the menu was in French, likely playing on guests' expectations of elegant dishes with the highest standards of global cuisine.

"It became very popular among the elites to hire a French chef to run the kitchens. It was seen as a mark of upscale living, a sure-fire way to impress guests."

"I don't mind where a cook is from, so long as they make great food," I said with a smile.

"I hear Ewan is pretty good in the kitchen," Maude whispered, a twinkle in her eye.

"Once. He made Gertie and I dinner once." This wasn't the place or time to discuss my possible burgeoning affection for our local antiques dealer. "Now, what else is in this box of historical records?"

That was smart, Julie. Deflection of an awkward, probing comment using tantalizing archival records. Well done.

Sherry was on it. She quietly pulled out some more paperwork from the box. "More itineraries, ship logs, dinner dance tickets, paper doilies with the ship's logo, a few snaps from the bow and ... the grand finale, one detail picture of a sparkling clean loo."

Maude and I were surprised.

"What on earth did they need a photo of the toilet for?" I asked.

Maude quietly laughed. "Health and safety?"

"Seriously?" I asked.

"I have no idea. Mind you, I'm no expert on ocean liners. Reading a passenger list certainly gives me no great insights into the inner workings of a large ship and her crew," Maude said.

"Hmmm. Well, it's either someone's idea of a joke or it has a meaning in the wider context of these records."

"And that's why archivists don't like to break up record collections, correct?" Sherry asked.

"Indeed," Maude said. "A lot of understanding is lost if a collection is split up and sent to different repositories."

"What year are we seeking?" I asked.

"We know for Lady Adelaide's ticket that it was 1931. I checked each month of that year just to be sure. Errors, changed plans, missed connections ... It's always wise to give your research a bit of leeway on both sides of your best date."

"Right," Sherry said.

We each took a ledger and went through the passenger list. There were hundreds of people listed for each voyage. These records were certainly available online, but since we were already here at TNA, it was fun to consult the original documents. It took over an hour to read each bound copy of passenger lists. We waded through first-class, second-class, and third-class. We examined every record of who dined at the captain's table, which musicians entertained during the evening and which passengers rang up alarming bar tabs on dubious credit.

Nothing.

Lady Adelaide's Simon wasn't anywhere to be found.

"Do you think Simon travelled under a false name?" I asked.

"Possibly, but harder to do in the 1930s compared with previous decades. United Kingdom booklet passports already existed, plus with the Communists and Fascist scares, identities were scrutinized a lot more closely," Maude said.

"Plus, why would Simon need to conceal his identity?" Sherry asked.

"To escape Lord Roycetonne. Maybe that was the plan all along. Travel under assumed names," I said.

"Possible. But don't you think that Lord Roycetonne's reach would have infiltrated the ship owner's boardroom so he could track down his daughter and her wayward fiancé? Lord Roycetonne didn't seem like a man to ever cross," Maude said.

"No, definitely not. And I imagine Lady Adelaide paid dearly for being found out," I said, thinking back to the expensive, forlorn suitcase we'd found in the secret coal cellar.

"Her marriage to the Marquis. For name, not for love," Maude added. "Ladies, I think we've exhausted the search for today. We can look at more passenger lists online back at the GGRS." She stretched then covered a polite yawn.

We set about neatly repacking the box of records, every document going back inside in the order it came out. This was both professional as well as courteous to the next researcher. There was nothing more frustrating than ordering up a set of records the online system listed as neatly arranged into five subfolders, only to open up the subfolders and find a disheveled mess.

"I'll take the records box back," I said. I picked it up, leaving the other two ladies at the table. Walking over, I entered the records pickup and drop-off counter area where one signed for envelopes and boxes for on-site research. I came into the room at the exact same time as another researcher, a pleasant looking man in his sixties.

"Please go ahead of me," he offered. "Your box looks far heavier than my little folder here," he said with a smile, showing me the slim folder tied with archival-safe tape—like flat string—under his arm.

"Thanks very much, there is a lot of paper in this box," I said.

We shared a grin as I sat my box on the counter and we waited for the desk staff to help us.

"I'm glad they have such rigid security here now," he said.

"Agreed. We need to protect records from theft so everyone has a chance to enjoy them," I said.

"I hope they send that London woman to jail for a long time. Imagine stealing a letter handwritten by Queen Elizabeth the First and flogging it online after cutting off the TNA repository stamp. Shameful," he said with a frown.

I was caught off guard. "Oh, did a theft just occur?"

He shook his head. "It happened about eighteen months ago. The initial trial finished two months back and it's on appeal."

"Really? I hadn't heard." Mind you, with Aunt Edwina's treasure hunt not in the too distant past, and the opening of GGRS, I'm not surprised we missed hearing about it. Frankly, I was still amazed I remembered to get dressed each day.

The man came closer to me. "It caused quite a stir here. I'll show you ..." He scrolled on his mobile phone and brought up a photo of the accused.

My mouth hung open wide. The accused went by a different name but it was clear: the archives thief was none other than sketchy genealogist Hayleigh Grables-Muncton.

***

GGRS Electric Bus. Early Evening.

Our volunteer driver Harvey was true to his word and distributed sandwiches and drinks from a cooler. As he drove, we munched away, contemplating what we now knew.

Maude spoke first, someone we could count on for a logical assessment. "Well, it explains why Hayleigh didn't want you to visit TNA, Sherry," she said.

Sherry was clearly horrified. "I cannot believe it. To think I signed a contract with somebody pilfering archives from the government. It's shocking."

"Hayleigh should be taken off the road, so to speak," Maude said, half serious.

And who could blame her? Hayleigh was a fraudster.

"It's not like we run background checks on all the GGRS visitors, but really–" I started.

"Maybe we should," Maude said.

"The online article also said that Hayleigh stole £5,700 pounds from a family history society over a period of years. Her husband is a solicitor who was also caught diverting trust funds from a deceased person's will into his own personal coffers," I reported.

"And they ran this scheme for three years?" Sherry asked.

"It would've been much longer if they weren't caught," Maude said.

"Justice is needed and swiftly," Sherry said. She was incredibly indignant and rightly so. "I feel terrible at having brought this woman onto your research site's premises."

"Well, Hayleigh and her husband are both permanently banned from TNA and their sentences are pending appeal. However, there is something we can do in the meantime to assist and I happen to know just the man for the job," I said.

"It's nothing illegal, is it?" Sherry said. She thought on her statement for a second or two. "Although at this point, I'm so angry with Hayleigh that maybe we could bend the rules a bit."

Maude patted the top of Sherry's hand. "Let's not get down into the mud with Hayleigh. I'm sure what Julie has in mind is an elegant way of telling Hayleigh that her behavior is absolutely unacceptable to the honest researchers and education we support at GGRS."

Chapter 25

The Major was delighted to receive my call and beetled over to GGRS as soon as he'd extricated himself from a medal ceremony at a local cadet academy where he gave a history lecture earlier that day.

We sat in my office at GGRS. He listened to my horrified recounting of Hayleigh's crime, and then thought about it for a moment.

"I must say, that woman is no better than hot vinegar soup."

I smiled. "That's a new analogy."

"Well, she's not even fighting fair, surreptitiously stealing archives and trying to profit from her misdeed. Shameful." He bristled at the thought and I was sure I saw his porkchop sideburns quiver. In fact, his moustache got in on the action too, so much so that I was worried it might become permanently askew.

"Major, do you recall how you led home base when we had to convince my ex to follow a fake lead away from the real treasure hunt Aunt Edwina prepared?" I asked.

"Operation Salt Cellar. Of course, how could I forget? Our results were legendary. Only last week I was speaking with the Duke of

Conroy about our success and he invited me for tea to recount our exceptional work."

Good. I knew the Major could be counted upon.

"How would you like to mastermind another operation, only this time you'd be out in the field?"

"In the field? Me?" His eyes lit up and he leaned forward, of course without hunching an inch.

"Yes, you," I confirmed.

"Indeed, I'd be enthused. What exactly did you have in mind?"

"A polite yet firm takedown of a thief. Something that tells her deviousness is not wanted in our world. Hayleigh doesn't know you so you're the perfect stealth operative for us."

"So outwardly everything appears the same but with a smart twist at the end to ensure she knows her place is elsewhere?"

I nodded. "Exactly."

"Very well. I shall name it Operation Hot Chocolate." He thought on it for a serious moment. "And with the plan I'm formulating, I will need someone with intelligence, fortitude, and lightning fast fingers on the keyboard." He cracked his knuckles for emphasis.

❀❀❀

GGRS Café.

We found Landry sitting at a table by himself, squirreled away at the back. The café smelled like freshly baked bread, warm chocolate chip muffins and blackberry tea. It was homey, welcoming and divine. The winning Christmas coloring contest entries were hung on the wall inside a confetti decorated frame for proud parents and visitors to admire. The chairs and tables were comfortable and spaced apart with plenty of distance so there would be no impediments to walkers, canes, scooters or prams. Over the past few months, our café had become quite a hit with the locals. Some people stopped in just for a snack and a chat, not even wanting a tour, to do research or take a walk. To each their own, I said. The more people through our site, the more opportunities we had to share the word about all that the Greymore Hall estate had to offer.

I approached the tall Texan who was furiously typing into his laptop. He had a smile on his face.

"Ahem, enjoying your work?" I asked in a teasing voice.

Landry looked up. His smile almost qualified as an unabashed grin. "Good morning, Julie." He got up to pull a chair out for me, ever the gentleman.

"Landry, I'd like you to meet Major Barry Whitcombe, retired," I said, stepping aside so the men could engage in the exercise of seeing whose grip was the firmest. Unsurprisingly, they had to call it a draw.

"Call me 'Major'. Everybody else does." My military friend spoke in a firm, friendly manner.

"Sounds fine. Thank you for your service," Landry said.

"We need your help, Landry," I said as the Major and I both got settled in chairs opposite laptop man.

"After all you've done for my family history questions so far, the only answer possible is a resounding 'yes'," Landry offered.

"That's very kind. Don't you want to know the request first?" I asked.

"No, ma'am. Just tell me what you need me to do," Landry said.

The Major explained the takedown of the rogue genealogist we wanted to enact.

"Thieving archives from TNA? That's pretty brazen ... and wrong," Landry said.

He looked at the Major. "Are you sure this Hayleigh woman doesn't know you, hasn't seen you before?"

"Positive. The last time I was here was for the Christmas shindig," the Major said.

"How could I forget. You and Harvey gave us a sleigh ride to remember," Landry said.

"Glad you enjoyed our surprise."

"Bingo and Jim are now the gift that just keeps on giving. I heard the youth group is having a fantastic time taking care of the newly retired horses," Landry said.

The Major clasped his lapels with pride. "Yes sir. And it is a most gratifying sight, seeing youth work together on a positive project."

Landry turned his laptop to face us. We both saw Bertie's premium chutney jars covering Landry's screen.

"Still working on solving chutneygate?" I asked, half-expecting a chagrined look back from Landry. Whomever Bertie had sold his cases of product to, it looked pretty doubtful that he would ever collect on the unpaid invoice.

Landry got a funny look in his face. "I am no longer working on that project."

"Did you have to give up because it was too much of a challenge?" I asked. "We would, of course, understand."

The words 'give up' appeared to give the Major reason to fidget.

Landry noticed. Then he spoke. "Of course not. I said it's off my project list because the deed is already done."

"You have Bertie's money back?" I was shocked.

"The whole kit and caboodle," Landry said.

"But I thought they were some dastardly outfit hidden beneath cloaks of internet layers all across the world?"

"They were." Landry looked satisfied. "They tried rerouting their IP address through eight different countries, using phony names, addresses, everything."

"So how did you track them down?"

Landry chuckled. "I won't bore you with the details, so let's just say I found the gap in their armor."

"That's impressive, young man," the Major said. He clearly enjoyed learning that Landry had already defeated one enemy.

Landry closed the lid of his laptop. "Cybersecurity is my business and I take the time to really educate myself on it."

The Major leaned in closer. "In other words, fools are those who think they can squirm out of your clutches in a dueling keyboards scenario."

"Well–" Landry looked a bit embarrassed at the high praise.

"You're very talented Landry, well done," I said, "Bertie will be so pleased."

Landry handed me his mobile phone, text from Bertie on screen. I read:

Absolutely brilliant and my most humble thanks. B.

Underneath Bertie had attached a photo of himself at his estate shop, standing in front of a towering pyramid of jars of mango chutney for sale. Scotford Castle's owner now had his dignity back.

"Imagine stealing from a duke," the Major tut tutted.

"I know. It's inexcusable," I said.

Then the Major got a steely look in his eye. "Now, about the help I need to politely escort an underhanded researcher from the GGRS premises ..."

✳✳✳

GGRS. Two Days Later. 'Operation Hot Chocolate'.

The Major invited Hayleigh on site under the guise of needing her help with his own Scottish ancestral research. Maude and I gave him a printout of his true family tree; the Major did actually had six generations of Scottish ancestors. He'd been quite enthused about naming, designing and also leading implementation of the stealth plan. 'Wholeheartedly' was his frequent response.

When Hayleigh arrived, we greeted her, then Maude and I got busy at the front desk. There were a few other visitors present and we all carried on with our regular business. The corners of our eyes, however, were kept trained on what Hayleigh and the Major were looking at on screen.

I walked by to catch the drift of their conversation. I wasn't trying to snoop ... well, all right, I was.

"I cannot find my ancestor in the parish register, census record or local craft guilds," the Major said, playing the role of exasperated researcher to the point of perfection.

"Have you tried a newspaper search or immigration records?" Hayleigh asked.

Not bad advice. It sounded sensible. So if Hayleigh knew these next steps were truly helpful, then why would she need to resort to stealing one of our nation's treasures? Perhaps it was greed, a devilish monster that was just too powerful for some people to resist.

What a shame.

Hayleigh had vastly strayed outside the ethical boundaries followed by all good genealogy and family history researchers.

"I'm afraid I'm not very good with computers," the Major said in an apologetic voice. "Perhaps you should give it a go ..." He shunted aside in his rolling chair and let Hayleigh sit in front of the screen. And with a near imperceptible wink—or was it an eye twitch—Operation Hot Chocolate was put into action. The Major prided himself on lightning effectiveness in dire situations and this would be a thing of beauty to behold.

We had left Landry in the café to keep things hush-hush.

Next, I saw Maude pick up her mobile phone, quickly read a text, then tap something on screen. Instantly the entire research site changed. By 'change', I mean that every single computer screen in the entire place now showed a photo of Hayleigh's public mugshot.

It was like the keyboard suddenly caught on fire right in front of the crook in our midst. She removed her hands like they were resting on hot coals. Hayleigh stared, stony-faced, at her mugshot. She reached to turn off the monitor. As she turned to look at the Major, she noticed that the same mugshot appeared on every other computer screen in the place, and we had a lot of them on site. Her face registered a combination of shock and indignation at being caught.

The Major issued her a stern look. "You cannot continue to ply your trade in good conscience. Gather up your things, cancel your so-called contract with Sherry Knox and don't ever come back here."

"But–"

The Major silenced her with a firm, unyielding shake of his head. "Don't ever scam anyone ever again, especially seniors. It's just not cricket."

"But–"

"Or perhaps I should call my good friend Constable Snowdrop to rectify this matter?" the Major continued.

With that, Hayleigh picked up her purse plus paperwork and slinked out without so much as a goodbye. When the door silently closed behind her, we all broke library protocol and clapped. Some of us even cheered. It was like a huge weight was lifted from our collective shoulders.

"I'd call that the walk of shame if I've never seen one," Maude said.

"I don't think that term refers to ... Oh never mind," I said. "The deed is done and the genealogical world can rest easier tonight."

And with that, Hayleigh the snake slithered out of our lives for good.

Maude got another text. She showed me:

Subject just left driveway. Coast clear now?

It was from Landry.

"Tell him yes," I instructed. "And also let him know he's earned free snacks at the café for the entire week."

❄❄❄

One Hour Later.

Ewan strode in, carrying a large binder. He made a beeline for me. "How's my favorite member of Oakhurst's newest crime-fighting team?" he asked.

I felt my cheeks go rosy. Now that I'd had a bit of time to think about what Ewan and I experienced up in Yorkshire, I was now convinced that this antiques dealer and I had a future together.

"Julie? He asked you a question," Maude said. She also took a five-pound note from Sherry. The ladies were smiling at each other. They had a knowing look in their eyes.

I frowned. "You're still not betting on us, are you?" Not too long ago, Maude had taken odds on how soon it would be before Ewan took me out for dinner on a date.

Maude shrugged. "Like Edwina once said, please forgive an old lady for her entertainments."

I looked at Ewan. "I'd like to tell her off, but she's just too sweet. Besides we need her at the research site for all her knowledge."

He looked me deep in the eyes. "I agree ... Julie, it's good to see you."

I felt a thousand sets of eyes upon us. "Ewan, we don't need to do this here," I said.

"There is a meeting room available," Maude suggested in a bright tone.

"Or perhaps they would be interested in the census record research training video," Sherry added.

Ewan raised his hands in defeat. "Ladies, if and when Julie and I go to see a film on a date, it will not be a family history training video. Give me a little more credit than that."

"Okay then, Mr. Romance," Maude said, leaning over the information desk and eyeing his binder. "What do you have there?"

"The furniture inventory from Roycetonne House. Not the trinkets, just the large pieces. Harriet and I have been working on it with help from Mr. and Mrs. Neebles."

"Mr. Neebles too? I thought he was the gardener," I said.

"Yes, and oddly enough Lord Roycetonne decided to store all the furniture from the nursery and one of his dining rooms in the carriage house. Only Mr. Neebles knew much about it. And thankfully there was no rot or woodworm in any of the pieces. Top quality, all of it."

The room went silent.

"Landry's in the café," I said in a reserved tone.

"I'm not angling to sell any of his antiques," Ewan stated.

I just glared back at him.

Maude approached. "Ewan, I'd tread very carefully with this topic."

"Else risk having to sit through a three-hour film about the earthworm's lifecycle courtesy of Bertie's latest rotational grazing agricultural committee," I warned.

Ewan's face fell. "I believe I should make myself scarce."

Chapter 26

Roycetonne House. 9:00 a.m. Next Day.

It was as if locusts had descended upon the great manor house. Not pests, however, but a throng of like-minded volunteers wearing sensible shoes and carrying canvas bags with emergency tissues and a brolly. Landry had promised a full week's breakfast, lunch and snacks onsite. GGRS was providing the daily shuttle bus. Our assignment was to assist the professional archivists, Bea Archibald and Naomi Murphy, on site with a preliminary sort through all the loose paper records. The group met in the front hall, the one with its overcrowded Victorian clutter and now-silent elegant fountain. Bea and Naomi were tidily dressed, ready for a good day's work. They had an air of competence about them, partly due to experience and also partly due to their specific education. Both were well-recognized experts in archival document cataloguing and preservation. Our volunteer team was in the best of hands.

Bea addressed the group first: "Thank you for volunteering to help us today. As Julie has already explained, this is an absolutely massive project. Our first order of business is to separate ourselves into pairs, where each set of two people is assigned a topic. We've already taken over some of the empty rooms across the hall and set them up with tables and archival-friendly supplies."

Gertie raised her hand. "We're sorting by topic, not decade?"

"Correct. It's always a hard choice, especially if the prior organization started one way. In this case, we started afresh. As our goal is ultimately to write a history of Roycetonne House, putting things into context regarding how this house operated, we're using topic as the main category definition. The fonds, however, will have detailed enough records descriptions so years can be pulled out from various topics as needed. Most researchers do come to an archives looking for a particular subject such as gamekeeping, house maintenance, menus, events or fine art. They get into that specific section first, then drill down to dates from there. Some of the bound volumes already have this type of organization, for example, the ledger books showing housekeeping expenses from when the house first opened up through to today."

"I'll bet Mrs. Neebles still does a really good job detailing those out every month," I observed.

"I wouldn't doubt it. She's the bedrock of this place," Bea said.

Naomi looked out at the group. "We've got the list of assigned volunteer pairs up front here on a sheet and have done our best to match you with a relevant topic."

"This is going to be absolutely fascinating," Gertie said. "Imagine, getting to go through 150 years of untouched archives."

And with that, we descended into the chaos with full intent of bringing order to a previous history so far left on hold.

Bea and Naomi had the work stations neatly arranged. Loose documents would get put into a general category at a table marked by the specific topic. The heavier items including books, ledgers, and albums were left on shelves for processing later on. All we were doing today was sorting by topic, trying to deconstruct the huge mountain of unsorted paper in the room that Lady Adelaide and Aunt Moyra had used for their office. Yes, it was a travesty to keep precious history in messy heaps. But, kudos to both ladies for having the foresight to recognize the importance of the history. The bottom line was that the mountain of documents was saved.

Gertie and I were assigned 'The Library'. Maude was stationed beside us at another table labelled 'Family: Personal Correspondence'. She smiled. "It's almost like an odd game of snap is about to commence."

"Match everything up to another paper and hope that we get an organized pile at the end," I said with gusto.

The way that the archivists had arranged things was that a few members of the youth group acted as 'runners', well, 'walkers' in this case because we had to be careful with fragile old documents. Bea or Naomi would look at a document and ascertain its topic as best they could. The runner would then take the document to the appropriate topic table. The volunteers at the tables would further sort documents into year and sometimes month. Indexing of detailed contents would be done at a later date during the preservation process. We were just here to get things roughly organized and ensure it wasn't such an overwhelming task for the experts.

"I am amazed at the pile of documents just left lying about," Maude said. "In all my years, I have never seen anything like it."

"We were shocked, too, when Landry opened the room on our first visit," I said. "It really did boggle our minds."

"That room will need quite the vacuum after we're finished. And look at all these lovely archival supplies. I feel like a child in a sweet shop with two-weeks' pocket money!" Maude beamed.

It really was an archivists' paradise. Landry authorized a generous budget and so the space was provided with a multitude of professional archival-friendly, acid-free folders, boxes, envelopes, ties, tape, supports, book covers ... Everything and anything possibly needed to get Roycetonne House records organized once and for all was here.

***

Six Hours Later.

All the volunteers had surveyed the now-empty hoarding room with satisfaction. Every single loose document was now on a topic table, ready for more detailed cleaning and sorting. We did, of course, leave everything on the tables when we went for our tea break. It was during tea and scones downstairs that Bea announced the most fascinating finds of the day:

"Thank you, everyone, so much for your help today. We've made incredible progress and I'm pleased to say that the mountain of documents is now in some semblance of order."

All the volunteers, both young and older, clapped and whistled with enthusiasm.

"I also want to let you know that we found three items of extreme interest in the piles," Bea said, turning to look at her colleague. Naomi had two pieces of paper and a small box in her hand. She handed them to Bea.

Bea opened the small box. She then held it up for us to see a beautiful gold stock pin, the kind that horsewomen wore over top of their white collared shirt to set off a dark hunting jacket. "We found one jewelry box that was hidden underneath the stack of home maintenance invoices from the 1940s. It's a curious design, because instead of a horseshoe which is typical of the equine set, this is three pineapples over top of a clay jug."

I raised my hand. "That refers to the racing stables. The three pineapples was the symbol that Roycetonne adopted from a racing stables up in Yorkshire. Of that I am certain because we—I—have stayed there and know a lot about its history."

Murmurs amongst the crowd.

Bea looked at me with curiosity. "Julie, the three pineapples ... were they on the racing silks?"

I nodded. "Lady Adelaide's fiancé was an expert horseman from that manor house in Yorkshire. They raced under the three pine-apples symbol until the owner ran into money troubles and gave up horse racing to economize. When Lady Adelaide took over Roycetonne House, she adopted their three pineapples symbol at her own stables. It was on all the jockey silks and if you look at some of the photo albums from after her father's death, you'll see them wearing them in the winner's circle. They were quite successful with thoroughbred breeding, training and racing up in Newmarket."

"So mystery solved," Bea said to the crowd. "It just goes to show what a bit of family history knowledge can help you understand when you're looking at artifacts from a great house."

The archivist continued on to the two documents that Naomi now handed to her. "The second interesting item is this invitation from Buckingham Palace, formally asking Lady Adelaide to step forward as a debutante. By that time in her life she was a poised, intelligent, well-educated young lady who was ready for society. Her father would've made sure she had every opportunity to find the right match."

Gertie leaned over to me again. "But Lady Adelaide chose love over the right last name. She had a strong constitution."

I nodded. "She had a strong heart."

We both looked back at Bea who had the last item in her hand now. "This one is particularly poignant to me because it is an unused first class ticket to America on one of the largest sailing ships at the time. It's poignant, because we know that the ship sank en route due to an explosion on board that no one ever really explained. There were rumors of sabotage but nothing was ever proven."

I looked at our team from GGRS and whispered frantically, "How come none of our research at TNA turned this up? Do you think Lord Roycetonne would have gone that far?"

"Hardly worth blowing up an entire ship over one wayward fiancé," the Major said in a blunt voice. "If Simon was that bad, surely there were other means Lord Roycetonne had at his disposal."

Maude leaned over. "The records must've been incomplete, or perhaps not all of them were donated to the facility. I can't see this being misfiled, the event was too important."

"We need to get back to the research site and do some more digging here. We need to know if Simon was onboard that ship or not," I said.

Everybody agreed with me. Before we called it a night, I went over to Bea and asked to see the gold stock pin. As I looked at it closely, I saw the jug imposed behind the three pineapples. I had seen this design before but I couldn't place it. I would have to think on it for the night and hopefully it would come back to me. Knowing how weary we all were from our big day of document sorting, I wasn't counting on coming up with anything intelligent on the bus journey home.

❊❊❊

Roycetonne House. Next Day.

I had a spring in my step. Nothing could deter me. As soon as the bus unloaded our team, back again for a second day to help catalog albums and ledgers, I disappeared into the hedge maze outside.

"Julie?" Gertie called out as she hurried to keep up with me. "Whatever on earth–"

"Trust me on this, Gerts. I know where I've seen that jug and pineapples design before." I hurried over to the sundial in the center, now surrounded by Mrs. Neebles' Viking Gods carvings. I crouched down underneath. "Look."

"We found the pickaxe symbol here, the one that led us to the secret coal cellar, remember?" she said, a bit confused.

"True. But we didn't look at the obvious." I'd remembered the reference location on the bus ride over here. I brought her around to the back of the instrument and pointed down. There, in the heavy base, were three pineapples etched into the metal. But there was no jug.

"I think Lady Adelaide put pineapples everywhere in Simon's memory," she said.

I thought on it for a moment. She was right. Lady Adelaide had indeed mourned the loss of her true love for the rest of her days. I then felt around the base of the sundial with my hands. "So why the hinges?"

"What hinges?" Gertie asked, peering closer.

"These tiny little ones that disappear into the base? They're almost imperceptible. Look." I scrabbled around some more in the cold pebbles—gloves were helpful—and stopped when I felt a latch. "Open sesame, perhaps?" I lifted it up, we heard a click and a secret compartment opened up to reveal a folded piece of paper inside. It looked perfectly preserved, dry and I could see the telltale loops of Lady Adelaide's careful penmanship.

"Oh my. Should we fetch Bea?" Gertie asked.

"Yes. I'll stay here. And tell her to bring the official archives camera."

❅❅❅

Five Minutes Later.

I wasn't fidgeting because of the frosty morning. I was on edge because of the mystery about to be revealed. It was proper to wait for the archival expert to see what we'd found, and then advise how to remove it. Obviously the paper had to be unfolded and examined; overeager hands plus the wrong technique, however, could render the fragile message indecipherable.

Bea squatted down beside me. "We're lucky. It looks to be in perfect condition. Imagine that, out here in all this cold and damp for decades, yet it looks as if it was only placed here yesterday. That particular metal container has out-of-this-world resistance to weather." She leaned forward with a pair of tweezers, picked up the folded note, then carefully dropped in into an archival-safe bag. "There. Safe and sound."

"Can we open it onsite?" I asked, excited and breathless.

"Let's get it back inside and see. If we do open it here on the estate, then I want to take a photo right away in case something tears, fades or shrinks while we're examining it."

Back inside the house, the paper was deemed safe enough to open. Naomi snapped a few digital photos as soon as the paper was unfolded and flat enough to read. We saw the Roycetonne House moniker at the top of the page, and a note from Lady Adelaide:

Please tell Simon I love him with all my heart but my plan to escape with him is foiled again. My father has me under lock and key. Tell Simon to go to America and make a new life without me. My father will hound him incessantly here; take his money and go. Be happy. Don't tie yourself to a woman who has a tyrant for a father.

Simon, I love you forever and always. L.A.R.

"This must be how Lady Adelaide communicated with the trades-man who acted as go between her and Simon," I said. "But her last note wasn't received."

"Perhaps the tradesman was discovered, too, and banned from the property," Gertie said.

"How sad. It sounds like Simon was paid off to leave by Lord Roycetonne."

"What a tragedy. And you said you couldn't find Simon on the ship's passenger list?" Bea asked.

Gertie and I both shook our heads.

"It's odd. Either he traveled under an assumed name OR he never sailed," Bea said.

"That's what we're going to research some more back at GGRS. But Mrs. Neebles did promise to show us the family cemetery. That may offer some clues," I said.

"Okay, I'll stay here with Naomi and the team. Let us know what you find," Bea said.

＊＊＊

Mrs. Neebles held her husband's hand. They'd both offered to take us out to the family cemetery, and the five of us—the Neebles, Landry, Gertie and I—stood with deference as we looked at the two tombstones. One was for Lord Roycetonne, the other for his wife.

"And you mentioned that no one else is buried here?" I asked.

"That is correct. There are no other memorial markers either, not that I've ever seen," Mrs. Neebles said.

"That's odd. You'd think that if Simon died, Lady Adelaide would have at least had a monument erected in his memory," Landry said. "She loved the man like no other."

"Let's think on this for a moment. The three pineapples were for the horses. Simon was a horseman. Has anyone checked the old stables?" I asked.

Blank looks all around.

"Well, then let's go and see right now," I said.

Ten minutes later we were inside the stables that were left as if in a time capsule. There were lovely curved metal railings dividing loose boxes, inlaid brick aisles and ample storage for tack, grooming and first aid equipment.

"Simon says ..." Landry started as he pointed up to a three pineapples symbol over each stall door.

"What was her favorite horse's name? I saw it in her diary a few times," I said.

"Maggie. Short for 'Margaret's Whimsey', her registered name," Mrs. Neebles confirmed, her husband nodding in agreement.

"Hmm. Don't think that's a clue. What else, pineapples, Yorkshire ..." I pondered aloud. "Remember the jug underneath the three pineapples on the pin. That means water."

"Or wine. Or olive oil," Gertie said.

Then the answer finally came to mind. I grinned. "Nope, water. I'm positive now. Follow me."

✳✳✳

Long Portrait Gallery. Ten Minutes Later.

We walked past the ancestors' portraits, noting that tights were an exceedingly popular legwear choice. We reached Lady Adelaide's portrait at the end of the hallway and I posed like her. "See, she's looking over her shoulder at a stream."

"So?" Gertie asked.

"So, she's not looking, she's subtly guiding those in the know."

"You mean the portrait is a secret map?" Landry asked, incredulous.

"But only for those she trusts. Obviously hanging this in front of her father felt safe to her. I think it's a coded message for us to go find something."

"But what?"

"First, let's figure out where to go. Is there a stream on site?"

"I saw one on the house plans, that I do recall," Landry said.

"And what's nearby?"

"I'm not sure. There's some outbuilding up there, but I don't know what it is."

Mrs. Neebles cleared her throat. "May I hazard a guess?"

"Please," I said, losing my Lady Adelaide pose.

"I am familiar with the stream on the estate. The outbuilding is a small grotto, a place of worship built into the hillside. I do not believe Lord Roycetonne was aware of its existence. You see ..." Mrs. Neebles hesitated.

"Yes?" I said with slight impatience.

"Only the staff and Lady Adelaide ever knew about it."

"What about Moyra?" Landry asked.

"It was built before her time here," Mrs. Neebles said.

"Why didn't you say something before?" Gertie asked with a gentle voice.

"I just didn't think shells had anything to do with this mystery. But knowing that we're after pineapples, well, things are starting to make a whole lot more sense," Mrs. Neebles said.

"Keep your shoes and coats on, folks, we're going out on another walk," Gertie said in a cheery voice.

Half an hour later we reached the semi-frozen stream. Mr. Neebles had joined us, and led us to the hidden door around the back of the small hill, somewhere concealed behind a thick set of laurel hedges that were allowed to grow a bit overzealous without looking jungle-like. Someone had this area well-managed to be hidden enough, yet not too messy to warrant a complete pruning therefore revealing what it hid behind the dark green leaves.

He led us through the tangle and we came to a narrow wooden door. It looked like elves lived here, inside some sort of rammed-earth home deep in the heart of nature. The door was well worn on the edges and handle, as if burnished to a gleam from frequent use over the years. Given the fact that Lady Adelaide had died in her nineties, if this was her special place, then it was understandable.

Mr. Neebles turned on the light and when our eyes adjusted to the dimmed warm glow, we gasped.

There, surrounding us on all four walls plus the domed ceiling, were seashells glued to every available surface. White, cream, light and dark brown, faded blue. Long, round, pointed, smooth ... all perfect, none worn or broken by tumbling over rocks in the sea. Someone had spent a lot of time selecting them on the sea shore.

"How close is the nearest beach?" I asked.

"Oh, about an hour or so by car. Longer in the summertime with all the tourist traffic," Mr. Neebles said with confidence.

"Can't see Lord Roycetonne letting his daughter spend oodles of time at the beach picking up shells," I said.

"I wonder if she had staff do it, or bought them in bulk," Gertie asked. "She'd need a lot to get the pineapples just right."

"Pineapples?" the rest of us all said in unison.

"Over there." Gertie nodded in the direction of the rear of the shell grotto. We moved closer and then saw what she meant. At eye level on the wall was a small door with shells arranged in the shape of three pineapples.

"Well, I never," Mrs. Neebles exclaimed.

"Never been inside here far enough to notice it was a door," Mr. Neebles said.

Landry walked over and found a tiny handle to the door. He pulled and carefully opened it to show a gleaming brass plaque inside. There, on the plaque, was the inscription we'd been searching for:

> *For Simon -*
> *In memory of a great romance.*
> *Love springs eternal.*
> *With all my heart. L.A.R.*

"Is this him buried here or just a memorial?" Landry asked.

"No one can be sure. We need to find Simon on a passenger list to know. It's hardly likely she'd have his body shipped home from America if that's indeed where he went," I said.

"Besides, we know that Lady Adelaide is buried in the churchyard, not here at Roycetonne House. That was in Moyra's will, to always ensure fresh flowers were placed on Lady Adelaide's grave located there," Landry said.

Gertie gave all of us a serious look. "We need to get back to the research site and find Simon on a passenger list. Landry, it's critical to figuring out what really happened to your ancestors."

Chapter 27

GGRS. Next Morning.

Maude, Gertie, Ewan, Constable Bud Snowdrop, my father and I gathered round Landry. The tall cowboy stood before us, a rather surreptitious grin on his face. "There's a reason I invited Bud here to meet with us this morning."

This was the policeman who'd issued me a parking ticket not all that long ago when the Major and his friends parked a museum exhibition tank in Greymore's back meadow. The wrong meadow, at that, I might add. He'd also ticketed Gertie for a ridiculously minor parking infraction.

This meant that Bud wasn't our favorite arm of the law here at Greymore Hall. In fact, he wasn't an arm at all. Perhaps a thickened, yellowed toenail. He looked as though he knew it too. I considered Christmas an aberration because I was only convinced to invite him due to the snowstorm preventing him from attending his first choice venue.

Landry continued. "There's an historic reason and it only came to light yesterday as we were doing more records sorting and organization at Roycetonne House."

It was a moment.

An incredibly deep, pondering, wondrous moment.

Landry smiled. "Yesterday, we discovered that Bud's grandfather did a huge favor to Lady Adelaide. In fact, he showed her the highest level of ethics ever possible."

I leaned over to Gertie. "This is a total surprise."

"A good one, I hope," she said. "I haven't liked any of Bud's prior surprises."

"He was polite at the Christmas dinner table, I will give him that," I said.

"Sure. But his girlfriend was the one who kept the party going. Bud was likely tallying up the parking tickets he could issue with all of us trapped at Greymore during the snow storm."

"Maybe he's redeemed himself through his ancestor," I said.

"That doesn't count, and you know it," she said with a glare.

Landry took a piece of paper from Maude; it appeared to be a photocopy. "Seems as though Lord Roycetonne wanted Simon Chester arrested on a pretense of theft."

Horrified murmurs raced through the research site.

"Did Simon really steal?" Maude asked.

"Yes, his daughter," I joked, "that's what Lord Roycetonne was upset about."

"That's kidnapping, not stealing," my father said. "Wakey, wakey."

"People, please." Landry calmed our excited voices with a raised hand. "For the record, the charge of theft wasn't justified. We found a handwritten witness statement from Simon and also one from

Lord Roycetonne. It was clear that Simon, the alleged victim of this concocted set up, was telling the truth."

"What did Lord Roycetonne accuse him of stealing?" I asked.

"Theft of a ruby necklace belonging to his late wife," Landry explained. "But when Mr. Neebles found it hidden in a grain bin, the jig was up."

"How on earth did Mr. Neebles know where to find it?" Maude wondered.

"It turns out Mr. Neebles is a light sleeper. He saw Lord Roycetonne messing about in the stables' feed room late one night and thought it odd. So when the police, led by none other than Constable Bill Snowdrop, came to investigate the ruby necklace theft, Mr. Neebles' input was critical. They found the necklace with Lord Roycetonne's fingerprints all over it and none of Simon's. Game over."

"It's disturbing Lord Roycetonne would stoop so low to stymie his daughter's love," my father said, giving my hand a caring squeeze. He and I knew all about how one bad apple on the family tree could spoil things for everybody else.

Landry agreed. "Bill Snowdrop wasn't falling for the ruse. He denied Lord Roycetonne his pound of flesh and wrote it all off as a misunderstanding."

"I'm surprised Lord Roycetonne didn't try to cross the policeman's palm with silver," Dad said.

Landry nodded. "I doubt a bribe would be recorded in his firm's official account books. It was likely hidden under something innocuous like 'gardening fees' or something like that."

"As in prune away the potential son-in-law," I whispered to Gertie. "Yikes."

"I suppose what I'm trying to say here is a roundabout and belated thank you to Bill Snowdrop. Unfortunately he passed away a few years back." Landry looked at Bud. "Bud, your grandfather did the right, honorable thing and saved an innocent man from being unjustly punished by a bitter man with great influence. Standing up for one's ethics and what's right is one of the most admirable things a person can do. Thank you."

Bud looked a bit shocked and also gleeful. Perhaps he now felt befriended by the group.

Maude had insisted we invite him for Christmas dinner and he'd behaved himself. Perhaps it was time to let the parking ticket saga go. I strode over to him. "Well done, Bud," I said. "I had no idea."

He spluttered, obviously not expecting my gesture of kindness. "I-I honestly didn't know. But the police report doesn't lie. A copy was found amongst the records at the manor house, at least that's what Landry told us."

"And that was the proof that Lady Adelaide no doubt wanted on file for historical posterity," I said. "Defiant until the end, albeit in a rather unorthodox manner."

Bud peered at me like an owl hiding in a camouflaged thicket. "The department, uh, removed my parking ticket quota."

"Ah, so the Greymore crew is safe to roam the streets once more?" I asked.

"Yes. But just don't go over the speed limit." He was almost pleading with me.

"They didn't?"

He nodded, glum. "I now have the latest speed check camera in my car. Three digit fines are coming to Oakhurst."

I slung a casual arm around his shoulder. "I hear the café's got some great donuts this morning. Interested?"

**

One Hour Later.

Landry, Maude, Gertie and I sat in a meeting room at the research site. There was obviously more to discuss, but Landry was quite uncomfortable with this next part.

He shifted slightly in his chair as he held an archivist's file in his hand. "This is something I didn't want to share earlier with everyone in the room. I thought they should hear my compliment to Bud's family, however, this next one isn't kind. This file contains a contract that Lord Roycetonne had Simon sign confirming his departure to America. Permanently. I'm wondering if it was a transportation-type punishment like prison ships." He looked to the group for help.

Maude was all over that one in an instant. "First, let's look at the dates. Simon left England we presume, in the 1930s. Convicts sent to America on what was known as 'transportation punishments' ended in 1776 with the American War of Independence.

They used Australia as a convict transportation destination after that time up until 1868."

"I read up about those prison ship hulks used to store prisoners in, what was it, the eighteenth or nineteenth centuries?" I shuddered. "Rat-infested, flea-infested, terrible conditions. The lodging was punishment itself."

"Those were moored ships—retired and considered floating prisons—not the seaworthy ones taking people abroad for resettlement," Maude explained.

Landry opened the file. "Very well then, you ladies have corrected me on my history facts. But there's no changing this. Lord Roycetonne and Simon Chester both signed this document I have here in my hands."

"What does it say?" Gertie asked.

Landry sighed. "In a few sentences? That Simon is to leave England and stay in America. He will travel on a first class ticket on a different ship from the one he had chosen for Lady Adelaide and himself. The ship was named 'The Pearling Swift'. Money and land was granted to him in America, enough for him to set up like a proper gentleman in the horse breeding industry. Simon agrees to never come back and to have no contact with Lady Adelaide."

We all sat in fairly stunned silence. It was odd that one person could control another with such strict conditions, yet it appeared to be what happened. Lord Roycetonne was that adamant about protecting his daughter's future so her hand was given to an aristocrat rather than a horseman from far more humble origins.

Maude added an explanation for us. "Simon was a Remittance Man. There were plenty of men not wanted by their families for various reasons and who were paid to settle abroad. They received a one-time payment or sometimes a monthly stipend."

"So Simon traded love for money?" Gertie said.

"I don't think it was that easy. We weren't there in the room when the document was signed. There may been threats made," I said in a soft voice. "We just don't know, and far be it for us to make assumptions about what stress Simon was under when his signature was put on paper."

"The paperwork's on Lord Roycetonne solicitor's letterhead. And the signatures match other ones we found in the family paperwork," Landry said. "Looks legitimate to me."

"Right then," Maude said, summing up a situation like she always did when guiding us toward the next required genealogy assignment. "We now need to find Simon on that exact ship's passenger list and see if he actually made it out of British waters."

Half a minute later we were all clustered around the screen at a computer carrell. Maude had a genealogy website up, one that housed passenger lists. "Now, remember that we only know the passenger's supposed name," she advised.

"Why would he change it?" Landry asked.

"Possibly to hide from Lady Adelaide," Maude said. "The ticket may have been booked that way, passport shown but recorded in secret? Perhaps something Lord Roycetonne's wallet greased the wheels on? Famous people are known to travel under pseudonyms to protect their identities."

"We can get the list of passengers on the ship and what class they were in," Gertie said.

"And what about arrivals? Just to confirm he got there?" I asked.

"Possibly. Just don't angle for the trio," Maude said.

"What trio?" I asked.

"Departure, passenger and inbound arrival lists. It's rare to have all three." Maude nodded. "One can only expect digitized records going back so far. If we need items not yet online it means another trip to TNA or even the National Maritime Museum at Greenwich."

Maude was such a treasure, a real wealth of knowledge. I was so grateful for her expertise.

"Now let's just see who we can find in first class." She scrolled and clicked her way through the screens. She brought up a souvenir booklet of the big ship's passengers, including senior crew and first, second and third-class passengers. Even menus and dining times were included. "Bingo," she said with a great deal of satisfaction.

"Just like our shire horse," I joked.

"Oh, I'm sure he'll be thrilled," Gertie said with a smile.

"It's quite shocking everyone had access to a passenger list. With today's privacy laws, there is no way that would happen," Landry said. "Trust me. Cybersecurity man speaking here."

"Ladies and Gentlemen," Maude said with a grin. "Allow me to invite you to cast your eyes upon none other than Simon Chester's appearance on The Pearling Swift." She rolled back from the desk to let us crowd around the screen much closer.

"You can increase the font size ... here we go," Maude said, using the mouse to make the lettering large enough for us to see without squinting.

"Where was the ship sailing to?" I asked.

"Louisiana."

"And can we find what Simon did next?" Landry asked.

Maude shook her head. "Not from a ship's passenger lists, I'm afraid. With all the cloak and dagger surrounding Lady Adelaide and Simon's relationship, I'm surprised we've got this much. We can check he disembarked at the port in Louisiana, but then he's on his own."

"Perhaps look at it from a different perspective," I suggested. "Maybe Lord Roycetonne wanted people to know Simon was long gone. That quelled rumors and made Lady Adelaide available for the arranged marriage."

"Well done, Julie. Now that's thinking like a true genealogist," Maude said. "One has to consider the social context of the time, not just names, dates and places."

I settled back in my seat, amazed at the compliment. It meant that all those hours in class and studying my family history textbooks were paying off in a quite helpful manner. Score one for the newbie!

Chapter 28

—

Roycetonne House. Next Day.

This was now a matter of the utmost importance. Once a genealogical mystery appeared, it was impossible to ignore. We were back at the manor house, this time with even greater purpose. Now that we knew Simon had made it all the way to Louisiana, it gave us something else to search for in the papers that were now a lot more organized on-site. By now, the archivists had placed each category of assorted paperwork into labeled boxes to keep things more sorted and together. We headed for the one labeled 'shipping' and took out all of the contents, dividing them up amongst us.

"Now, it's very important we put these back in the same order in which the archivists have left them," Maude advised. "We don't want to undo any of the good work they've already done."

"I still can't get over it. 150 years' worth of archives all stockpiled in one room," Gertie said, shaking her head. "It really is unbelievable. Such a treasure."

"Right you are, so let's dive in," Maude said. She and I were tasked with the shipping records from Lord Roycetonne's office. Gertie and

Landry were tackling Lady Adelaide's diaries. We all dove in to try and figure out what really happened in the past.

About twenty minutes later, Gertie came up with the first clue as to what actually happened. She held up a yellowed newspaper clipping that just floated out of a diary page. The tape used to secure it to the diary page had long lost any of its stickiness. In fact, the tape was so brittle that it fell apart in one long strip, detached from the newspaper clipping. It was definitely not an archival-safe method of preserving documents. Honestly, it was better to photocopy the newspaper article for preservation because the original newsprint paper was flimsy and full of rougher fibers that also had a higher acid content.

"Look what I found," Gertie said with an excited voice. "It's a big clue. Also really sad."

We all gathered around her, letting Maude get closest. Maude read aloud:

Tragedy at Local Thoroughbred Breeding Farm
Louisville, Kentucky
January 17, 1932

Legendary Kentucky thoroughbred racehorse breeding farm Silas Eeeks Stables was the site of an unfortunate accident yesterday evening. After a prized stallion bolted from his enclosure, jumping the five rail fence, horseman Simon Chester was fatally struck by a moving car as he tried to get the stallion away from the road. Farm manager Barney Watson expressed his sincere condolences to Simon's family and confirmed that a new perimeter fence is being installed at the farm to prevent another tragedy such as this from happening. The stallion was eventually recaptured with the help of two other grooms from the property. The horse only suffered a few minor abrasions on his front legs.

All of us sat in silence.

Landry was the first one to talk. "Well, we now know where Simon went from Louisiana. But to be hit by a car after all that strife beforehand, what a waste."

I was reminded of how another GGRS researcher's ancestor was killed in a tram accident back home after a distinguished overseas military career.

"It must've broken Lady Adelaide's heart," I said. "Surely she must've longed to follow Simon to America at some point, but his death would've put an end to her dreams."

Gertie nodded. "You called that correctly. Lady Adelaide's diaries are filled with pages and pages of how inconsolable she is, how she refuses to leave her room, refuses to eat … She went into mourning for weeks and said she wanted to leave the estate."

"How soon did her father make her marry?" I asked, curious at how cruel Lord Roycetonne really was to his daughter.

"Well, we have the wedding album we can look through," Maude said. She went over to the shelf and pulled down the wedding album.

"Here. Lady Adelaide was married eleven months after this article was printed."

"Once again, her father's desire for a united society front and a speedy forgetting of Simon was all he had in mind. I can't even imagine how it affected Lady Adelaide's mental state," Gertie said. "I think I would've rebelled."

"Remember, it was different times back then. Lady Adelaide would have gone somewhere to recover, a respite home. But where?" Maude coached.

"A kind relative?" I suggested.

"That would be about her only hope. That, or to a secret friend. But we know she stayed at Roycetonne House and did her father's bidding."

"Wait." Gertie flipped ahead eleven more months in the diary to the wedding day. Lady Adelaide wrote:

> Father, I will do as you bid. But know I have made a permanent mark in this world with Simon, one you cannot erase. You tell me to now let Simon rest, yet I cannot. My time away under the guise of healing from shock was well-deserved. And I shall take that secret to my grave. L.A.R.

Maude sat down, even slumped. "Well that just about proves it, then. Landry, you have a more exciting piece of genealogy here than you expected."

"Really? How so?" he asked.

"A permanent mark? She was away eleven months?" Maude looked him in the eye. "My dear man. Lady Adelaide went away to have Simon's baby in secret."

❋❋❋

The rest of the day was consumed with plowing through other family papers to find any female relatives or friends of the family. Find a close one, and we would head to the census for that village or town, likely finding the presumed hostess. We were lucky we had so much source material. The problem was it would take hours and perhaps days to plow through it all. Yet, we were undaunted. Lady Adelaide's story was so poignant that it had to be uncovered.

"There's a big gap in her diary starting eleven months before her wedding," I said.

"More telling clues," Maude assessed. "Let's try some other original sources apart from the diary pages."

"Such as?" I asked.

"Original sources are those created by the subject or her relatives at the time of an event. Official papers or photos of the family. Derivative sources are those created later or by others such as a research project, book or index. For example, if Landry wrote a book about his family, his book would be considered a derivative source."

"What do you suggest?" I asked.

"Birth certificate," Maude said with certainty. "The birth would have to be registered and the parents' true names listed. They're indexed online and it's easier to find a birth certificate than a christening in a parish register that may not be digitized or indexed yet."

Maude accessed the online birth index and searched 1931-1933, covering a possible late registration. She searched under both 'Moyra' and 'Moira' as well as both 'Roycetonne' and 'Chester' surnames. Nothing. No suitable entry.

"Well, it is possible that she was entered under a false name, but more likely the local registrar failed to send his copy to London before the indexes were compiled. It happened frequently."

A collective groan emanated from our little group.

"Don't worry," Maude said, "we'll try the parish register for a christening instead. Luckily all the names are unusual."

"How about family photos from her childhood? Maybe there's a favorite aunt or cousin?" Gertie suggested.

"Well done. Fabulous idea. Now we're thinking about multiple ways to prove someone's family history."

Maude gestured us over to the shelves and we each hauled down a photo album. There were the obligatory formal portraits, the photos of the servants outside the service entrance doors, the children with ponies, tea with society ladies on the lawn and ..."

"Whatever on earth ..." Landry trailed off as he gazed upon some baby pictures.

"Find something?" I asked.

"I don't know. I have to get my laptop. One moment." He was back in a flash with it and opened a subfolder of pictures on the hard drive. He flicked through a few then brought up a picture of a baby girl in a lace trimmed dress. "It's her, I'm sure of it." He placed the laptop on the desk next to the photo album he'd been tasked with searching through. "Tell me if you think these photos are identical."

They were. The bonny baby was all smiles and gums as she peered into the camera, a tiny stuffed toy giraffe in her hand, lace-trim-mings in the exact same places on the dress. Even the flowers on the wallpaper in the background were exact.

"It's a match," Maude declared. "Why do you have the photo on your laptop?"

"It's a photo from the first catalog my grandfather printed. We started out selling farm implements, stoves, radios and clothes, you see. That's where he made his biggest profit margins." Landry said.

All of us saw the photo in the album and compared it with the one on Landry's laptop screen. The photos were the same. Perfect.

"So who is the baby?" I asked.

"Let's see if whoever put these photo albums together had a knack for family history." Maude had on her white cotton gloves and sat in front of the photo album. She gently removed the photo from its four corner holders and turned it over to see what, if anything, was written on the back. "We're in luck," she said.

We leaned in close and saw that someone had written on the back: 'Aunt Agatha's child'.

"Landry, do you know who Aunt Agatha is?" Maude asked.

He shook his head. "I have no idea. Aunt Moyra never mentioned an Aunt Agatha to me."

"I think she's the lady holding the baby in the picture beside this one," I said, looking at the same child in both photos. "Maybe this is who Lady Adelaide ran to for help."

"Like a substitute for her own mother who had already passed away?" Gertie asked.

"Something like that. She would've needed someone to run to," I said. "Where were these photos taken? They might help us narrow down the local archives where we need to search for more information."

"You don't think there will be anything in these papers?" Landry asked, looking at the boxes and albums surrounding every four corners of the room.

Maude shook her head. "I doubt Lady Adelaide would've left any evidence of that here on site. Back in those days, an illegitimate child was seen as a great embarrassment for any aristocrat. Lady Adelaide's pregnancy had to be concealed at all costs. Were her new husband to find out, the wedding would've been off and they would have been outcasts from society. That would have greatly terrified her father, likely why he agreed to her leaving under the guise of recuperation."

"Is there anything on the back of Agatha's photo?" I asked.

"Let's just have a look," Maude said. She slipped out the next photo beside the baby picture and turned it over. On the back, lightly written in pencil, was written 'Aunt Agatha'. "Not exactly inspiring, is it?"

"Is there anything in the background of these photos that gives away where she was located?" Gertie asked.

"Well, it's a large white building, and it appears to have a royal statue in the center of a lawn ... We're possibly looking at Greenwich, and I'll bet the family was there for a day out, a picnic perhaps, under the radar without all the primping required at a manor house. They were just trying to be ordinary people. Look at how they're dressed. No airs or fancy clothes on the adults in the group photo here. It just looks like five adults out for a picnic with a lovely baby."

"Does that narrow it down to the city we should be looking for? Or the town or the village?" I asked.

"Hmmm, that's a bit tougher. In the 1930s, one could get to Greenwich from many places in England within an hour or two. It's a touristy spot because of the observatory and Maritime Museum."

"Don't forget the café. They have one on site that serves great snacks," I said.

"Oh, you and your snacks," Gertie said with mock impatience. "I want to find out who these people are. Is there nothing else in the photo albums?"

We poured over the pages nearest to Agatha and the baby photos. One in particular caught our attention; it showed Agatha outside a larger country house. There was a picture of the wrought-iron front gates with a polished wood sign: Mistytwines Cottage. Windfordly."

"Some cottage," Gertie said. "The house looks like it has eighteen bedrooms."

"Likely the country house of an aristocrat. Landry, can you look up the name of that house? I'm guessing that they wouldn't subject a baby to a long trip before a picnic. My guess is that this house is somewhere close to Greenwich."

Landry did as he was asked and soon came up with a result. "Here it is. Mistytwines Cottage. Owned by Lord and Lady Comptine and located in the southeast of the royal borough known as Greenwich. I'm searching the Comptine family ... aha, it was Lord Samuel and Lady Agatha Comptine. Lady Agatha was Lady Adelaide's mother's sister."

"So Lady Agatha was actually Lady Adelaide's real aunt?" I asked.

"Looks like," he confirmed. "It says here on her profile that Lady Agatha sat on the hospital board, was known as a woman with a strong constitution and employed a significant amount of common sense."

Gertie looked at Maude. "We need to prove that baby in the photo was Lady Adelaide's. Can we look in the local parish register for the church closest to Mistytwines Cottage?"

"Great minds think alike, my dear," Maude replied. She took over on the keyboard from Landry and accessed one of her genealogy websites. She looked up 'Windfordly' and got the name of the church, 'Saint Evan's'. Next she went to Saint Evan's parish registers and found an index. This church was definitely ahead of others because it appeared to be indexed right up to 1980, likely the result of an enthusiastic family history researcher who lived in the vicinity. For all we knew, it could've been Lady Agatha herself who initially spearheaded the effort.

After a few more minutes of scrolling, we found the christening entry we were looking for: Moyra Roycetonne. Mother: Adelaide

Roycetonne. Father: Simon Chester. Not taking any chances, we matched the index to the actual handwritten record. Both gave the same information.

Landry pushed his chair back from the table. "Adelaide actually used their real names. Pretty gutsy. Did she not think her father would find out?"

"Either she didn't care or she assumed they were far enough away that nobody would ask questions. Remember, back in the 1930s, there was no internet, mobile phones or free telephone calls in England," Maude said. "In fact, most houses didn't even have a telephone."

"But how did they explain the baby to the servants at Mistytwines Cottage?" I asked. "Surely somebody would have talked."

Maude smiled, a pert, understanding smile "Ah, not necessarily. Lady Agatha sat on the hospital board of directors. That meant she had involvement with treatment of the poor as well as unwed mothers. It would be perfectly acceptable and viewed as kind for her to take in a foundling or an orphan under her own wing as an act of benevolence. That's likely how the baby was explained. Lady Adelaide would just wear large poufy skirts to hide her condition."

"And what about Lady Agatha's husband?" Landry asked.

"Perhaps he was benevolent as well," I said. "Did they have children of their own?"

"That's the way to think about it," Maude said. "If they were childless, then that opens up a whole new set of reasons for them to take in Lady Adelaide and Simon's child."

It hit me all at once. "But Lady Adelaide went back to Roycetonne House to marry the Marquis. The couple had two daughters but there were never any photos or mention of the baby in her diary since she came back. So she just abandoned her child with Lady Agatha?"

"It was likely to give the child the best possible chance of success in life. Do you really think an illegitimate child would have thrived under Lord Roycetonne's nose?"

Landry was silent. He sat there, shaking his head. "I cannot believe it. Aunt Moyra never breathed a word of this to me, ever. Now it makes sense why she left her beloved up in Yorkshire to come back and nurse Lady Adelaide. She was doing what all good daughters would do: take care of their mother."

"And Simon?" I asked gently. "What about him?"

"I think we have some more work to do," Maude said, "starting with Landry's own family history."

❖❖❖

After Lunch.

Landry sat at the table in the sorting room, scribbling out a rough family tree. Maude took pity on him and handed him a blank pedigree chart. "Use this," she said. "It keeps all the generations in order."

"Thanks. I was getting my generations intermingled." He looked at her with grateful eyes. "Once I get my head wrapped around this, I'm putting it on the computer."

Gertie and I watched over his shoulder.

"What do you know about your grandfather Sheridan?" I asked.

"I was always told he was born and bred in Texas. I've seen his grave there too, closest cemetery to his business. That's how he wanted it," Landry said. He pulled up the incorporation papers for the catalog business his grandfather founded.

Landry continued. "The first products made by the catalog company were handkerchiefs under the S.A.M. brand. I now reckon that stands for Simon, Adelaide and Moyra. After all we've learned on our family history journey, I think my grandfather Sheridan was paying tribute to Simon but I sure don't understand how they are related."

Maude shook her head. "I'm afraid the records don't support the familial ties you've been told. I found your father's birth certificate and it confirmed that Travis a.k.a. Big Daddy was Keith Galfinch and your Aunt Moyra's son. Travis is indeed your father."

"But what's the connection between England and Texas?" Landry asked.

"Sheridan's father owned that Kentucky racehorse stables where Simon died. Out of respect, Sheridan kept in touch with Moyra through the years and offered her son a job when the time came. Sheridan treated Travis like an adopted son, and Travis even changed his last name to 'Jackson'."

"Whew. Just goes to show my original assumption that Lady Adelaide was my grandmother was way off," Landry said. "I'm glad we took the trouble of proving it with the correct records."

"Indeed," Maude said. "As far as I can ascertain, the family wanted the real family lineage hidden as it would only raise questions about Moyra's own parentage. Lady Adelaide didn't want that with her father still looming, even as a ghost."

"So, after all this I really can only offer one explanation," Landry said.

"Yes?" I asked, Maude and Gertie listening.

"Roycetonne House and all its history are part of my heritage and I want to do everything in my power to protect and preserve it," he said.

We all cheered with joy. It was a long journey to get here, but we'd done it together. Now history was saved and Landry had a better appreciation of his family's legacy. And what a special one it was.

Chapter 29

Private Box, Grandstand, Horse Racetrack. Next Saturday.

Landry invited the key people who helped figure out his family history. Ewan, Gertie, Maude, Bertie, Harriet, Mr. and Mrs. Neebles and I were all there. We had togged up in our racing day finest, most of it borrowed or dug out from the back of a closet. Most family historians didn't wear dresses, heels and fascinator hats with half-veils, berries and feathers to the research site. Overall, the researcher's style was more comfortable, dress-in-layers clothing, ready to tackle even the most recalcitrant of building HVAC systems. It was fun to dress for a day out, and as we overlooked a fantastic racecourse from high up in the building, everyone reflected on what a treat it was to be here on such a lovely, sunshine-filled day.

We sat at a large dining room table laden with silver and fresh flowers. Outside on the private balcony was an ample stack of racing programs. The scent of money was in the air, yet we didn't let that deter us. After our recent family history work, we all knew to look beyond the glitter and fast horses. What really mattered was knowing one's true roots and what legacy to leave the next generation.

Landry stood and raised his glass of champagne. "Thank you friends for coming here today. It's my pleasure to treat you to a day of finery, just like my ancestors at Roycetonne House would have done. I'm trying to connect more with my past and this helps me do it. I appreciate everything you have done to get me here today, and also for making this lughead understand how important genealogy really is. Until I was proven related by blood to the Roycetonne family, I didn't understand the value of what Roycetonne House offered, well not beyond the monetary value, that is." He gave a long look to Harriet and then to Ewan. "And to our lovely auctioneer and very competent antiques dealer, I must give you my heartfelt apologies. It is my full intent to keep the entire Roycetonne House collection together."

Everyone at the table cheered. Perhaps we were a little boisterous for the people in the private boxes on either side of ours. We were likely making them wonder what on earth all the noise was about because the races hadn't even started. Never mind. Landry's decision needed celebrating.

He continued. "I wanted to let you know about my plans. I've decided to live part-time in England and part-time in Texas. As you know, my cybersecurity business is fully mobile. I can't give up the Lone Star State altogether, yet I feel obligated to make sure Roycetonne House has a bright future, the one that I'm planning for it."

There was a momentary pause, a chance for us all to wonder what on earth he was thinking of doing. Most of us were still basking in the warmth of his announcement milliseconds ago about not selling off the furniture and fixtures. It was hard to believe that there was more good news to come.

"I'm well aware of the expense of running Roycetonne House. I also realize that my grandmother Moyra, thanks to her mother Lady Adelaide, left me a massive inheritance. It's my belief that those who are privileged need to share that privilege with the less fortunate. Based upon the mental anguish that Adelaide and Moyra both experienced during their lifetimes, I would like to help prevent others from experiencing the same heartache and pain. To that end, I will be making a formal public announcement next week stating that Roycetonne House is going to be repurposed as a combination mental health facility as well as art therapy center. All the correct medical authorities will be consulted and grant approval of our detailed initiatives before we open our doors." He looked at me specifically and toasted me again. "As a painter, Julie, I'll be relying on you to help me design the art therapy studios."

"Of course," I said, speaking a bit louder than normal to ensure I could be heard over the intense applause. "What a heartfelt idea. It's a lovely tribute to your family. It ensures your legacy will continue for many decades to come."

"I'm glad. Part of the house will, of course, become a museum and I'll make sure all the precious antiques and trinkets are behind protective cases and velvet ropes, just like you've done at Greymore Hall. Harriet and Ewan, I'm relying on you to set me straight on that count. I'll also take a note out of Bertie's book for Scotford Castle and perhaps the Duke would be willing to give me a few pointers?"

"It would be my honor," Bertie said. He toasted Landry back with his own champagne glass.

"Now, on a bit more fun note, I also want to let you know that I have founded a new stakes race here at this very racetrack called the 'Lady Adelaide Stakes'. I am resurrecting the horse breeding venture started many years ago by my own ancestors, and I hope to import some Kentucky thoroughbreds to my small but mighty starter stables that I will re-open on the Roycetonne House estate. I think my motto will be, 'he only has two horses but boy did they try hard'."

Everyone laughed. Landry then invited us to enjoy the meal and an afternoon of fun. The mood was light and casual, warm and cozy, mainly because we were with friends who had everyone's best interests at heart. We were there to focus on a community that needed help, and that extended into the wider part of the country where mental health needed to become a priority, More rapid access to treatment was needed. When one had mental health issues, seeking a counsellor or psychiatrist was imperative, yet the waiting lists were too long. Roycetonne House would provide a much-needed bridge between patient and healthcare provider; with Landry's vast inheritance, everything, from staff to facility, would no doubt be top-notch.

In the midst of the frivolity, Gertie banged a spoon against the side of her glass. It wasn't exactly formal protocol, but we were all friends here. Even Bertie smiled. She spoke, "What will happen with the agony aunt column? Are you going to continue writing it yourself?" she teased.

"Well, I reckon I'll have my hands pretty full with the new Roycetonne House museum, therapy center and my cybersecurity business. I'm already guessing I'll need to hire about fifty more people. An agony aunt column isn't really in the cards for me."

He looked around the table at everyone assembled.

"I didn't say the agony aunt column was over, however," he said. "I am pleased to announce that Mrs. Neebles will be starting a new role at Roycetonne House, taking over the column with a bit more modern spin and practical advice."

Mrs. Neebles piped up. "Now before everybody says I'm too old, I'll have you know that my niece—a nurse—has shown me how to work social media. She and I are going to do this together and it's going to be a hoot."

"Well done, Mrs. Neebles!" Landry said. The housekeeper looked awfully pleased.

"So the column won't be anonymous anymore?" Gertie asked.

"No, it will not," Landry said. "I had a discussion about it with the newspaper editor and it just seemed more forthright to announce that it will be an aunt and her niece doing the work in cooperation. They also quite like the idea of pairing a chainsaw carving housekeeper with a nurse."

"Sounds like those occupations go hand-in-hand," Ewan whispered to me as he leaned over from across the table. His eyes caught mine and the spark was there yet again. Our fingers brushed as he passed me the salad dressing.

As we began to eat lunch, I looked around the table, so pleased with what we had accomplished. We had saved a family's legacy, sorted and secured an immense archival collection and most of all offered help, friendship and solace to others in the community. Overall it was a job exceedingly well done.

Epilogue

─────

Gordon Mumbles Obstacle Course.
Spring Thaw. 6:00 a.m.

It was a pretty sad sight indeed. Gertie and I were lined up at the fourth obstacle of the course, a wall made out of ropes that the men were expected to climb. The ropes were made into squares used for footholds. At the top of the rope wall was a wide, horizontally-placed tree trunk that one slung each leg over and then climbed down the other side. Of course, at the bottom of the rope wall was a large mud pit. Sloppy and deeply puddled. This was typical of the entire course. It was a rough and rugged five-mile adventure, not for the faint of heart. It was set out in the middle of nowhere, surrounded by bush and forest. It had that stoic, almost military feel to it, likely due to the owner being a veteran of the military service.

I looked over Gertie. "You sure you don't want to bet on this?"

She shrugged. "There would be no point. We would both want the same bet, i.e. they're never going to finish."

"Ewan was pretty certain this would be a cakewalk for them," I said.

Gertie gestured at the muddy path to our left. We saw three weary and trail-battered men limp their way towards us. They had started out so bravely, using the rope swing over a mud pit, clambering under scads of barbed wire and then ziplining 200 feet across a small chasm. But with twenty progressively tougher obstacles to go, it appeared that the course had already gotten the best of them. Ewan got to us first, bent in half, panting. Bud Snowdrop was a close second, his pudginess slowing him down a little but more likely due to the red scrape on his forearm. Fred Todling loped along behind the other two, and I had to admit that he looked a lot more comfortable dictating a legal deposition request than he did on this physical obstacle course. Heck, Fred had even looked more comfortable in his broccoli and cheese ballet performance costume.

We waited until Bud and Fred caught up to Ewan.

I cleared my throat and then checked my watch. "So gentlemen, how's it going so far? You do know that you're being timed?"

Ewan righted himself and grimaced. "I give up. You win. I had no idea–"

Gertie was all over this. "Ewan? Giving up in front of your beloved Julie? What does that say about you?"

Ewan grinned at Gertie. "That I have a brain and value my health?"

We all laughed. I looked at Fred and Bud. Both of them appeared ready to burst a lung at any moment. "Gentlemen, do you agree with Ewan too?" I asked.

I got a rapid nodding of heads. All three men were busy looking for the way out, one that didn't involve clambering over the remaining obstacles on the course. I pointed to a tiny little exit sign, dark green painted with white letters. It was like an oasis beckoning to them in the middle of a desert.

"You do know that there is penance for quitting," I said.

"Anything. We'll do anything. Just get us off this course," Bud spluttered. The poor man looked exhausted. Not exactly reassuring to know that he was the law enforcement supposed to tackle fast-footed robbers if they ever penetrated the safety of our quaint village's bubble.

"I must say, when you invited me for a nice day out in the country with a little bit of light exercise, I hadn't expected this. My extensive, unsurpassed legal radar went up when the host made us change into these camouflage exercise uniforms," Fred said.

It was true. The men were all clad in clingy exercise tops and bottoms plus loaner thick-soled, black lace up boots. If the uniforms were supposed to make the men more agile and fit, it didn't have the intended effect. The men looked exhausted.

We heard the slap of a riding crop against a boot and the Major appeared in our line of view. "What's with this? There is no waiting on this course. Back to work, men! This is what we trained for!" His moustache and pork chop sideburns quivered as he issued the order to his three weary recruits.

"We can't go on, Major. I'm sorry. It's over," Ewan said.

"Good grief, Ewan. What were you thinking?" the Major asked. "You cannot start something you don't finish. Not in my camp."

Ewan's shoulders sagged. "Major, I'm done in. Tuckered out. I didn't read the brochure closely enough and it's all my fault. My sincere apologies, but none of us are fit enough to continue."

The Major was about to say another word of annoying encouragement, but I thought it best to step in.

"Don't worry, Major. I've already got some extra harsh duties ready for them back at Greymore Hall. In fact, you will enjoy watching it from the comfort of a lounge chair while enjoying tea and scones."

"Well then, perhaps you have figured out the solution to this most odd day," the Major said. "Imagine men quitting an obstacle course. When I was younger I would have gone round twice with vigor, ahead of the pack. Ahead of the pack, I tell you. In fact–"

I put a gentle hand on his arm as he gestured at the towering rope wall. "Major, they've already started to head back to the bus."

"Ah. Perhaps we should follow."

"Precisely."

❊❊❊

Greymore Hall. Back Parking Area. Next Morning.

The Major, Gertie, Maude and I each sat on a comfy lounge chair and munched on scones slathered with butter, strawberry jam and clotted cream. We also had perfect cups of tea. The sunshine was lovely and the glorious yellow buds of daffodils had recently burst open to showcase the flowers' happy trumpet faces. As they swayed in the slight breeze, our view was obscured by three men in wellies. Ewan lugged buckets of water, sponges and brushes. Fred Todling heaved an industrial vacuum up the path. Constable Snowdrop wore ski goggles.

"Rather a motley crew, don't you think?" the Major said rather haughtily, taking a nice sip of tea.

"Indeed," Gertie said, leaning back in her comfortable chair. We were all tucked underneath warm car blankets to ward off any early spring chills.

The laborers? Not a chance. There was zero chance of them standing still long enough to catch cold. They had too much work ahead of them.

Now that the snow was all gone and the weather had cleared, the team from the obstacle course fiasco was called to task. Today, they were cleaning the vehicles belonging to Gertie, Maude and I. They'd already spent time writing the latest research site newsletter and transcribing a lengthy eighteenth century divorce court witness testimony record. Today was vacuum-fest and then the penance was over. Mind you, the rest of us still held the memories firmly in our minds. Ewan, Fred and Bud all togged up in camouflage exercise uniforms was not an image that was easily erased or forgotten.

The Major was really getting into reforming his disappointing recruits. "Put your back into it, man! Lift up those floor mats! That's where a lot of the dirt hides!"

Fred shot the Major a look of slight disgust but acquiesced. The rest of us thought that the Major rather enjoyed his position of power, barking out directions from his lounge chair.

"You can't beat this, Gertie, hey?" I said, putting my hands behind my head and leaning back against the cushion.

"You'd better be careful they don't have a payback strategy plan. Three men scorned? I'd be on the lookout," she replied.

"I think the remorse is genuine. Ewan's even gone the extra mile and is taking me out for dinner tonight."

Maude, Gertie and the Major all exclaimed together, "Finally!"

Ewan happened to overhear them and looked up, a wet sponge in his hand. He took it as a signal for him to work harder so he applied even more soap and rubbed the sponge against the vehicle with more vigor. All of us laughed.

"I suppose it's been a long time coming," I said.

Gertie gave me a canny look. "You two have moved glacially slowly on this romance. Novels have been written, edited and published in the time you two took getting organized."

"I know. I just wanted to make sure the research site and Aunt Edwina's legacy were all secured before I got distracted."

Fred slipped in a soapy puddle and fell down, pulling Ewan on top of him. This was better than a ringside ticket to the circus.

"I can see what you mean," Gertie said.

At that very moment, Ewan's eyes met mine and he grinned. Sure he was making up for a bet that he lost in a pretty horrific way, but it was all in good fun. I was here with my friends and there was no place else I'd rather be.

❋❋❋

Julie's Front Door, Converted Barn,
Scotford Castle Estate. 7:00 p.m.

I opened the door to see Ewan standing there, freshly scrubbed and hair combed, wearing an expensive sports jacket and coordinated trousers. In his right arm he had a huge bouquet of cream, pink and lavender roses. In his left hand he held a box of chocolates.

"My, you have gone all out. Thank you, Ewan. Perhaps we should do this more often," I teased as I welcomed him inside.

"Well, I thought I might as well do everything correctly for once. The last time we ate a meal alone was when I got you locked in the moving truck and sent up north on a lengthy, unwanted journey."

"Yes, your little sojourn to Yorkshire was a bit off the calendar."

His face fell. He looked a little nervous. I decided to smooth the path.

"Ewan. I'm joking. It's all fine."

"Oh, good." His face changed into a look of relief. "Are you ready to go? By the way you look lovely," he said, commenting on my sunshiny yellow floral dress and matching bag.

It was clear he was trying really hard but making it far too obvious.

Much to his surprise, I shunted him back outside and closed the door. Then I quickly re-opened the door, watching his mouth gape open like a fish. "Ewan, let's start again. Thank you for the flowers and chocolates. You look nice. I look nice. We're friends. Let's just go out to dinner and have a good time, okay?"

"I'm glad you said that. I've been feeling short of oxygen ever since I left my house," he admitted.

"Well there's no need to get all worked up about it. It's not like you haven't met me before. For goodness sakes." He helped me on with my coat, I locked the door behind us and we started to walk towards the car.

"I'm just getting all these words of advice from Fred, Bud, the Major, you know how it is. Wear this, say that, do this. I feel a bit like a marionette on strings."

I nodded. "I've had the same advice from Maude and Gertie and–"

Ewan stopped me right there. As we stood together on the path, he turned to look at me, gazing deeply into my eyes. "Julie, you know how I feel about you. I'd like to take you to dinner and discuss our future together. Not as historian and antiques shop owner, but in a more romantic sense."

There was a moment between us and I went with it. "I'd like that, very much."

The moment was still there.

He bent down and gently pressed his lips to mine. We held the kiss and I could sense that this was just the beginning of many more promising times ahead for us.

I pulled back, ever so gently. "Now, if I were to ask you to make a quick stop on the way to the restaurant, would that be a problem?"

"Does it have anything to do with a solicitor or police constable?" he asked.

"Not directly."

"Not directly?"

"Well, you see, I promised Bertie that I would leave my latest watercolor at the research site for him to collect. The problem is, he just phoned to say he was delayed and Fred's offered to drive it over to Scotford Castle, but he doesn't have a key to get in to GGRS."

"Can't your father let him in?"

"He's out playing cards. Jacques and Maude too."

"Alright, then I guess we'll make that stop. The restaurant reservation will hold."

"Thanks." I slipped my hand inside of his and knew that Ewan was a keeper. When he gave me a caring look and gently squeezed my hand back, I was absolutely certain.

THE END

Thank you for reading! Please leave an online review and/or rating at your retailer of choice.

Acknowledgements

———

Over the years, we have accumulated a library full of reference books on topography, geography, geology, history, aristocracy, manor houses, military, ecclesiastical buildings and archeology. To write even a single nonfiction book is an immense achievement. Thanks are due to the authors who have done painstaking work, producing such engaging reference materials. Their dedication, sometimes to incredibly specific, detailed topics, is commendable.

As always thank you to Penny, Brenda and Val – fact checkers and beta readers who are so generous with their time and talents. To Wolf Wenzel, graphic designer extraordinaire. Thank you for sharing your lifelong talent for the Aunt Edwina series covers. Thanks also to Bethany Brown of The Cadence Group for her enthusiastic, unwavering guidance in the publishing process, as well as to Gwyn Flowers at GKS Creative for interior design work. Aunt Edwina would be impressed.

About the Author

Lynne Christensen is a world traveler who enjoys visiting museums and archives. She grew up roaming around graveyards in Europe with her genealogy-loving parents in search of elusive ancestors. A lifelong learner, she earned both Master of Business Administration and Bachelor of Commerce degrees plus has multiple years of experience in marketing and corporate communications. Her writing is published in numerous magazine articles, case studies, advertisements and technical manuals. She lives on the West Coast of Canada in a house full of fascinating books.

Northleo
WRITING INC.

www.auntedwina.com